DAY OF RETRIBUTION

a novel by

Tom Trench

Stepping
Stones
Press
Ltd.

This is a work of fiction.
Names, characters, places, and incidents
either are the product of the author's imagination
or are used fictitiously. Any resemblance to actual events,
locales, organizations, or persons, living or dead, is entirely coinci-
dental and beyond the intent of the author or the publisher.

www.tomtrench.com

ISBN: 0-9746122-6-X

In loving memory of my mother, Ruth Ansley Kimbrough
Any writing ability that I may possess was passed down to me from
my mother, along with the values that have shaped my life.

Acknowledgments

The path taken in getting this book into your hands has been long and winding, with many setbacks and disappointments along the way. Without the encouragement of friends and family, this story may have forever remained untold.

First, I wish to thank my wife, Judy, who not only served as my inspiration for Leah Coleman in this story, but who continued to believe in my writing even as I began to doubt. She was the one that took the first version, as recorded on micro-cassettes, and transferred it into a manuscript format. There is no doubt she at times wanted to do bodily harm to me during that frustrating process. And for the record, the pen name I have chosen is taken from my father, Thomas Trench Kimbrough, a two fisted, blue collar, family man.

Upon hearing my idea for this book, Bob Krulish, a friend and mentor, was the person who strongly encouraged me to put it down on paper. My children, i.e., Amy Hand, Carol Hiatt, Janet Miller, my son, David, and his wife, Nancy, read one or more of the drafts and gave advice where needed. Janet's husband, Gary Miller, provided expert input pertaining to the psyche of one of the characters, Alex Carter. Trinda Cole did an initial editorial review. Tom Pruden served as my confidant during the early stages of this process. T.J. and Tamara Dickerson and Pastor Scott Hogue read the manuscript, and as those mentioned above, gave me hope and encouragement to persevere.

Finally, I wish to thank Linda Lane for offering editorial suggestions for the final draft of this book. After I had received numerous rejection letters from both literary agents and publishers, she was willing to help me when no one else would.

Glenn T. Kimbrough

"He that sows the wind . . .
ought to reap the whirlwind."

Rosewell Dwight Hitchcock
(1817—1887)

Part 1

The Wind

CHAPTER 1

Week Two Begins - Monday, July 15, 1996

The sun dropped below the horizon as David hurried to make the most of the little daylight left. Driven by a sense of urgency, he plowed through the dense underbrush toward the big, moss-draped cypress. The only sound other than the ground crunching under his feet was the jangling of the empty fish stringer that hung from his belt. Only a little further to go...and he was there.

His sigh of relief ended in a gasp as he looked down into the black, tannic-stained water. Where was his boat? Grabbing the nylon rope that had secured it to the tree, he found the loose end that lay in the shadows. It had been severed.

His heart pounded. Adrenaline coursed through his body. How would he escape the snake-infested island now? Then he heard it. A low snarl from behind escalated into a piercing scream that shot through him like a bullet. Pressing himself hard against the cypress, he tried to melt into its dark form.

"Not so sure of yourself now, are you? You're mine...and it's payback time."

David's breath froze as he watched a man dressed in a black wet suit emerge from the twisted vines a few feet away. Even in the deepening shadows, he could see revenge glowing in his stalker's eyes.

Like a deadly serpent poised to strike, the man never took his eyes off David's face; but for a brief moment the glint in his hand

9

snatched David's attention. The last shards of twilight filtering through the trees caught the blade of the large knife he swung back and forth.

What now? David could try to wrest the weapon from the man's hand and risk being butchered in the attempt. Or he could dive into the murky water below and risk being attacked by the ever-present alligators lying along the river's edge.

Suddenly, as though he had read David's mind, the man raised the knife and lunged toward him.

David Coleman bolted upright. His ragged breath came in pants that chased his racing heart. Sweat dripped off his tensed body. Several seconds passed before he realized that it had only been another nightmare. For the third time in a week, Alex Carter had violated his sleep.

"This has to stop!" he hissed into the darkness.

His wife, Leah, stirred at his side. He lay back down on the sheet now cold with perspiration and took slow, deep breaths to calm his throbbing heart. Staring into the darkness, he heard the old clock in the family room downstairs striking out the hour, five o'clock in the morning.

Grateful to escape the terror of his nightmare, he let his thoughts travel back in time to a night many years before. He had been twelve then, lying beside his dad under heavy quilts in the cold bedroom of his grandmother's farmhouse in Mississippi. He could still see the shadows darting back and forth across the ceiling as the glowing coals in the small fireplace collapsed into ashes.

Remembering the hours-long struggle to get to sleep, he'd finally given in to the anticipation of his first hunting trip and waited impatiently for the morning's first light. Every hour on the hour, the old Seth Thomas on the mantle had struck. In between the hour counts, the rhythmic sound of the pendulum swinging back and forth ticked off the passing minutes. Even though he had tried to catnap between those strikes, he'd come to the conclusion that the thought of killing his first deer was too exciting for sleep to come.

He'd been both expectant and fearful about what the day might bring. That morning, like this one, held the possibility of death.

Enough was enough. He decided to get up and face the dreaded day rather than deal with the possibility of another nightmare. Without disturbing Leah, he reached out to turn off the alarm, swung his feet over the side of the bed, and slowly stood upright. He listened for a moment to the peaceful sound of his wife's breathing before groping in the darkness for the shorts he had tossed aside the previous evening. Then he tiptoed downstairs.

Stopping at the bottom of the steps, he faced the mirror on the wall. The glow from the night light in the hallway illuminated it just enough to reflect his shadow. Having once been a college linebacker, he prided himself on being able to hold his own with men half his age. Through the years, he had lifted weights and, on most days, found the time to jog a couple of miles. His two hundred twenty pounds were well proportioned over his tall frame, and it was apparent from the way he still carried himself that he had once been a force to be reckoned with. For that matter, he still was. Leah told him he was more handsome than ever, but he knew his youthful appearance was yielding to the years. That realization bothered him, but so did having to admit to himself that he was more vain than a man his age had any business being.

Turning away from his image, he disarmed the security system and flipped on the kitchen light. As soon as his eyes adjusted, he headed for the coffee maker that he'd prepared the night before. Like most engineers, David Coleman was a creature of habit. Pressing the start button, he waited for the familiar sound of the water bubbling up and into the strainer. Satisfied that the process was underway, he headed for the back porch. At the door he switched off the motion sensor floodlights.

The warm, muggy air of the July morning in Tampa invigorated him. Unlike many who moved into the area, he liked the humidity. Its warmth held a softness quite different from the arid heat they had grown accustomed to in the West. The buzz of insects reminded him again of how glad he was that the porch was screened.

The Hillsborough River flowed lazily past the rear of their property. Woods to either side constantly threatened to take back the ground he had cleared when the house was built and kept the gardener busy doing what David no longer had time to do.

An array of brilliant pastels in the eastern sky broke through the trees to announce his favorite time of day. He was a morning person, and the sounds of awakening life helped relax his still-tense body. The quacking of a duck followed the splash of a fish striking the water's surface somewhere downstream. This was what he needed to keep him sane when the day fell apart, and somewhere along the line it *would* fall apart.

Leah had told him on numerous occasions that she could tell when he hadn't taken this time to prepare himself for the day. He knew it to be true.

Reflecting on the high ethical standards that had brought him to the confrontation that would take place in a few short hours, he tried to remember that they had served him well during his college days, throughout his marriage, and should continue to do so in the years beyond. Unfortunately, not everyone appreciated those standards. In particular, Alex Carter didn't appreciate them. He knew Alex was a troubled man. Right now, however, that didn't seem of significant consequence, because he was also a man capable of great violence.

Trapped by the thought of what might happen later that morning, David pondered what action he should take…but no answers came. Only the words of his father as they had tramped through the woods during that first deer-hunting trip passed through his mind.

"Remember, son, that the world says 'might makes right.' But let me tell you a better way…right makes might."

David was right about Alex and what had to be done, no doubt about that, but would being *right* give him the *might* to get through this morning unscathed? He shook his head and tried to redirect his thoughts to the present. It didn't happen.

"Remember the golden rule, boy. You treat folks the way you want to be treated, and they'll 'most always do right by you."

"Alex Carter must be the exception to that rule," David muttered aloud. If only he could talk to his father one more time. Some of the old man's wisdom would sure come in handy right now. But his dad's fatal accident years before had forced David to face the reality of death—and ultimately to question the purpose of life itself. After their emotions hit bottom, he and Leah had determined to work harder for the things that *really* counted. For a while they did, and they enjoyed more than their share of prosperity and happiness. Then, abruptly and for reasons beyond his control, David's successful business failed and with it the dreams they had shared.

After that, everything had been a struggle, or so it seemed to him that morning as he thought of the dangers that awaited him. Even the memories of what life had been like during the years of prosperity had faded, crowded out by the battle to survive in the hostile corporate world.

Sitting on the porch and listening to the sounds of life around him, he knew he was no longer the man he had once been. *Funny how a life-threatening situation inspires introspection*, he thought with a cynical laugh. True, he had recouped some of his financial losses, but the man inside—the family man, the spiritual man—had paid a price. He'd reached that same conclusion many times since his business failure—and now as all those other times, he would push on and make the best of the situation at hand.

His father's words on the last day they were together came back as clearly as though the old man were standing on the porch beside him.

"Keep one thing in mind, son. It doesn't matter so much how you die...what really matters is how you live."

How *had* he lived? Had he really lived at all? Or was his a dawn to dusk existence that ended in restless sleep, only to be repeated the next day? For sure, he'd missed out on a lot. Life had become hectic, complicated, and those important things he and Leah had vowed to put first had somehow fallen by the wayside. At least they had for him. Now he just wanted to get through this morning, to go on living.

The muscles at the back of his neck burned, a sure sign of stress. He needed a smoke, a vice he justified by indulging only on weekends. Today would be an exception to that weekend rule. Going to his study, he chose a pipe from the rack and carefully packed it

13

with his wife's favorite black cherry blend. After lighting it and allowing the savory aroma to waft into his nostrils, he went back to the kitchen and removed two cups from the cupboard. The one for Leah he set on the counter along with a spoon, sugar bowl, and jar of creamer, a gesture she had once told him made her feel loved. The other he filled for himself. Returning to the porch, he sank into his favorite chair. His pipe never tasted better than it did with that first cup of coffee.

Just as he was finishing his second cup, Leah appeared in the doorway. Once again her beauty captivated him, as it always had. Their special relationship had evolved over the years as each came to value the other over self. It seemed that into whatever chambers his mind wandered, she was always there.

"What time did you get up, Hon?" She yawned. "I didn't think you'd ever quit tossing and turning. I thought you were going to wear a hole in the sheets." Walking over to him, she kissed the top of his head and sat down in the chair beside his.

"Why didn't you let me know you were awake?"

"Because I didn't want you to try anything. Once a night is enough for a man your age," she teased with an amused smile.

She had always been beautiful, and now, in her forties, she seemed lovelier than ever to him. She had inherited her olive complexion, high cheekbones, and black, arching eyebrows from her Italian mother, who was still a striking woman for her age. In the glow of the morning sun, David could see strands of gray beginning to appear, contrasting sharply with the dark brown hair spilling down across her shoulders. Even after bearing their three children, she had managed to retain a very seductive figure. In his eyes, she was still the southern belle he had married in their youth. Wherever they went, he watched the eyes of men follow after her in admiration and, most likely, he suspected, a bit of desire.

"Hon, when did you get up?" Leah asked for the second time.

He gave her a blank look, then realized he'd ignored her question. "Sorry. Guess I'm more preoccupied with this mess than I thought. A little after five but, as you already know, I didn't sleep very well."

She reached out and slid her hand into his.

"Honey...," he said in a soft voice, gently tightening his grip on her fingers. "I don't want you to overreact to this, but I'm going to carry my pistol this morning...just to be on the safe side." He knew what her reaction would be; he also knew what he had to do.

"No, David. No! I don't want you to. It scares me to think about that." Tears welled up in her dark eyes. "I don't even want you to go in today. Can't you just stay home and let Landon handle this thing with Alex?"

He hesitated, then shook his head. "I don't think I could do that. I'm partially responsible for this problem, and I wouldn't feel right if I weren't there." He patted her hand. "I won't respect myself if I dodge this. Neither will my staff."

"But—"

"I'm going in. That's all there is to it. And I'm taking the gun." He knelt down beside her, gently wiped away her tears, and kissed her. "Everything will be all right, I promise...but much as I hate to leave you, I've got to get ready. Landon will be here at six-thirty, and you know how he hates to be kept waiting."

He stood up, returned to the kitchen, and shoved a piece of bread into the toaster. While he waited for it to pop up, he looked at the bright, cheery wallpaper he'd helped Leah hang on one of those rare Saturdays when he wasn't buried under his work. They'd moved often during their married life, but this house, decorated with her special touch, was his favorite. He buttered the warm toast and consumed it in four bites.

At the bottom of the stairs, he paused in front of the mirror. The stress-filled face looking back at him offered no comfort at all. As he had done a lot lately, he vowed under his breath to take some of his accumulated vacation days after this crisis passed. Then he found himself wondering whether he would be standing before the mirror tomorrow morning...or whether he would be just another tragic statistic on the evening news.

After a quick shower and shave, he headed for the closet. His suit needed to fit loosely enough through the chest so the small automatic wouldn't create a bulge, but not so loose that it sagged. He tried on several coats before selecting the brown one. For a moment he considered wearing the clipped holster that attached to his belt in the back, but he dismissed the idea as being too risky. He had never worn the holster, and it didn't have a keeper strap to secure the pistol in place. The gun could slide out and fall onto the seat in Landon's car, which would be disastrous. Not only did he not have a permit for carrying a concealed weapon, he knew taking a firearm onto company property was a major violation of policy, an offense that, if discovered, would cost him his job—regardless of the circumstances. Landon Walters, his boss and a senior executive with the company, would discharge him in a heartbeat if given the opportunity.

When he was finally ready, he again stood in front of the mirror at the bottom of the stairs, inspecting himself from various angles to make certain the bulge wouldn't attract attention. As small as the pistol was, it still pulled his coat downward and slightly to one side. Placing his personal organizer in the opposite pocket and unbuttoning the coat helped. It was six-fifteen.

For the next fifteen minutes he paced back and forth in the foyer, contemplating all the scenarios that could happen in the meeting with Alex. No telling what that man might do in a fit of rage...or later, when thoughts of vengeance took over.

He worried about Alex's wife and children, at least the daughter still living at home. If only there were a way to help the man salvage his roles as husband and father...but given some of his other problems, it was unlikely the marriage could be saved. It was also too late to salvage him as an employee...and David had long since given up on their friendship.

Once more he considered the dangers awaiting him at the office and, without conscious intent, patted the bulge in his jacket. Alex Carter was a dangerous man, of that there was no doubt.

Unfortunately, Alex wasn't the only person David feared.

CHAPTER 2

At exactly 6:30 Landon's small Mercedes pulled into the tree-lined drive of the Coleman home. David turned from the window and hurried to the breakfast room where Leah was sitting.

"Landon's here. I've got to go."

"Honey, be careful. You're the only man I have, you know." She rose to meet him. He saw her fighting to hold back her tears.

"Call me when it's over, will you? Promise me."

"I will. Everything will be fine, trust me."

They had been together for most of their lives. Suddenly, he was overwhelmed by the intimacy they shared, the kind that few couples ever experience—at least based upon his observation of friends they had known over the years. He felt her fear. Only once before had he known her to be so terrified, and that was the night eight years ago when their two teenaged daughters hadn't come home. Leah had known in her heart that something terrible had happened, and she'd been right. The girls, who were now grown and married, had been in a vehicle accident, and one of their friends had been killed. He heaved a sigh of relief that their youngest, a son, was attending the University of Miami. At least he and the girls were out of harm's way.

He looked back at the love of his life, his soul mate and best friend. Through the years, they had kept few secrets from each other, and Leah was aware of almost everything that had occurred at Expressway over the past week. She also knew the danger.

"Can you tell that I'm packing a gun?" he joked, doing his best to make light of the situation.

"Do you really need to carry that thing?"

"I hope not, but if things get out of hand, we'll all be glad I've got it."

"Please be careful." Her eyes once again welled up.

"I will, and try not to worry. I'll give you a call as soon as it's over."

She wrapped both arms around his neck and melted into his embrace. Her body felt so good under the cotton shirt that had once been his. He couldn't remember what life had been like without her. The soft fragrance of her perfume still lingered from the night before as he kissed her on the neck. She was the centerpiece of his world. He kissed her again before gently pushing free from her embrace. Would this be the last kiss they would ever share?

At the front door, he picked up his briefcase and stepped out onto the porch, trying to look as calm as possible.

"I love you," she said, "and I'll be praying for you."

"You do that. I'll need all the help I can get." He paused and gave her a last, longing look. "I love you, too."

David knew Landon would be watching him for any signs of unusual behavior. Although David had reported to Landon for more than six years, their relationship remained uncomfortable. His initial attempts to befriend the man had not been reciprocated, and he'd finally concluded that their impersonal association was typical of what most executives preferred. David walked around the rear of the car to avoid the possibility that Landon might notice the slight bulge at his chest.

July and August were steamy months in Tampa, due in part to the scorching midday heat followed by afternoon thunderstorms. On that particular morning, not a hint of a breeze stirred. Long strands of Spanish moss hung limply from the large oak trees framing the driveway. On any other day David would have driven his van into the office, but Landon had suggested at their meeting on Saturday that they ride together, presumably to discuss and finalize details for the meeting with Alex Carter.

After David placed his briefcase on the floorboard in front of his seat and they exchanged the customary but meaningless greet-

18

ngs, Landon shifted into low and eased forward down the driveway. It was David's first ride in his boss' new 380 SL, although the little ragtop had been widely discussed around the office for the past two weeks. The leather bucket seats and electronic dashboard array reminded David of the cockpit in one of the company's private jets.

After adjusting the air conditioning that was blowing into his face, David ventured a comment intended to start the conversation on a positive note. "Nice car, Landon, real nice. Is this yours or Carla's?" He wondered to himself why Landon, with two young children, would have bought a coupe.

"Oh, it's mine. She still has the Cherokee, and it's perfect for hauling the kids around."

David considered the impracticality of a coupe, especially at those times Landon was off hunting in the Cherokee, but decided against pursuing the thought. "How'd the weekend go, or what little there was left of it?"

"Not too bad. We went to early mass yesterday, and then I played golf in the afternoon."

David smiled at Landon's reply. It was so typical. His answers were always closed-ended, forcing the other person to keep the conversation going. Over the years, David had also noticed how Landon would reply, "Not too bad" rather than "good," or he would say, "I don't disagree" rather than "I agree" when someone made a positive statement. He'd come to the conclusion that such responses reflect a lawyer's thought process. To them, answers apparently should leave room for rebuttal if necessary. As an engineer, David's approach to everything was different from Landon's, especially his aggressive style of management.

The two men were also opposites in personality, David thought, somewhat ruefully. He looked for the humor in most situations, and when he laughed, it was contagious. Landon, on the other hand, seemed to hold himself above humor, except for an occasional quip, which was done, for reasons known only to Landon, in a Cajun dialect. David viewed himself as spontaneous and open. He never hid where he stood on a matter; in fact, he was always willing to voice his position and would do so without being closed-minded to an opposing viewpoint. In contrast, he found Landon fiercely private, opinionated, and stern.

"How did you score?" David ventured.

"Pretty well, but not my best."

"How was mass?"

"Just like every other mass."

When David was with Landon, he felt compelled to make conversation despite the fact that the other man expressed no desire to indulge in chitchat. He and Landon had been out of sync ever since David had joined the company. At first David told himself it was their age difference or perhaps because he had more managerial experience than his younger boss, but that didn't explain Landon's hostility toward him.

Throughout his career, David had always been able to strike a harmonious chord with people, but with Landon that had not been the case. Now he wrote it off as a personality clash, long ago giving up any notion that their business relationship would ever grow into friendship. That's why it had surprised him when Landon suggested they ride together that morning. In truth, he thought, Landon's suggestions were never intended as suggestions, but rather orders couched as suggestions. Unfortunately, David had learned that lesson too late for his own good.

"How about you?" Landon finally asked. "Did you and Leah do anything exciting?

His boss' unexpected attempt at carrying the conversation forward caught him by surprise, and he hesitated a moment before answering. "Not really. I caught a few bass Saturday afternoon. We went to church yesterday. I really just wanted to hang around the house and spend time with Leah."

Leaving the housing development in which they both lived, Landon turned west onto Highway 301 and after a few miles, south on Interstate 75. David tried not to fidget. The man was driving well below the speed limit, seemingly oblivious to both the traffic passing on his left and the nondescript scenery of scrub oaks, pine trees, palmettos, and an occasional stand of cypress on either side. Typically, the drive took David about thirty minutes, but at Landon's current pace, it promised to take longer that morning.

When it became apparent that Landon was not going to take the lead in discussing the meeting with Alex, David broached the issue. "Landon, I still think Alex may lose control when you confront him this morning. We should be prepared for the worst, and I don't think we are."

"You're overreacting. I've never seen any indication Alex will react violently, if that's what you're thinking."

"I hope you're right, Landon, but the picture that's been painted by almost everyone I've talked to over the past week raises a lot of concerns. And last night I received a phone call that makes me even more nervous." Staring at Landon but getting no response, David continued. "I don't know how he found out about our investigation, but a man who used to work with Alex at Chemtrac called to tell me about an incident in which he and Alex were involved. He introduced himself as Mike Joiner, Alex's replacement as manager of environmental services. Anyway, after Alex was demoted, he accused Joiner of getting his job through unfair tactics. He told me that he tried to prove otherwise, but Alex would hear none of it.

"According to Joiner, not long afterwards someone threw a Molotov cocktail through the window of his new home, only in this case, the bottle contained ethyl mercaptan, the chemical used to add odor to natural gas. It stinks worse than rotten eggs and is quickly absorbed into most materials. Everything in Joiner's house had to be replaced—carpeting, drapes, clothing, everything. Even the wallboard. Fortunately for the Joiners, they were gone for the weekend."

He paused, expecting Landon to respond. When he didn't, David continued. "They were never able to find the guilty person, but rumor was that Alex did it. Soon after that incident, Alex resigned to come to work with us here in Tampa. The only connection they could make to Alex was a high school buddy who worked for Georgia Natural Gas who would have had access to the chemical. Alex, of course, denied it. But Joiner said that Alex's wife, Maggie, told a friend that he had done it. By then he'd left town, and Mr. Joiner decided it was in his family's best interest to let the matter drop. He said that anyone mean enough to have done that was probably capable of filling the bottle with gasoline the next time."

Landon's continued silence annoyed David. It was as though the man were devoid of spontaneity. As seconds turned into minutes, David became aware of Landon's cologne, a fragrance he hadn't noticed before, nor did he recall having seen Landon's navy, pinstriped suit. He almost commented about both, but then chose not to. He stared instead at the driver's profile, as though by mental telepathy he might force Landon to acknowledge that Alex did pose a distinct risk. He also noticed that the speedometer read fifty-five miles per hour.

"That doesn't prove anything," Landon finally said, acting as though there had been no lull in the conversation. "Someone else could have done it and then started the rumor about Alex. Chemtrac had recently been acquired, and there were a lot of organizational changes taking place. I also understand the new owners were battling the United Chemical Workers to get the union voted out. It could well have been a reprisal related to the union activity."

"Maybe so, but it looks mighty suspicious to me, especially in view of Alex having just been replaced by Mr. Joiner...and the statement attributed to Maggie. All I'm suggesting is that we don't take Alex too lightly. I have personally seen him lose control, and I'm convinced he has some kind of emotional problem."

A few more awkward moments passed before Landon replied again. "And just how do you think Joiner found out about our investigation and got your name?" For the first time he gave David a quick look. His expression was clearly one of ridicule.

"I wondered about that when he called me. In fact, I specifically asked him that same question."

"And?"

"His answer was, 'Someone is concerned for your safety and asked me to call.' Then he hung up."

"Any idea just who this mystery guardian angel might be?" Landon replied with a sardonic smile.

Anger rose in David's throat, and he clenched his jaw to stifle the impulse to lash out at Landon for compromising his objectivity because of his friendship with Alex. Clasping his clammy hands together in lieu of choking his boss, he decided that Landon was baiting him and stared out the window while he regained his composure. He forced himself to wonder whether the cattle he saw grazing in the distance were purebred Brahmas or some crossbreed whose genes were better designed to cope with the Florida heat. And then he reformulated his response.

"My guess is that it's Maggie. She's about the only one it could be. She obviously knew about the bomb-throwing incident, and she might well know something about our current investigation. It's pretty clear that Alex has found out we've been conducting an investigation into his business affairs."

"You're assuming the Georgia incident actually happened, which may or may not be the case." Landon replied. "We can check it out easily enough, but even if it did happen as you say, there's nothing to connect Alex with it. Why would he have done it? He would be the first one suspected, and the man's too smart to put himself in such a compromising position. What could he have hoped to gain? He'd already been reassigned, and such an act would not get him his old job back."

"The only motive he would have had was revenge," David answered, "if he thought this Joiner—assuming that's his real name—had actually done him wrong. Alex wouldn't be the first man to seek revenge on a person he blamed for his downfall." David sensed from Landon's expression that he had already dismissed the matter. "Just don't say I didn't warn you."

"It's not me that needs the warning. You're the one I see worrying about what Alex might do," Landon snapped.

David stared out the window at the trees, meadows, and signboards with which he had grown so familiar over the past few years, but his thoughts were not about the scenery. The sun hovered over the horizon now, directly behind Landon, creating a silhouette of his sharp, chiseled features and setting his glasses ablaze. Then he noticed that Landon was holding the steering wheel in a death grip. Did he feel the concern that he refused to admit, even to himself?

"Landon, when I wasn't on the phone last week, I did some research into workplace violence. Are you interested in what I found?"

"Go ahead," Landon responded. His jaw tightened. "But as I said on Saturday, your imagination is running away with this."

David watched the speedometer climb to seventy miles per hour. Cars that had passed them were now being quickly overtaken.

"Nonetheless, it wouldn't hurt to give it some serious thought because over two million people were attacked in the workplace last year, and about half of them in a southern state. There are five characteristics typically common in workers who go off the deep end, although a person may not display all of them. First, it's usually a male in his thirties or forties, and frequently the guy has moved from job to job. Alex is in his early forties but hasn't changed jobs that much. Second, the person has a sort of fascination with weapons."

"So do half the males in this country," Landon interrupted, casting a quick glance with eyebrows raised in David's direction, "especially in the South where hunting is synonymous with manhood. I would say that you have more of a pattern for moving from job to job than he does. So far, I'm not impressed."

"Third," David continued, "the person may enjoy reading mercenary-type magazines, and fourth, he typically has a fascination with violent movies. I've been told Alex owns a library of action movies, especially those that are violent and kinky."

"I don't know or care what kind of magazines he reads, and as far as movies go, the biggest hits are typically violent. The American public has an appetite for violence. I would discount both points. So far, I'd say you're zero for four."

"Number five is a direct hit," David persisted, "and it's also the characteristic most common in workplace violence. The worker displays paranoia and thinks he is being mistreated. On this one, there's no doubt. Alex always feels that any criticism, no matter how constructive, is unfounded. He takes everything personally. He has told numerous people around the office, including me on several occasions, how he is falsely accused and wrongfully treated. He's convinced I've told lies about him behind his back. He gets defensive anytime his actions are questioned. But most important, the guys who work with him have flatly stated he could become violent, and their opinion is not subject to debate."

24

This time Landon didn't pause before answering. "Sorry, but I don't buy *any* of it. Furthermore, you should disqualify yourself as a judge in this particular case. Judges have to be impartial and base their decisions on factual evidence. You're far from being impartial when it comes to Alex Carter. And as for evidence, you don't have any."

"Landon, you'll be making a big mistake if you don't go into this meeting with vigilance, both for your safety and for the employees who could be exposed. I'm strongly advising you to take appropriate precautions. We could at least inform the local police that there might be a problem."

Landon shot David a withering glance. "From where I sit, I see *you* as the one suffering from paranoia. If you want to leave town for a few days, as I suggested on Saturday, feel free. No one will blame you. Personally, I'm not worried about Alex. And if there is a problem, I have more confidence in Bruner than the police."

Following the exchange, neither man spoke as the Mercedes slowed down along with the other traffic approaching Tampa. From the beginning almost every conversation between them had been combative. David wondered why he should have expected this one to be any different. Over the years he'd made numerous recommendations, which Landon initially rejected and later was forced to accept. It was common knowledge that the only advice Landon valued was that given by other attorneys or by the division's president, Jim Hargrove.

David suspected that he was the highest-ranking manager to understand the magnitude of Landon's shortcomings as a person in charge. Since joining Expressway, he had repeatedly been shocked by Landon's naiveté, especially about decisions involving personnel. The man seemed to form his opinion of a job applicant based solely on a résumé, but he'd shown no aptitude in evaluating the individual in a face-to-face interview. He was indecisive on the one hand and impulsive on the other. To a great extent, those weaknesses had contributed to the current crisis they now faced with Alex. And David sat squarely in the middle of it.

What did he know about the friendship between Landon and Alex? It was common knowledge the two frequently spent weekends hunting together. He'd been told that Alex was one of Landon's closest friends, in spite of the difference in their social status. Would the man sitting next to him pull the plug on his friend? Nothing in his past performance suggested this would be the case. Instead, Landon would no doubt hold it against him for being the one that brought the matter to the forefront.

Sensing he was once again fighting a losing battle, he decided to let the matter drop. Landon would have to learn the hard way. David hoped and prayed that no innocent people would end up paying with their lives for the man's stubbornness.

Even at that early hour, traffic slowed their progress. When they finally reached the downtown area, they were nearly blinded by the sun's reflection from hundreds of east-facing windows in the office buildings. What a contrast, David thought, to the darkness that awaited them. Suddenly, the loaded pistol weighed heavily against his chest, as heavily as his intention of using it, if need be, on a man he genuinely liked. Pondering the matter further, he convinced himself he was doing what any reasonable man would do under similar circumstances. Yet, the troubling thought persisted.

After passing downtown Tampa, Landon exited onto Memorial Highway and then turned north onto Eisenhower Boulevard. Along either side stood one glass building after another, each beautifully landscaped and sparkling like a diamond in the morning sun. For most commuters, it was the start of another beautiful summer day.

To David, beauty was the farthest thing from his mind.

CHAPTER 3

Landon and David were executives with Expressway, a division of Pyramid International. As the country was coming out of the great depression in the mid-thirties, Charles Gavin, a gifted chemical engineer from a well-to-do family, had founded the company. Gavin had the rare combination of aptitudes that would have assured success in any field. He had the mind of a visionary, the courage of an entrepreneur, and the business instincts essential for success.

During the first thirty years, technical expertise had driven the company's success. With the retirement of Mr. Gavin, the directors recognized that the industrial economy had peaked and that further growth would come from diversification. The new president needed an understanding of corporate law, coupled with good business savvy. Pyramid's general counsel, Steve Snelling, proved to be the ideal choice. Under his direction, Pyramid grew from a two-billion-dollar regional company to a twenty-billion-dollar international conglomerate.

In the chain of command, Landon Walters reported to Jim Hargrove, president of Expressway, and Hargrove reported to Steve Snelling, president and chairman of the board of Pyramid International. As executive assistant to the president, Landon provided oversight for both the legal team and the environmental department, over which David was manager.

Throughout Expressway's history, environmental issues had held a relatively low priority, as was true for most gasoline marketers. In the late eighties, that casual attitude had come to a radical end.

Gasoline manufactured at Pyramid's refineries was transported by pipeline or rail cars for storage in large tanks located at their bulk plants and terminals. From those storage tanks, it was trucked to Expressway's convenience stores, where it was unloaded into large underground storage tanks. Over the years, gasoline had spilled onto the ground during these deliveries, and in many instances, it had leaked from the rusted tanks into the earth surrounding them.

On December 22, 1988, a federal regulation was enacted requiring companies owning underground tanks to install equipment to prevent leaks. The regulation also required that any existing contamination be cleaned up. Alex Carter had been hired as a backup to David, since he had the environmental experience that David lacked, as well as knowledge of environmental laws, a vast and highly complex field. Alex, supported by a staff of young project managers, was responsible for hiring consultants to manage the remediation projects at the Expressway sites. Of Expressway's twenty-seven hundred stores, over half were contaminated. The typical cost for cleaning up a site was $150,000 and required five years or more to complete.

Contaminated marketing sites were not a problem unique to Pyramid. Beginning with its initial use as a fuel for automobiles, gasoline was typically stored in underground steel tanks. In those days there was little or no awareness of the possible environmental problems that could result, specifically those related to contamination of ground water ultimately consumed by the general public. Gasoline retailers and thousands of private and governmental agencies that operated their own vehicle fleets historically stored their inventories underground. Most tanks eventually rusted. Until the quadrupling of gasoline prices during the oil embargo of 1973, it was a very cheap fuel—so cheap that when inventory shortages disclosed a leaking tank, many companies chose to simply write off the product rather than make the sizable investment necessary to replace the tanks. The need for the federal regulation in 1988 developed from this environmental failure.

Pyramid was recognized by most of those in the know as a well-managed, progressive company. During the seventies, it was named several times by *Fortune* magazine as one of the ten best-managed companies in America. Its success was largely due to its talented executives and the company's aggressive management style.

As part of Pyramid's benefits program, most managers were paid substantial salaries, with key managers also receiving generous stock options. Such options became vested after a certain number of years. If the company was successful and the value of its stock increased, those options could later be sold at a profit. Since no taxes were paid until the options were sold, managers often held onto the options for years, hoping for their long-term growth in value. The options served as a strong incentive for managers to stay with the company, plus serving as an inducement for them to work long hours, take calculated risks, and work together as a team. Their strong sense of ownership led to higher profits and increasing stock values.

In 1990, the company decided to reduce its excessive overhead by downsizing. Competitive pressures had begun to undermine the market leadership Expressway had previously enjoyed, and many companies, including Pyramid, opted to cut expenses by eliminating personnel. In some cases, other companies were paid to provide the services previously provided by the managers whose positions had been eliminated. Those left behind were expected to take on added responsibility without a proportionate increase in compensation. Fifty- and sixty-hour workweeks became the norm. No one dared to challenge those decisions for fear they might be terminated. Although the cutbacks produced impressive gains in the company's earnings, many experienced managers viewed the decisions as short-term expedient and long-term foolish.

Prior to the establishment of the Environmental Protection Agency in the late sixties, operating policies within the industry were dictated primarily by profit maximization or union contracts rather than by corporate concern for the environment. With the enactment of the Underground Storage Tank Regulations, such policies had to be changed. Congress understood that all things being equal, businesses would usually compromise environmental protection in favor of profits. Thus, many environmental laws included provisions for personal fines and imprisonment for individuals convicted of violating those laws. The enforcement branches of federal and state regulatory agencies were charged with exposing violations and prosecuting those responsible. Preferably, the highest corporate officer involved was indicted in order to send a message to other companies that it didn't pay to violate environmental regulations.

Realizing the personal and professional risks of such violations, presidents of corporations either opted to become very involved in environmental matters or to take the opposite approach and have a subordinate accept the responsibility and risk. At Expressway, Jim Hargrove had elected to shield himself from harm's way by having David Coleman report to Landon Walters. Thus David, a professional engineer with many years of project management experience, reported to a man who had no experience in project management or working closely with engineers.

Given a different mix of personalities, such an organization might have been successful. In Expressway's case, the personalities of the senior environmental team mixed like oil and water.

CHAPTER 4

At seven-fifteen Landon pulled slowly through the entrance gate directly east of the office and turned north into the parking lot of Expressway, Inc. When David had worked at Pyramid's home office in Houston, he disliked the big city. Pyramid's headquarters was just one tall building surrounded by similar edifices built to enshrine man's success, separated only by concrete and humanity. Parking had been a daily hassle, followed by the dreaded walk to the office. He could still remember making his way through street people who had quickly sized him up as an easy mark. Although he would never have been accosted because of his size, the panhandling had always made him uncomfortable. Was it more compassionate to refuse to give financial aid to those who asked, or take the easy road and fund their addictions? He had never really resolved the matter, thus the daily ordeal only heightened his dislike of Houston.

By contrast, Expressway's Tampa office sat in a twenty-acre, park-like setting surrounded by spreading oaks, palms, and meandering blankets of flowering plants. As peaceful as the grounds had always seemed, on that particular morning David longed to be anywhere else, even in Pyramid's concrete jungle.

The building faced east toward Eisenhower Boulevard. Like most of the buildings in the area, it featured a glass curtain exterior, its tinted windows outlined by bronze frames. The entrance drive wrapped around a landscaped area boasting a one-hundred-foot oil well and then turned north into the employee's parking lot.

In spite of the impending crisis, or maybe because of it, David allowed himself to be drawn into the beauty of the four-story facility.

To the south, ponds reflected a stand of cypress trees in the distance. Neatly manicured lawns and landscaped flowerbeds complimented clusters of palm trees that had been transplanted from south Florida pasturelands. Picnic tables along jogging paths that wound through the grounds welcomed any who wandered by.

Overhead, seagulls floated on the early morning breeze that was blowing in from the nearby bay. Others scurried about like squadrons of soldiers, running to and fro in the parking lot in search of food. Near the building's entrance stood an impressive sign bearing burgundy on white lettering: *Expressway, A Division of Pyramid International*.

As the two men walked toward the office, David took Landon by the arm and not so gently turned him so they were face to face. "Landon, are you sure you don't want me to handle this meeting with Alex? After all, he does report to me, and I've had to confront him before on some difficult matters. I just want you to know that I am willing to do it."

"No, we settled that Saturday morning. But thank you for offering...again." Landon pulled away and turned back toward the office. "It would be too awkward, especially in view of the problems you two have had."

Though not surprised by Landon's response, David had felt inclined to make one last offer. He had his own idea about the real reason that Landon had decided to handle the situation himself.

"But—"

Before David could finish, B. J. Bruner, the senior security officer for Pyramid International, met them. Bruner had been in town for the past week, since being dispatched from Houston as soon as the accusations against Alex had surfaced. He was an ex-Vietnam Green Beret who appeared quite normal to most observers, but who, David knew, was far from normal in almost every respect. It had been a long time since anyone had called Bruner by anything other than his last name. In fact, no one knew what B. J. stood for, and when asked about it, his standard reply was that Bruner was all they needed to know. He was a loner, and most were satisfied leaving him to himself.

"It's about time you got here," Bruner said, as he greeted the two with a handshake a bit too strong for David's comfort. He gave Landon a penetrating look. "Are you sure you're ready for this?"

"As ready as I'm going to be, but I'll be the first to admit that I won't be sorry when it's over," Landon said matter-of-factly. "I don't see that we have any other choice in the matter."

Bruner turned to David and winked. "How about you, big fella? Think you're up to this?"

"No problem here. All I've got to do is watch for Alex. Once you have him in tow, I can get back to my real job. I'm more than happy to leave this kind of business to an expert like you."

"Bruner," Landon said, "are your men in place?"

"Yes. Every entrance is covered. There's no way he can enter without one of my guys grabbing him."

Bruner appeared upbeat, even exhilarated. David considered the possibility that he relished the idea of violence and the opportunity to display some of his unique skills. Although the Vietnam conflict was long past, David had no doubt that Bruner could still handle about any problem that came his way.

On each corner of the building were high-resolution cameras that provided panoramic views of the grounds. Other cameras inside the building allowed the security officer at the front desk to monitor the corridors. The monitors changed as the system automatically switched from camera to camera.

Uniformed security personnel were on duty, twenty-four hours a day, seven days a week. After regular business hours, a card reader at each door allowed authorized employees to enter the building while recording the individual's name and time of entry. During normal business hours, an unmarked security vehicle periodically cruised the parking lot. Regular security staff carried two-way radios; however, Expressway policy prohibited even the security personnel from bearing firearms.

Bruner gave David his cell phone number and hurried to catch up with Landon, who was already making his way toward a small conference room across the lobby. Stopping at the elevators, David pressed a button. The doors in front of him opened.

Fast, efficient elevator service was just one of the many features which had been designed to impress visiting dignitaries, shareholders, and potential investors. The lavish ambiance also encouraged ambitious young managers to pay the ransom for success, whatever the cost, to someday be assigned an office on the fourth floor—the executive floor.

Under Pyramid's close direction, the architect had taken into account every possible detail. In addition to providing the upscale office accommodations for its four hundred occupants, the building featured a well-equipped exercise facility, complete with four air-conditioned handball courts. For those wishing to run outdoors, asphalt trails wound through the trees and around the ponds. Separate steam rooms and dry saunas were provided for men and women. The building contained a cafeteria catered by Marriott, a barbershop, a travel agency, and a small clinic managed by a nurse practitioner. The company had spared no expense to prove that it was committed to the total well being of its employees.

Should a security event occur, a keyed access program would control access to the fourth floor. During such periods, admission to the executive offices required either a special key to activate the elevator or the security guard at the front desk could authorize access remotely. Doors leading to various stairwells could also be electronically locked to prevent entry to all floors from the stairways; however, the doors could be opened from the inside simply by pressing the panic bar.

If the situation involving Alex developed into a crisis, the system would be activated.

When the elevator doors opened on the fourth floor, David hurried through the beautifully appointed reception area, oblivious to the oriental rugs, parquet flooring, leather furniture, and rosewood desk. For Expressway employees, being assigned an office on the fourth floor represented the ultimate measure of success. For David, impressed as he normally was by the elegance of the furnishings, having a responsible job that met his and Leah's financial needs meant far more. And on that morning, his thoughts were elsewhere.

He'd carefully considered where he would wait to watch for Alex's arrival so as not to arouse the curiosity of others who might arrive early. If he observed Alex doing anything out of the ordinary or heading toward one of the side entrances, he would immediately alert Bruner. Since his own office provided only a partial view of the parking lot, it had been decided that he would use Landon's. Not only did his superior's office afford a full view of the lot, it was also more private than his own.

After placing his briefcase at the end of his credenza, David headed straight for Landon's office. The offices between his and Landon's were usually assigned to aspiring attorneys or admisistrative assistants competing for their chance at stardom, power, and fortune. During Landon's tenure at Expressway, he had once occupied the very office now used by David.

Because of the early hour, David entered Landon's office without having been seen by anyone except the watchful eye of the video camera constantly scanning the hallways. He closed the door behind him. The office was twenty-foot square, second only in size to Jim Hargrove's. The size of one's office and its furniture package were strictly dictated by company policy to reflect the importance of the position.

David shook his head. Landon's office was a mess. His desk and both credenzas were buried under stacks of documents. On the floor behind the desk, more piles of documents bore yellow tabs stuck to the top page, identifying the subject matter beneath. The two cor ner walls were fixed-glass panels starting three feet above the floor and extending to the ceiling. Mini-blinds were standard decor for exterior windows and available upon request for any glass-paneled interior walls. On one of the interior walls hung more diplomas and certifications than it seemed any one person could have possibly earned. The centerpiece of these documents was a black-on-white picture of Franklin Delano Roosevelt. Landon had placed the picture directly opposite his desk. It almost seemed that FDR could make eye contact with the man in the chair and oversee the work in progress.

By standing at the end of the bookcase and behind the circular table in the corner, David found he could see the entire parking lot without being observed from the corridor outside Landon's office. Although a narrow glass panel extended from the floor to the ceiling next to the door, the viewing angle from the outside hallway did not include the corner where he would be waiting. David knew that no one, not even Landon's personal secretary, would open his closed door without Landon's permission, and he was otherwise occupied at the moment.

David stood at the window, sweat beading on his forehead. He felt the dampness in his armpits as he adjusted the blinds so he could observe the parking lot without the risk of being seen. Alex drove a dark blue Blazer, his baby, as he liked to call it. On most days he arrived around seven-thirty.

Staring through the blinds, David realized that he was smiling at the absurdity of the scenario. There he stood, hiding in the office of the heir apparent to the president, carrying a loaded pistol, and contemplating the possibility of shooting another human being before the day was over. *I've seen movies no better than this.* It seemed too incredible to be really happening.

He glanced at the wall clock. Only a couple of minutes had passed since he positioned himself as sentinel, but it seemed like forever. The events of the past week kept flitting through his mind like clips from an old movie. What had started out as a routine exit interview with Peter Everett had taken over his life. Not only did the situation now threaten his very safety, but that of everyone who would arrive at Expressway's office that morning.

Only ten days before, David had scheduled the interview to finalize paperwork on Peter Everett. So much had happened since that meeting that even he was having trouble keeping up with the revelations that had been uncovered daily. In no way had he expected to open a Pandora's box, one that no one would be able to close in time to avoid the whirlwind of devastation that followed.

CHAPTER 5

The Crisis Begins - Friday, July 5, 1996

Peter Everett arrived at David's office for his exit interview at two-thirty in the afternoon. For the first half hour, David accounted for the items on the termination checklist. First, he collected all company property that had been issued, beginning with Peter's credit cards. As he read off each item, Peter placed it neatly along the edge of the desk. AT&T, American Express, Avis, Hertz, Peter's personally coded Expressway ID, Delta, United, and Eastern were all present and accounted for. Next, Peter placed his laptop computer and pager on the desk. He was then asked to sign a statement declaring that his decision to leave Expressway was a voluntary separation. Finally, he signed papers that informed payroll of his decision to cash out his retirement and thrift plan accounts, while continuing temporary coverage of his medical insurance.

With those matters settled, David smiled at the younger man. "I don't mind telling you, I'm going to miss you. You've been a real asset to the team." Although he had tried to avoid showing favoritism, everyone knew they enjoyed a special chemistry. David appreciated the fact that Peter had never taken advantage of their friendship, and Peter valued David's interest in his career. As usual, the two men seemed to enjoy just being together. Peter was a brash, good-looking young man, only a few years older than David's son. Perhaps that explained their special relationship.

Peter grinned. "For the most part, I've enjoyed working here. I like to think I've had a part in helping to restore our environment a little. You know, undo some of the damage we've done to Mother Earth." After pausing for a moment, he continued on a more somber note. "I wish I could have reported to you instead of Alex, but I understand how those things work. I do appreciate everything you've done for me, David. I haven't met many men like you. I want you to know I respect you very much, I really mean that."

"Those are kind words, but it's I who should be thanking you. You have a great future ahead, whatever you end up doing. Just remember to put yourself in the other person's shoes, and try to see things from their perspective if you can."

"I'll remember. Goodness knows you've reminded me often enough," Peter replied with an impish smile. He rose, walked to the window and after a moment, returned to his chair across from David.

"You must be excited about your new career with your father-in-law. Everyone in the office envies the opportunity you have."

"You bet I am. I'll miss the project work, but this is one I can't pass up."

"Well, if you ever change your mind, tell your father-in-law that I'll take the same deal he gave you, no questions asked."

The two men sat there in silence. It was a bittersweet moment for David. He genuinely cared for Peter, and Peter seemed to feel the same toward him. Although Peter was only moving to Orlando, a hundred miles away, David knew the closeness they had enjoyed could not be sustained, given that they would now be following different career paths.

Finally, the silence became awkward and David rose, indicating that it was time to move on. It was a cue that he frequently used to end a meeting, but Peter remained seated, his smile fading into a look of concern.

"David, before I leave, I need to let you in on something."

"Oh, like that tip you gave me on the Derby last year? What a nag! I was beginning to wonder if the poor thing would even make it around the track." David laughed, suspecting that Peter was setting him up for one last joke.

"No, it's not like that. I really did have an inside tip on that horse, but they had to change jockeys just before post-time, and that changed everything. Anyway, what I have to tell you is no laughing matter."

David stared at him. Was Peter baiting him or was he serious for once? He had no desire to be suckered again by his young friend. "Yeah, right. You couldn't keep a straight face at your own mother's funeral."

Peter rose, closed the door, and returned to his chair across from David. This was totally out of character for the free spirited young man. "It's about Alex." David's expression didn't change. "Alex is on the take from SSI. He's getting kickbacks for business pushed their way."

"You're not kidding are you? If you are, *don't*." Peter shook his head, his lips drawn tight. "Is he getting paid in cash or what? Are you sure? Do you have any proof?" The questions, crafted to cut to the chase, poured out without pause. Peter turned and glanced at the door, as though making sure of their privacy.

"You don't seem that surprised," Peter said with a wry smile, his voice now barely above a whisper. "I thought you would be more shocked. Were you already aware of it?"

"No. But I've never trusted him. What exactly do you know?"

"Not a lot, for sure," Peter replied, again giving the door a quick glance, "but I do know he and Cliff Hawkins, SSI's president, are thick, really thick, if you get my drift."

"Really thick, as meaning what?"

"Cliff is gay, David, and my guess is that he and Alex are...you know."

"Alex and Cliff Hawkins?" As this disclosure and its ramifications sunk in, David's expression changed to one of disbelief.

"You've got it. In fact, several of the managers at SSI are gay. Alex and Cliff talk several times a day on the phone. You can always tell when it's Cliff because Alex closes his door and speaks really soft. It's pretty obvious once you know what to look for. With anyone else, he uses his speaker phone and talks so loud everyone in the office can hear."

David's thoughts raced ahead, processing all the implications of what he was hearing. "But I thought Alex fancied himself as a lady's man." David rose and started pacing back and forth behind his desk. The consequences to the company and to him personally were as serious as they could get. Because Alex reported to him, he would be implicated by association if nothing else. Seeing such anguish on David's face, Peter walked over, placed one hand on David's arm and his other on his shoulder.

"I'm not saying he doesn't like the ladies, at least he talks a big game, but I've never seen him do more than just flirt. My guess is that with women, he's all bark and no bite. With Cliff, on the other hand, there's always something going on. Anyway, Expressway's getting ripped off by those guys."

"I *really* don't want to believe this," David said under his breath, turning to sit down as the weight of Peter's accusations achieved total impact.

David watched him choose his words with apparent care. "Cliff meets Alex for dinner pretty often, and they both like to party. I've heard that they've taken vacations together, maybe outside the country. The Blazer Alex drives, as I understand, was a gift from Cliff, as were his bike, his boat, and who knows what else." He hesitated. "There could be more of your staff involved than just Alex. That's about all that I know, boss. You'll have to take it from here." "Boss" was a term Peter affectionately used with David, but only when they were in private and relating informally to each other. David allowed the liberty since he was, in fact, everyone's boss in his department.

"I don't know what to say, Peter. I never suspected anything like this. Why didn't you tell me sooner?"

"I was afraid to," Peter replied. "Too much chance of my getting the boot. Make no mistake, Alex is one vengeful person. If he finds out I've told you this, there'll be hell to pay."

"I need to tell Landon. There's no way I can keep from reporting this information. Do I have your okay?"

After a long moment, he nodded. "I guess you have to do what you have to do, but keep me as the source confidential if at all possible. I don't want that vindictive nut knocking on my door in the middle of the night. When Alex is drinking, he gets ugly mean. I've seen it before, and it's scary. The more he drinks, the louder and meaner he gets. With enough booze, he thinks he's invincible. That idiot would take on King Kong if given a chance."

"I'll keep you out of it to the extent that I can. As you know, Alex leaves tomorrow for a week's vacation. That'll give us a chance to look into this matter without his suspecting anything."

Peter turned to open the door and then hesitated. "Since it's my last day, do you mind if I cut out early? I'd rather not hang around any longer than I have to."

"Go ahead and take off. Once I tell Landon about this, you know where it's going to lead. If true, it's going to be a bombshell."

"Yeah, and I hated to be the one to cause you this grief. But on the other hand, I couldn't just walk out and leave you in the dark. Sooner or later this business was bound to come to light. I wish I had said something a long time ago, but I didn't feel that I was in a position to rat on Alex without risking my livelihood. But that was my call and, right or wrong, it's the one I made. When you tell Landon, make sure he understands that Alex will come out fighting like a wounded bear. I wouldn't put anything beyond him."

"I'll make that as clear as I can, you can rest assured. I appreciate you bringing this to my attention," David said, extending his hand. "Good luck, my friend, and give my regards to Michelle."

Peter grinned and nodded. Ten minutes later, David watched him leave the building, get into his BMW, and drive away.

Then he headed for Landon's office, walking past the secretary without stopping for his normal friendly greeting. Once inside, he closed the door and began recounting to Landon everything Peter had said. True to form, Landon showed no reaction and only asked a few questions for clarification. He then instructed David not to repeat a word to anyone.

As David turned to leave, Landon asked, "How would you rate Peter's performance? Is he someone you would rehire?"

"I would score him extremely high. He's done a great job, and he'll be hard to replace," David responded. "Why do you ask?"

"I didn't ask you to critique his performance. I asked you whether you would rehire him," Landon snapped back.

"In a New York minute."

"I certainly wouldn't. He should have reported this long ago, but he didn't. In my book, that displays a clear lack of loyalty."

"He had good reason to protect his own interests in this situation," David answered. "After all, he did report to the man."

"Well, that may be *your* opinion, but I can guarantee you one thing, he'll never work for this company again. In fact, I may decide to fire your entire staff, at least anyone having knowledge about this and who failed to report it, assuming of course, that Peter's allegations are substantiated."

"There are circumstances which—"

"Not in my book!" Landon yelled. "There's only what's right and what's wrong, and I, for one, will not compromise my principles for anyone. Send me his termination papers. I'll add my own comments about his performance."

Recognizing that further discussion would be a waste of time and only serve to infuriate Landon further, David turned to leave.

As he opened the door, Landon continued, "Did you understand what I said?"

"Yes, sir," he responded without breaking stride. "The papers will be on your desk first thing Monday morning." *Some things never change,* David thought, *especially between that jerk and me.*

Time and again that had been the pattern between them—Landon barking out an ultimatum and David having to accept it without the opportunity to discuss a difference in viewpoint. The more David thought about it, the more frustrated he felt. He had honestly tried to understand Landon, but he was no closer to knowing how to communicate with him now than he had been years before, following their first argument. Once again he found himself wishing he reported to someone else. Any non-lawyer would do.

CHAPTER 6

Saturday, July 6

It was not unusual for Landon to be driving to the office on a Saturday morning. However, on that particular day it wasn't by choice. It may have been sunny or overcast; he was too deep in thought to notice. He was thinking about the conversation that had taken place the previous afternoon with David. Since Jim Hargrove was leaving for a trip to London on Sunday, Landon had called him at his home on Friday evening to request a meeting. If Peter's allegations were true, the situation could develop into a serious problem for Expressway, not to mention jeopardizing Landon's own career. The sooner it was dealt with, the better.

Turning into Expressway's entrance, Landon saw about two-dozen cars in the lot. Some employees would be working, or giving that impression to the senior managers present, while others would no doubt be taking advantage of the exercise facility. Jim's BMW was already parked in the space reserved for the group president. He pulled into the next space just in front of a sign bearing his initials. He dreaded having to admit to Jim that a problem such as this had developed within his department, especially the day before the Hargroves were to leave for their long-awaited vacation. After checking his telephone for overnight messages, he headed straight for Jim's office.

As he walked down the familiar hallway, he rehearsed again what he would say, attempting to keep it from sounding like an all-out crisis. It could get to that, but for the time being it was simply an allegation that needed to be investigated. It might not amount to anything.

"Jim, is this a good time or shall I come back later?" he asked as calmly as he could, leaning into the open doorway of Jim's office.

"Landon, come on in. I'm just going through this pile of mail. It can wait. Seems like everybody waits until I'm leaving to think of stuff that needs my immediate attention. What's on your mind? I believe you mentioned something about Peter Everett's exit interview."

Before responding, Landon closed the door and sat down in the same brown leather chair he always chose directly across the desk from Jim. Both men were casually dressed, Jim in shorts, golf shirt, and tennis shoes; Landon in tan slacks and a white dress shirt unbuttoned at the collar. "Pretty excited about your vacation, I would guess?" Landon asked, not caring one way or the other.

"You've got that right, my boy. We've wanted to visit England for years, but never seemed to have the time. My wife is English, you know, and is she ever looking forward to visiting her relatives, most of whom she hasn't seen in over ten years."

"Will you be staying in London the entire time?"

"Oh, pretty much, in and around the area. We plan to make a couple of one-day excursions, but our primary purpose is to visit with family. Americans could learn a lot from the English, especially in the areas of culture and social etiquette. But much like children, we don't want to take direction from our motherland. The English are so proper and all that, you know, but in some ways I rather enjoy it."

Jim's excitement made it that much harder for Landon to drop the bomb. Landon had always respected Jim and owed a great deal to him. After all, he had personally hired Landon sixteen years before. It had also been Jim who had moved Landon quickly up the corporate ladder, promoting him over other talented young attorneys in the organization. Regardless, Landon decided to get to the meat of the distressing matter.

"Jim, as I mentioned last night, I have some potentially troubling information…and I feel especially bad since this matter involves one of my areas of responsibility."

44

Jim's jovial expression vanished before Landon's eyes. He looked at Landon with a penetrating stare, and the attorney realized that the timing couldn't be worse. He also knew that Jim had a short fuse and that he had suffered two heart attacks in the last few years. Red splotches began to appear on the man's throat and cheeks, and it occurred to Landon that if he weren't careful, he could be responsible for bringing on a third one.

"Go on, I'm listening." The man's effort to maintain his composure was written all over his face.

"Yesterday, Peter Everett, one of our remediation project managers, met with David Coleman and made an allegation that Alex Carter has been taking kickbacks or perhaps accepting bribes from at least one of our consultants."

"Which one?"

"SSI...Scientific Solutions Inc. Them for sure and possibly others."

"And?"

"I'm not sure at this point what exposure we have, but it could present a difficult problem for us. The allegation implies issues that go beyond kickbacks. According to Peter Everett, Alex may also have some 'other involvement,' shall we say, with the president of SSI. David and I have known for some time that they were good friends, and I was somewhat uncomfortable with the relationship. In fact, I voiced my concern to David a number of times, but he apparently chose not to deal with it. At any rate, an allegation has now been made, and we will need to investigate it immediately. Alex is on vacation for the next week. By the time he returns, I want to be able to take whatever action may be appropriate."

"Let's fire him and be done with it!" Jim responded without hesitation, a response Landon had anticipated. "If he's taken money for doing the job we're paying him to do, I'll fire his ass myself." Jim paused for a moment. "What did you mean about 'other involvement' with the president...or whatever it was you said?"

On different occasions through the years, Landon had counseled Jim concerning the firing of different executives who had made the mistake of crossing Jim or who'd seriously erred in judgment.

Landon had seen how quick Jim was to sever relations with long-term, loyal managers, and those experiences had taught him to tread lightly at moments like this. Sweat beaded on his brow, his mouth felt dry, and his own heart rate picked up. Leaning forward in his chair, he hoped that his body language conveyed the message that he was in control of the situation.

"First let me assure you that if we confirm that kickbacks have taken place, we will terminate him immediately, possibly even pursue criminal charges." Landon voice was smooth and measured. "It's this 'other involvement' that could complicate things…something we must be extremely careful in addressing." Knowing Jim's prejudice against people of all persuasions other than his own, Landon struggled to find the best way to tell him the rest of what he knew. He had hoped he would be able to finesse this part without Jim's involvement, at least for the present. Taking a deep breath and speaking as calmly as he could, he pressed on. "Peter told David that the president of SSI and several of the staff there are homosexual. He implied that Alex might also be involved in their…uh…extracurricular activities."

"What do you mean homosexual?" Jim exploded. "What the hell are you saying, Landon? Surely, you're not telling me that a multibillion-dollar company like Expressway is playing footsies with a company like that? That's all we need…having some two-bit reporter tie Expressway in with…," he sputtered, raising his hands in air and then slamming his fist on the desk.

Landon knew the discussion had skyrocketed out of control. He *had* to keep Jim from losing it completely, or worse yet, dropping dead right there in front of him.

"I know that's a concern and one we have to be very careful in addressing. The press could have a field day with this if we assume a worse-case scenario, but we must remember that federal discrimination laws prohibit us from allowing anyone's sexual preference to be considered in our business decisions."

Again Jim slammed his fist down, this time even harder than before. "Don't feed me that crap. I wasn't born yesterday, you know." His face grew red. His eyes bulged. "Just why, may I ask, are we

46

working with that type of firm? There must be a hundred, no, a thousand blue chip companies out there who would give their right arm for a chance to do business with Expressway. Yet here we are, spending tens of millions with some unknown bunch of crooks who...who...." He shook his head. "And if that isn't bad enough, one of our very own managers could be cavorting with them."

"Jim, we only found out about this yesterday," Landon said in a soft voice, hoping his tone would defuse Jim's rising fury, "and David said it was the first he'd heard about any of it."

"That's ridiculous! From what I read in the paper and see on television, most of these guys—and I use the term loosely—are proud of what they are and go out of their way to flaunt it."

Jim stood and came around the desk. Landon could count his pulse by watching the throbbing arteries in his temples. They were protruding so prominently that he half expected to see one explode any minute. Bending over, his face only inches from Landon's, Jim glared at him with a look of disbelief and disgust.

"Let me get this straight, Landon," he said, his foul, hot breath filling the other man's nostrils. "You're telling me we have signed contracts, which you no doubt initialed, with this renegade bunch of queers? You're telling me that we have walked arm in arm with these guys, or gays, for the last however many years without even knowing what they were? You mean to tell me they've been milking the cow right under our nose, and our staff of experts wasn't sharp enough to even suspect that something was amiss? You mean to tell me we don't do background checks on the companies we are paying a king's ransom to? What the hell kind of department are you running here? I don't mind telling you, Landon, I find this absolutely beyond belief!" With that, Jim straightened up and shuffled back around the desk, falling into his chair as though exhausted.

Landon was speechless. He had seen Jim angry on numerous occasions, but never anything like this. He didn't know how to respond. Sure, he had reason to be disappointed and even angry that his hand-picked protégé had let him down, but Jim's hatred for groups he felt to be inferior was his problem, something Landon couldn't change. Unfortunately, he also knew his superior's bias when it came to this particular alternative lifestyle could be more problematic from a legal perspective than either the kickbacks or the 'other involvement.'

For a long moment he just sat there absorbing Jim's tirade, trying to think of a suitable response. He also knew that he needed to distance himself from the mess as quickly and as far as possible. In the final analysis, his concern for Jim's heart took second place to his own professional survival.

Jim stood again and began pacing around the office, muttering expletives under his breath. The back of his neck reddened with every pounding heartbeat.

"I think we can cut our losses and keep it out of the papers if we play our cards right." Landon knew he was grasping at straws.

Jim looked out the window. "Can you even begin to grasp what this could do to Expressway?" he asked, turning back to Landon and leaning across the desk. "To Pyramid International? To my reputation? To *your* career? Hell, we'll be the laughing stock of the entire company! Landon, I find this in-com-pre-hensible! Where the hell have you been for the past however many years? I thought you were on top of this program."

After waiting to see whether Jim was going to continue, Landon responded in his most reassuring, professional voice. He remained seated rather than run the risk of bodily contact with his boss. "Before we pass this up the line, I think we need to investigate the matter fully and determine the facts. Right now, we have no proof, only Peter's allegations as reported by David. Remember that David has never liked Alex. Peter hated him, as well, and may have trumped up these charges just to make trouble for him."

"As the saying goes, where there's smoke…. I've been around the block enough times to know that's true. So until we can prove these allegations as false, we'd damned well better proceed on the assumption that they're true. Hell, this could be just the tip of the iceberg. I must say, Landon, this is some *bon voyage* you've brought me." Jim was breathing deeply, obviously attempting to calm himself.

48

In genuine concern, Landon asked, "Do you need to take something for your heart? Can I get you a glass of water or anything?"

"Don't worry about me, pal." Contempt hung on every word. "You obviously have more than you can handle just doing the job I'm paying you to do, and paying you quite well, I might add."

Neither man spoke for a few moments. Landon continued to ponder how they might extricate themselves from this matter. He glanced at Jim, who seemed to be breathing more normally now. The red splotches had begun to fade.

"I suggest we call in Bruner," he offered. "He's the best man I can think of for handling the investigation, at least initially. First thing Monday, we can start contacting some of our consultants to determine how extensive this problem may be. At this point we can't rule out anything. If Alex has, in fact, taken kickbacks, it's not beyond the realm of possibility that some of our other project managers have, also. David himself may even be involved."

"Hell, I hope he is!" Jim replied, for the first time showing a positive response. "That troublemaker came in here on Steve Snelling's recommendation. Neither you nor I wanted him. He was forced on us. If we can prove he's involved, I will lay this mess right on Steve's doorstep. Not that we won't still catch a lot of the blame, but it would sure help to cut our losses. I want David's telephone tapped today. I want a recording made of every conversation he even thinks of having. I want his office bugged. I want to know every word he says! If he even coughs, I want to know it."

"I can arrange that," Landon said confidently, relieved that the focus had shifted from him to a plan of attack. "I'll call security this morning, and by Monday I'll have everything in place. If he's involved, we'll find out." Hesitating to consider the implications of what he was agreeing to do, he cautiously continued, "You know that policy dictates that we get approval from Steve before tapping an employee's phone."

"To hell with company policy! You've got my okay. That's all you need. Do it! Even if Coleman isn't involved, I *want* him involved. I want that man out of here, do you understand?"

49

"I'll get right on it. Is there anything more?"

"I want you to stay on top of this until it's one hundred percent resolved. I'll leave instructions with my secretary once I get to London on how to get in touch with me. I want to be kept informed about *anything* having to do with this."

"Yes, sir!" Landon replied, returning Jim's fierce glare with a look of embarrassment. "I just want to say I couldn't regret anything more than having let you down like this. I can assure you that this matter will receive my undivided attention. Please try not to let it ruin your trip. I'll do everything possible to get this resolved with a minimum of publicity."

"If I may, Mr. Walters, I'd suggest you do whatever it takes…whether it is possible *or not*. I'll expect to hear from you sometime next week. If necessary, I'll cut my trip short and handle this thing myself."

As Landon stood to leave, his knees buckled. Reaching for the doorknob to steady himself, he struggled to still his trembling hand. Jim's uncontrolled outrage and snide accusations had shaken him to the core, resurrecting feelings he had not experienced since childhood.

"Oh, and Landon," Jim added. "I don't want a word of this to get out. Tell Bruner not to discuss it with anyone. Tell him I'll personally brief Steve to the extent he needs to be informed. If any of this leaks out, I'll hold you *personally* responsible. Not that I don't already."

"I understand." Landon headed toward his office, touching the wall along the corridor to stabilize his shaky gait.

As he slumped in the plush leather chair behind his desk, his head was spinning. He was in real trouble. His career could already have been damaged beyond repair. At best, he had lost Jim's confidence, which he might be able to restore, given the time. At worst, he could be shuttled off to a dead-end position somewhere or perhaps even fired.

It had occurred to him at one point to tell Jim about Peter's concern for his safety and David's opinion that Alex was capable of violence. He'd decided, after Jim went ballistic, that it would be

50

better to discuss those issues at a later time…if at all. Jim had already approached overload. Bringing up the possibility of workplace violence might prove to be the last straw.

After regaining some of his composure, Landon picked up the phone and dialed the corporate security number.

"B. J. Bruner, please. This is Landon Walters calling."

"Just a moment, please, Mr. Walters."

After a minute or two, Bruner answered. Landon briefed him on the situation and asked that he get to Tampa no later than Monday morning. Before ending the conversation, he passed on Jim Hargrove's explicit orders that he would personally handle any communication with Steve Snelling regarding the matter. For his own protection, he also told Bruner that telephone taps and listening devices were being installed on Jim's authority.

With the wheels now in motion, Landon sat in his office, staring blankly at the picture of FDR. Suddenly, all of his accomplishments since joining Expressway, actually for his entire life, seemed meaningless. Landon had always done his best. He was bright, dedicated to his job, a man of integrity. Now his future, and that of his family, was in jeopardy over the secret actions of others. *How could David have allowed this to happen?*

Finally, he let himself consider his intense disappointment in Alex. Then he grew increasingly angry at his friend's betrayal. The man was well paid. He had friends throughout the company who really liked him. Landon had wished many times that Alex had been given David's job…not that David hadn't done okay. In fact, if he were forced to be honest, he would have to admit that David's performance up until then had been better than expected. Yet, Landon had never felt that David gave him the respect he deserved or that he received from others within the company. So competent or not, David came in a poor second to Alex. Not only would Alex have been a much easier person with whom to work, he was a great deal more likeable.

Looking up at FDR, he felt very much alone, just as he had so many times as a boy after incurring the disfavor of his mother. But he was not one to bare his soul to anyone, so he reburied the

51

feelings, closed his eyes, leaned back in his chair, and sat there for a long time. Finally, he rose and headed for the door. His son had a ball game that afternoon and would be counting on his dad's being there. And he would be—in body if not in spirit.

CHAPTER 7

Landon Walters

In the early fifties, birthing a child out of wedlock was viewed as a family disgrace, and that was certainly true in Meridian, Mississippi. Landon's mother, Mary Lou Walters, became pregnant as a teenager and was then abandoned by the father. The shame she bore for her one great sin seriously scarred her self-esteem and changed her life forever, and indirectly, Landon's as well.

Economic necessity forced Mary Lou and her young son to live with her parents. Lacking marketable skills, the young mother took a job as a file clerk at the county courthouse that paid barely enough to cover their share of the household expenses. After the death of her father a few years later, the boy was raised by Mary Lou and her mother with little benefit of male influence. Although Landon was an only child, he was neither pampered nor given reason to think too highly of himself.

Her son was the most important thing in Mary Lou's life, and she committed herself to making amends for the stigma they each bore. Unlike many mothers who lavish affection upon an only child, she had difficulty expressing her emotions, perhaps fearing that by doing so she would once again expose her vulnerability. Although their family and friends did their best to support and encourage the young mother and her son, the kids who knew their secret were not so kind.

Early in life Landon was made cruelly aware that his family was different from the other families in the neighborhood, and not just because there was not a man in the house. "Bastard" was a term he heard whispered many times while growing up, and like other such children of that period, he developed an emotional wall that protected him from the ridicule.

Mary Lou also became hardened to their plight. Having made a grievous mistake, she was determined that Landon would not make a similar one. Thus he grew up in an overly strict, overly protective, and overly private environment.

From Landon's earliest recollections, whenever he asked his mother if she loved him, she would reply, "I love you when you're good." When he misbehaved, her response was to withhold all expressions of love. He soon learned to equate good behavior with acceptance and bad behavior with rejection. Seeking to always do the right thing became a way of life. On the other hand, he lived what he'd learned, reacting with intolerance when others failed to live up to his expectations.

Landon's ability to grasp abstract concepts and retain information was exceptional. As valedictorian of his high school class, he received a partial academic scholarship to the University of Mississippi. Although his mother could have applied for public welfare, she was too proud to accept charity. By the time he entered college, she had saved enough to pay the miscellaneous expenses not covered by the scholarship.

Since Landon was not physically gifted to excel in sports, he channeled his energies into academics. His achievements as a student were rewarded with expressions of approval and pride from his mother, further fueling his desire to excel.

Landon was a lonely child who had few close friends and never a serious girlfriend. As a tall, skinny teenager, he seldom dated, partly because it was a luxury he could not afford and partly due to his unique relationship with his mother. He maintained the highest grade point average in his class throughout his education and graduated from college with honors, receiving a degree in economics. Realizing that economics was too cut and dry to satisfy him intellectually, he then entered graduate school at Ole Miss to study law.

Following his second semester in law school, he spent his summer working for the firm of Dennig, Hartford, and Browser, assisting in research and taking depositions. Two experiences that summer persuaded him to become a corporate lawyer rather than pursuing criminal law. His first assignment had been to take a statement from a derelict accused of burglary. By investigating the public records, Landon had determined that their client had been dishonorably discharged from the army. The man had also served time in California for petty larceny. When asked about his military service and prior arrest record, his client lied about both. Landon was distressed by the realization that, as a criminal lawyer, he might be basing his defense upon lies. His unyielding standards and sense of personal integrity could not be compromised in that manner.

The second incident involved a man awaiting trial for brutally raping a ten-year-old girl. Moses Gilbert was a huge, red-faced man in his forties who towered above Landon, outweighing him by at least a hundred pounds. Moses was illiterate, profane, and carried scars from a lifetime of abuses. The meeting was held in a small windowless room at the state prison. The cubicle was steamy hot, without so much as a ceiling fan to stir the stale air.

When Landon asked Moses about the alleged rape, he denied the specific crime with which he was charged, but then grinned and confided that he had, in fact, raped grown people before, both men and women, but never a child. Repulsed and sickened by the thought of defending an admitted rapist, Landon would never forget how Moses had then leaned forward, placing his big, red face just inches from his own, and confessed that he had raped his cell mate only two nights before. Nor would he forget the fear that cascaded through him at the thought of being caged alone with such an animal, one whose hot, foul breath reeked of decay and rottenness.

Those two experiences convinced Landon that if law was to be his profession, it would not be as a defense lawyer. Yet, he lacked the assertiveness to be successful as a prosecuting attorney. Given his more contemplative nature, he concluded that corporate law would be his chosen profession. It would reward him financially and provide both him and Mary Lou the respect they had never had. The next summer he worked in the law department of Gulf Coast Oil and Gas. It was there that his decision was confirmed.

Upon graduation, he joined Expressway's Law Department in Tampa. He was reluctant to move away from his mother, but she encouraged him to take the job. His grandmother had passed away and Mary Lou was now quite content with her job and her social involvement in the community. The whispers had long since ended. With his impressive salary at Expressway, any financial need she might have would be easily met, and he could fly home as often as needed. He stood on the brink of a very promising career.

A mutual friend introduced Landon to Carla during his second year at Expressway. Carla was a third grade teacher still living at home with her parents. For the first time in his life, he truly connected with a woman. Even more surprising, she connected with him. They were complete opposites. She was gregarious, outgoing, and witty. He was quiet, intelligent, and private.

When they traveled to Meridian for her to meet his mother, he was understandably apprehensive. His concerns quickly ended when Mary Lou met them at the front gate and embraced Carla. From their initial meeting, the two women liked and respected each other. Carla became the daughter Mary Lou had always wanted.

Three years later the Walters had a son whom they named Landon Tyler Walters II, and four years later, a daughter they named Mary Carla. They were very much in love, financially successful, and, for the most part, happy. Although he worked long hours and traveled extensively, they made the most of their time together. Carla was content to stay at home and rear the children, just as her mother had done. They lived in a nice neighborhood, attended church, joined the country club, were active in various civic organizations, and made whatever sacrifices necessary to ensure that his job came first. Until the afternoon of July 5, 1994, life for the Walters family seemed to be perfect.

CHAPTER 8

Week One – Monday, July 8, 1996

As soon as he entered his office, David saw the flashing light on his telephone. He dialed in his personal access code and was not surprised to hear Landon's voice. The message was short and to the point.

"David, please be in my office at 8:15 for a meeting." The call had been placed at 6:30 that morning.

Arriving at Landon's office a few moments later, David found the attorney in serious conversation with a corporate security man whom he recognized as B. J. Bruner. David had seen Bruner on several occasions and knew of his reputation, but had never spoken with him. Bruner was a short, wiry man reminiscent of bull riders David had seen through the years at various rodeos. His Texas drawl complemented his overall appearance. His features were chiseled; his complexion, ruddy. Even though he smiled, his eyes betrayed an inner hardness.

"Good morning, David," Bruner said, as though they were old friends.

Sensing something dark and covert beneath the man's polished surface, David closed the door and sat down in the single chair nearest the door. Joining Bruner on the couch beneath the picture of FDR never entered his mind. "Good to see you, Bruner. I've seen you around, but I don't think we've ever met." Without waiting for a response, he continued. "I guess I'm not surprised you're here, and to be honest, I'm glad you are. Looks like we have a problem on our hands which may require your expertise."

Landon didn't bother with preliminary niceties. "I've asked Bruner to take charge of this investigation. He's already been briefed on the issues. I expect you to drop whatever you have scheduled and give this matter your undivided attention."

"No problem," David replied, glancing at Bruner.

Although few people outside the military knew exactly what Bruner had done in Vietnam, David had heard talk about the talents this man brought to the current situation. According to company gossip, Bruner had served with an elite Green Beret group of the Special Forces skilled in assassinations. He and one or two others in his reconnaissance unit were reported to have stolen behind enemy lines under cover of darkness to seek out the huts housing Vietcong officers. With blackened faces and camouflage attire, they would slip into the huts and slit the throats of the sleeping officers without so much as a sound. Where Americans were held captive, they would infiltrate the camps, quietly execute the guards, and release the prisoners. It had been said that Bruner was highly decorated for his actions on behalf of American soldiers.

The cessation of the Vietnam offensive had also ended the need for his specialized training, and he had been returned to the States. In 1980, he was hired by Pyramid International to provide security for the company's senior managers, a role made necessary by increased terrorism against American executives and their families overseas. It was well known that at public meetings and during international travel, Bruner was never far from Steve Snelling.

"Bruner will coordinate all aspects of the investigation into Peter's allegations," Landon said, staring coldly at David. "He'll need your complete assistance, especially in dealing with our consultants. I want this to arouse as little suspicion as possible, and I'm instructing you to refrain from discussions with anyone except as directed by me or by Bruner."

"I understand, Landon, but I'm sure people will want to know what's going on. With Bruner here, it's going to be obvious that something big is up."

58

"I know that," Landon snapped, "but those who want more information will just have to live without it. I want you to start contacting our consultants about anything they may know relative to kickbacks given to anyone in your department. Phrase your questions to avoid saying anything accusatory about Alex, something he could use against us later in a defamation of character suit."

"How do you suggest I do that?" David replied, looking to Bruner for support. "It won't take a genius to figure out we're investigating the man."

"We can't help that." Landon's tone confirmed his dislike for David. "I expect you to contact those with whom Alex did the most work. Simply tell them you're looking into certain rumors that Expressway employees may have accepted gifts or favors beyond a nominal value or participated in trips that were paid for by a consultant.

"Let them do the talking. If they mention Alex by name, pursue the questioning accordingly. Don't admit or confirm anything. Take accurate notes, documenting *exactly* what they say. I want to know who, besides Alex, may have received favors. I want to know if such favors were requested, or if they were made voluntarily. I want to know what was expected in return. I want to know why the gifts were made, the approximate value of each, and the time and place they were made. I want to know those who delivered the gifts and those on the receiving end. And I want to find out who would have firsthand knowledge regarding these transactions."

"Firsthand knowledge as opposed to what?" David asked.

"As opposed to hearsay. If we have to take depositions, I want to focus on those who were actually present, those who saw the transaction, who heard it, or who did it."

"Won't that be a bit tricky? Aren't we asking these people to incriminate themselves?"

"At this stage we will be merely soliciting information given voluntarily. If we end up taking depositions, they'll be properly advised of their rights at that time. I've asked Bruner to coordinate interviews internally with Expressway personnel who may have information. All information you receive, however trivial, is to be accurately documented and passed on to Bruner immediately. Any questions?"

David could picture the response of different consultants when asked about favors, knowing most would immediately suspect that they were in trouble with Expressway. They would no doubt also know that the investigation was targeted at Alex. It wouldn't take long for one of Alex's cronies to let him know questions were being asked. David glanced toward Bruner. He'd felt the man's stare boring through him since the meeting began. Bruner winked, smiled, and gave David a nod of approval.

"I don't have any at this time," David replied, turning back toward Landon. After a short hesitation, he continued. "Well, I guess I do have one. Should I contact SSI or leave them out of it for now?"

Landon pursed his lips, then puckered them in a pouting gesture. "For now don't call them. If we uncover evidence that clearly involves them, I'll send Bruner with a team of corporate auditors, unannounced, to their offices. Our contract with them gives us the right to make such audits during normal business hours. I don't want to alert them prematurely. Make it very clear to the others that it will not be in their best interest to disclose to anyone that we are asking these questions. If SSI finds out this investigation is being conducted, they'll have time to destroy some of the evidence. And they would probably alert Alex that he's under investigation."

"Fortunately for us," David added turning toward Bruner, "Alex has gone to Georgia for a week to visit his brother. By the time he gets back, we should have our facts together."

"Bruner, I want a written, daily report."

"Yes, sir, will do," Bruner replied in a drill sergeant's cadence.

Landon ended the meeting with a wave of his hand. David stood, motioned to Bruner to follow him, and headed for his office with Bruner trailing closely behind. When they arrived, Bruner closed the door behind them and began talking about what a great team they would make. The man was too friendly. David knew the game he was playing, but had no choice except to play along. Bruner told David how important he was to the investigation and how this was not intended to be a witch hunt, just an attempt to determine the extent of Alex's wrongdoing.

"Without your help, big fella," Bruner said, "this assignment would really be impossible to carry out, especially for an outsider like me."

Bruner stood beside David, watching as he opened a file in his computer that listed all the environmental consultants under contract to Expressway. He then printed out a copy for Bruner's records while proceeding to prepare a handwritten list of employees Bruner should contact.

"Just between us boys, what's your opinion? Do you think he's on the take?"

"I can't rule it out," David replied. "Although I've never seen any indication of..." His voice trailed off.

"Any indication of what?"

"I started to say I hadn't seen any indication that he was taking kickbacks, but in all honesty, I wouldn't put it past him. I've always been a bit bothered by the close ties he develops with his consultants. I personally don't believe in getting too chummy with the people I do business with. In Alex's case, he always seems to be looking for favors."

"Favors?" Bruner asked, eyebrows raised.

"Meaning he's all the time going fishing or hunting with those guys, going to ball games, out for beers, and so forth. I guess what I'm saying is that if a man like him has his hand out, sooner or later somebody is going to put something in it. Alex is in a position to award lucrative jobs to the consultants, and some would go the extra mile to make sure they stay in good with him"

"And you think they did," Bruner pressed, leaning over a bit closer and forcing David to stand in order to put some distance between them.

"I'm saying, I think that's possible. Alex has always had favorites, and he's pretty friendly with those people."

"Well, big fella, it's our job now to find out what he's been up to and just how friendly they've been with each other. Let me know immediately if you come up with anything interesting, and I'll do the same."

"Sure," David replied, forcing a smile.

He tried to mask his disdain for Bruner's buddy-buddy façade that hid his real purpose. After a parting handshake, Bruner spun around and headed for his new office, one that Landon had assigned to him only two doors down from David's.

David sat down at his desk and mulled over the meeting in Landon's office. Maybe he had just imagined a different attitude from Landon that morning, more assertive than before. Landon was always a bit curt; at least it seemed so to David. He knew his boss would be taking heat with something like this happening in his department. *With Alex reporting to me,* he realized, *I'm no doubt under suspicion myself.* The thought occurred to him that his phone might even be bugged, but he dismissed that idea as paranoia.

After considering his own vulnerability a bit longer, he decided that with Bruner on the job, perhaps his phone really could be tapped. Just to be on the safe side, he decided to use one of the phones in the lobby if he had something personal to discuss, including conversations with Leah. She would sometimes call just to tease him and whisper intimate suggestions into the phone. He figured it was probably a game other wives played with their husbands, but he didn't like the thought of Bruner or anyone else being privy to such personal discussions. Putting that unpleasant thought aside, he proceeded to contact the consultants on his list, starting with those he knew best.

By Wednesday, the investigation had turned up sufficient evidence to confirm that most, if not all, of Peter's allegations were true, and that others within the environmental group might also be involved, including Peter himself. David had been shocked by how many of those with whom he had spoken voiced similar fears about Alex. Several came right out and said they were afraid of him and believed him capable of violence. Others voiced the opinion that he was a very insecure person who was a master at manipulating those who trusted him. Some suggested that he was somehow dysfunctional psychologically. The consensus was that Alex possessed a mean, calculating, and vindictive nature. The pattern that emerged confirmed David's concern about the danger they might be facing and the gut feeling that he had long tried to ignore.

Bruner was in David's office later that afternoon comparing notes when the phone rang. "David Coleman."

"David, it's Peter."

David put Peter on the speaker and motioned to Bruner to stay quiet. "If you don't mind, I've put you on the speaker. I've been on the phone all week, and," he laughingly added, "I think I'm developing a cauliflower ear, but you're too young to even know what that means. How's the new job going, and how's Michelle?" He hoped to prevent Peter from asking whether he was alone.

"It's going well and she's fine. Thanks for asking. I've been thinking about our conversation last Friday, and I think it was a mistake to bring up that stuff about Alex. I want you to just drop it if you can."

"It's too late, Peter. I mentioned to you then that I'd have to share the information with Landon, and you were okay with that." David was relieved that Bruner was present. Not only did it verify in the presence of a witness that Peter had, in fact, made the allegations and done so voluntarily, it also established that Peter had given David permission to share that information with Landon. This could be important if Alex later sued the company for defamation of character by initiating the investigation. Or if Peter later denied having been the source of the information.

"I know what I told you, David, but I've been thinking. I'm really...." His voice cracked. After a moment, he cleared his throat. "I'm really afraid that once Alex finds out I talked, he's going to freak. He could drive over here and blow Michelle and me away. He's crazy enough to do it. He's a big hunter, you know, and vindictive as hell. I'm scared, and I don't mind telling you. When he's drinking, his personality changes...and not for the better."

David noted that Bruner was not taking notes during such a key conversation, which led him to believe that his phone probably was bugged.

"Peter, I'm afraid you've created your own problem," David said as gently as possible, making it clear that Peter had been the one to volunteer the information. "I've been talking with some of our consultants during the past few days, and several have said you

63

bragged to them about how you were going to take Alex down when you left. You know as well as I do how rumors spread in this business. We can't protect you from all the talking you've done. You did that yourself."

"Maybe so," Peter replied, "but if I hadn't told you, I wouldn't be in this bind. I don't want to have to live the rest of my life looking over my shoulder, waiting for Alex to show up and do goodness knows what to get even."

"We have uncovered enough information that we won't even have to mention your name when we talk with Alex," David reassured him. "We'll simply tell him that we've obtained information from several of our consultants that implicates him, and that's true. Peter, we will do everything in our power to keep you out of it. I don't know what else we can do at this point."

Peter again cleared his throat and coughed. "Okay, I guess that's the best you can do, but...anything you can do to protect us will be really appreciated."

"You've got my word on it. Take care of yourself and give my best to Michelle."

"Thanks, David, will do." With that, he hung up.

"He's really scared," Bruner said, as David switched off the receiver.

"Yes, he is, and so are a lot of others. Almost without exception, the consultants I've spoken with have said they would be concerned for their safety if Alex found out they had talked."

"We certainly can't rule out revenge," Bruner replied, "but I believe the severance package Landon plans to offer him will go a long way to buy his good behavior. As long as we don't completely cut his lifeline, maybe there'll be nothing to set him off. By the time the money runs out, he should be gainfully employed in another part of the country."

"Bruner, I'm concerned about my own safety, mine and Leah's. Alex has always blamed me for trying to turn people against him. With God as my witness, I have never tried to hurt the man. In fact, I've put up with more crap from him than I ever have from anyone else." Bruner's facial response suggested that he was reading more into that statement than was intended. Hoping to clarify

64

his meaning, David continued. "I've always felt that Alex is insecure, but I'd hoped that he would eventually accept me and that we could build a positive working relationship from there."

"Did you ever tell Landon how you felt?"

"Yeah, a few times I did, but Alex has always had an in with Landon. This will sound like sour grapes, but I always felt that I was the odd man out, or so it seemed."

David exhaled heavily, a gesture he frequently used for relieving stress. "If we fire Alex, as it looks now like we will do, I'm concerned about the first forty-eight hours for sure. But with the severance package you indicate that Landon will offer, it just might buy enough time for him to cool down and get a new start. If he doesn't crack right off the bat, and his wife sticks with him, he could be all right for a while. You know he and Maggie have had serious problems in recent years. In fact, they were separated for a time a while back. Alex has been battling a long-standing drinking problem, so you can see we're dealing with a man who may be nearer the edge than anyone realizes.

"I'll start getting more concerned around the holidays," David continued, "if he's still unemployed and running out of money. I just hope Maggie doesn't throw in the towel. If that happens, I think he could become pretty dangerous, pretty quick."

Bruner smiled broadly. It occurred to David that Bruner seemed to welcome the prospects of a confrontation with Alex.

"Can't worry about all that, big fella. Chances are none of it will happen. And even if it does, my guess is that he will blow his own brains out rather than coming after you three guys."

"He won't come after Landon. They're good friends. He would definitely go after Peter, and probably me. The only good thing going for Peter is that he's a hundred miles away. You know, out of sight, out of mind. Alex could knock me off any day of the week. He knows my routine. I'd be a sitting duck should he decide to take me out."

Bruner got up to go. "You worry too much. If it happens, it happens."

"That's easy for you to say," David replied with an uneasy smile.

With that Bruner walked out and headed down the corridor to make his afternoon report to Landon.

On Friday morning, David was at his desk organizing his notes when the telephone rang. "David Coleman."

"Hi, David, it's Alex."

"Alex, where are you calling from?"

"I'm back home. Just got in last night."

"I thought you weren't returning until Sunday."

"That was our original plan, but we decided to come back early. Julie found out she was going to miss a party Saturday night and, well, you know how persuasive girls her age can be with their dads." There was a short pause. "What's been going on this week, anything major?"

With that question, David knew Alex had been tipped off and was on a fishing expedition. It was totally out of character for Alex to call him directly. It had been his long-standing practice to always first call his secretary and ask her if David needed to speak with him, rather than having to deal with his boss unless necessary.

"Just routine company business. I've been working on a special project for Landon, but nothing other than that," David replied, choosing his words carefully.

"Do you want me to come in and give you a hand? I've got nothing going on here, and I'd be glad to do it."

"No, but thanks anyway. It's really a one-man job, and I'm about the only one that can do it. You enjoy what's left of your vacation, and I'll see you on Monday."

"Are you sure?"

"I'm sure...but thanks for the offer."

David hung up and headed for Bruner's office. Finding the office empty, he proceeded to Landon's. When he arrived, Bruner and Landon were having a whispered conversation, but since the door was open, he walked right in.

"Well, Alex knows we're onto him," he announced in a low voice. "He just called me personally to check in, and he has never done that before, not in all the time he's worked here."

Bruner smiled. "So much for the element of surprise. Guess we go to plan B."

"Plan B?" David asked.

"Just a figure of speech," Bruner replied. "I mean he could come armed, and we'll just have to be prepared for that possibility. It's no big deal."

"Bruner, I don't care what anyone else says about you, I like you," David joked, encouraged by Bruner's confidence.

"Goes both ways, big fella," Bruner responded as both men laughed.

Landon's somber expression remained unchanged.

"David, I want you to meet with Bruner and me tomorrow morning here in my office. Be prepared to provide me a full report on what you've uncovered, and then we need to discuss the meeting with Alex on Monday." After they had agreed on 9:00 o'clock, David excused himself.

The strain of the investigation over the past week had left him emotionally drained and physically exhausted. Knowing Alex was back and that he knew he was under investigation was more than a bit unsettling. *They don't pay me enough for this,* David thought; *in fact, they don't pay me enough, period.*

CHAPTER 9

Saturday Morning, July 13

The meeting on Saturday was definitely out of the ordinary. For Bruner, it seemed to be just another day at the office. Landon was seated behind his desk, Bruner on the couch. David took his customary seat nearest the closed door.

David summarized the results of his part of the investigation. "Landon, you're already aware of the gifts and trips which were paid for by SSI. From what I've learned to date, it appears to be the only company involved to any serious degree. Unless you have questions about those items, I'll move on to the incident Bruner has told you about involving Waterford Environmental.

"I talked the first time with Ed Rogers on Thursday. Late yesterday, he called me back with more details after apparently checking his facts out and probably checking with his lawyer on how much information to give us. You'll remember him, Landon...he's the business manager who handles our account with them. Tall, good looking blond guy with a New York accent. Anyway, Ed recalled an incident when they went hunting during one of Alex's business trips to Texas. According to him, they'd rented a Jeep to get back and forth between Austin and a cabin Waterford owns about fifty miles to the south. Someone backed into the Jeep and smashed the hood while they were in a bar that first night. When they came out and discovered the damage, the other vehicle was nowhere to be found. Ed had declined the insurance coverage offered by the rental agency, and they estimated the repairs could run a thousand dollars or more."

David got up, walked to the window, and looked out as he recalled the details. He had learned the hard way to be precise when talking with Landon. "Ed stated that when they saw the damage, Alex suggested that the costs be billed to Expressway. Specifically, he said that Waterford should submit an invoice for the repairs and bill them against one of the remediation projects, showing the charges as equipment rental. At first, Ed said, he didn't think Alex was serious, but when Alex kept insisting, Ed knew he wasn't kidding. He also said Alex told him it would be okay to include the expenses for the hunting trip as well."

"Was Alex drinking at the time?" Landon asked.

"According to Ed, he had been drinking heavily, but Ed also said Alex repeated the suggestion on two other occasions over the weekend, the last time being at the airport on Sunday. That time he was stone sober."

"Did anyone else hear him?"

"I asked that specific question, and Ed said that several other men in the group overheard Alex's comment and asked him later about it. Anyway, Ed said that what really convinced him Alex meant business was his detailed instructions, the precise language to use for passing the costs through so no questions would be asked. In Ed's opinion, there was no doubt Alex had worked this maneuver before."

"What instructions did he give?"

"Alex specified that Waterford should state on the invoice 'For rental of environmental equipment owned by Waterford.' Alex told him that he would initial the bill, and I would approve it. Expressway was to include the costs, along with other legitimate project charges, in a claim that qualified for state reimbursement. The state would then refund us the full amount. That way, no one would be out anything."

"Why would the state refund Expressway for our expenditures?" Bruner asked.

David returned to his chair and sat down. "A federal law that became effective in 1988 requires any company owning underground storage tanks to install equipment to protect against leakage of product

69

into the ground. Such leakage can get into the groundwater system and potentially poison someone's drinking water. Fifty percent of all the drinking water in the nation comes from underground water-bearing zones.

"In addition, it requires them to obtain insurance which guarantees payment for a cleanup, should that be necessary. Since there was no insurance available for this type of coverage at the time the law was passed, the law provided incentives for states to establish such programs. The insurance was to be funded by whatever means decided on by each state. In most cases, a tax has been added to the cost of each gallon of gasoline sold. As an incentive to the states to set up these programs, the federal government awards millions of dollars in annual grants. But this applies only to states having an approved insurance program in place."

"Wait a minute," Bruner interrupted. "You mean to tell me that the federal government set up a program that will refund Expressway the money we spend to clean up leaks from our own tanks? Since when did the government do anything to benefit big oil companies?"

"This program was intended to assist the small mom-and-pop operations. Individuals own and operate convenience stores or service stations that pump forty percent of all the gasoline sold in this country. Fortunately for us, the law didn't exclude large companies like ours. Since 1990, we've spent well over a hundred million dollars to clean up sites around the country. Before we're finished, we'll spend at least another couple hundred million. If we're lucky and the states don't bankrupt themselves with these insurance programs, we should get back over two hundred million dollars."

"That's incredible." After a moment's reflection, Bruner continued. "And how do we go about getting our money back?"

"First, we have to suspect or discover that leakage has occurred. Next, we hire a consulting firm, like SSI, to drill holes on our property so that soil and groundwater samples can be collected and analyzed. These samples not only prove whether contamination exists, but they're also important in defining the extent of the problem."

"Extent?" Bruner asked.

"That means the horizontal and vertical distance the gasoline has spread into the ground. Tests are conducted to analyze the characteristics of the soil so a system can be designed to remove most of what has been released. Some states allow us to simply remove the soil and replace it with clean material. Other states, however, require us to clean up the soil without removing it. That's called *insitu* remediation. During this process, we have to regularly report our progress to the appropriate state. Typically, an insitu project lasts for years.

"Once a remediation system has been designed to remove the gasoline, a corrective action plan must be submitted for state approval. Assuming our facility was operating in compliance with all the regulations at the time we discovered the release and our findings were reported in a timely fashion, state approval of this plan ensures us that most of our expenditures will be reimbursed."

Bruner shook his head. "You're telling me the state will actually refund us for cleaning up our spill with money they raise through collecting taxes?"

"That's exactly what I mean. It's a sweet deal for us, that's for sure. Unfortunately for the states, most of them had to set up these programs before they knew much about remediation techniques or how to manage the reimbursement programs. Many of the state regulators responsible for administering this program were not qualified to deal with the engineers and geologists employed by the oil companies and consultants. The consultants were quick to realize they had a window of unusual opportunity, a gold mine, so to speak. Some of the more opportunistic ones, SSI for example, saw that they could take advantage of the mom-and-pop operators, as well as the state agencies administering the programs. And they did.

"Those consultants designed systems far more elaborate than needed just to jack up the price. Their fee, of course, has been a percentage of the cost for the system. Some of them formed subsidiaries to fabricate and assemble equipment systems that are sold to the parent company, in essence to themselves, at a big profit. Then the consulting firm sells the system, along with their additional markup, to the tank owner, who in turn submits all of his costs to the state for reimbursement. Everybody makes out except the poor taxpayer.

71

The consultants get rich, the tank owner gets most of his money back, and the state passes the costs on to Joe Taxpayer, who picks up the tab. If that isn't bad enough, some consulting firms fabricate charges, especially to the smaller, unsuspecting tank owners, billing them for work that was never done and knowing that the chances of getting caught are somewhere between slim and none."

"Why didn't you stop doing business with such firms?"

"Good question. We've tried to do just that, but our learning curve has been only slightly ahead of the state's. Just trying to hire a staff and get our own guys up to speed has been a big challenge. But when we suspect dishonesty, we immediately terminate the consultant."

The room was silent for a few moments while David let Bruner process all he had just heard. Landon stared into space, looking more than a little bored with the degree of detail David was going into in order to educate Bruner.

"What's this got to do with Alex?" Bruner asked.

"It has everything to do with Alex," David replied, trying not to sound condescending. "He hires the consultants. He initials the invoices for payment, and he initials the applications for reimbursement to the states."

"Who actually approves the invoices and applications?" Bruner asked.

"I do up to a hundred thousand dollars," David said, "but only after Alex has placed his initials on the documents. Anything over my authorization limit goes to Landon for approval."

"Doesn't that set you up for being a party to fraud? How do you know that the work being billed and the applications for reimbursement are legitimate?"

"That's part of the problem. There's no way I can know for sure what's legitimate and what isn't. We hope that by hiring ethical project managers and working with reputable consultants, we minimize our exposure, but it's a risk we've all recognized. We have procedures designed to also provide checks and balances, but they can't totally eliminate those risks.

"I approve hundreds of documents each week, over fifty thousand dollars a day, for scores of projects across the country. If our project managers initial an invoice and Alex approves it and passes it on to me, I have to trust that the charge is legitimate. Unless, of course, I see something obviously out of the ordinary. With the workload I have, I can't do much more than rubber stamp these documents. I've complained to our auditors about this, and to Landon for that matter, but that's just the way the system has to work at this time, given my small staff. I have requested additional help and suggested that our auditing department take a more active role by auditing the program, but management hasn't felt the situation warrants more scrutiny."

Landon and David exchanged glances, but Landon let the comment pass unchallenged.

"Who prepares the reimbursement applications for Alex's review?" Bruner asked.

"The consulting firms do...here again because we don't have the staff to handle it and each state has different rules and procedures. Nice tidy little operation, wouldn't you say? The consultant designs the program, spends the money, and then applies on our behalf for the reimbursement. With Alex authorizing projects worth millions in profit to the consultants, you can understand why a firm like SSI would be willing to wine and dine him, or whatever else it takes, to stay on his good side."

The room was silent. Landon suddenly sat up and turned to face David. "Did you say Alex had proposed that the damages to the Jeep be passed through for state reimbursement?"

"Yes."

Both men looked at Landon and then each other, as though wondering where the attorney had been for the last fifteen minutes.

"This is more serious than I had first thought." For the first time Landon looked worried, obviously more so than before. "If costs such as repairs to the Jeep have been misrepresented to us and passed through by us to a state for reimbursement, the U.S. mail has been used to commit fraud. That constitutes a federal crime. And if a federal crime has been committed, we have no choice but to report it to the FBI. Need I say more?" Getting no response, he continued. "Until we determine the facts, we'll proceed on the basis that no such activity has occurred. However, if our investigation turns up irrefutable evidence to the contrary, and *I* will make that determination, the FBI will have to be brought into the case." Small beads of sweat formed on Landon's forehead.

David regretted not having done more to control Alex, but to press the issue further, given the relationship Alex enjoyed with Landon, would have placed his own job at risk. He had tried on several occasions to discuss his concerns with Landon, and each time he'd been rebuffed. Perhaps he should have gone over Landon's head, but it was too late now.

"If this hits the newspaper," Bruner said emphatically, "they will crucify us. I can see the headlines now. 'Expressway, a Division of Pyramid International, Indicted for Fraud by the Great State of Texas.' This thing could ruin us! By the time the FBI gets through nosing around, we'll be defending every deal we've made in the last twenty-five years. Our sins will be out there for all the world to see, like underwear drying on the old clothesline. Can you imagine where this could lead?"

"I could kill the good-for-nothing bastard," Landon said just loud enough to be heard. "Here I treated him like a…and all the time he was on the take. I wondered how he was able to live as well as he did. I just assumed…"

Sensing that he had not, at least as yet, been blamed for the fiasco, David ventured a comment he hoped would give Landon comfort. "As I mentioned earlier, Landon, from the people I have spoken with, SSI appears to be the only firm involved."

Landon gave him a wary look. "What do we really know about them?"

David glanced at Bruner before responding. "They are a Florida-based firm with headquarters in Orlando. They have offices in about a dozen states and normally are very competitive. In fact, they may be too competitive. About a month ago, we received notice from Cycla-Corp that they were initiating their due-diligence evaluation in preparation for acquiring SSI. In a subsequent conversation with them, I learned that SSI has not been very timely in paying their bills of late. Cycla-Corp is interested in diversifying into remediation

74

work. The acquisition by Cycla-Corp would serve to reduce our liabilities and should prevent SSI from going belly-up if, in fact, they're in financial straits. It seems to me that whatever we turn up in our investigation should be reported to Cycla-Corp, as it could affect their decision to go through with the deal."

"What have you already told them?" Landon asked.

"Not much, only that SSI is one of our primary consulting firms and that our relationship has always been good. I'm concerned that whatever we tell them could backfire on us. If we don't disclose the kickbacks to Alex at this time and then terminate our relationship with SSI after the acquisition, Cycla-Corp could sue us for collusion or something. If we do disclose that we're investigating SSI and they act on that information to withdraw their offer, SSI could come after us for damages. It's my understanding that Cycla-Corp's board will be voting on the deal in about three weeks."

"Your comments to Cycla-Corp definitely could be interpreted as encouraging them to make the deal. And as you just said, if we terminate relations with SSI after the acquisition, Cycla-Corp could have grounds for damages in a lawsuit. I wish you hadn't made any statements without first touching base with me." Landon's face darkened with each word.

"When I was contacted by Cycla-Corp, it was simply a routine inquiry to verify that our working relationship was as SSI claimed it to be," David shot back. "We had no indication at that time that there were any problems with SSI's business ethics. What was I supposed to say, that they do about half our work, but we can't recommend them?"

Landon glared at David with a look of suppressed rage that made even Bruner squirm in his seat. David had sensed Landon's hostility toward him for some time. Now the expression on the attorney's face revealed a hatred that could not be denied, and the animosity clearly exceeded David's fears. He'd rationalized that the younger man might be intimidated by his willingness to challenge certain decisions, or perhaps was frustrated by his own reluctance to make decisions. No doubt Landon's negative attitude toward him was due in part to certain actions Landon had criticized him for taking, and for which he was later commended by others.

"They've done excellent work for us, from everything I've been told," David continued. "I may be wrong, but I believe we have no choice but to advise Cycla-Corp about our investigation. Who knows what else we may uncover? As sure as we're sitting here, Cycla-Corp will back out of the deal, and we'll be held responsible by SSI."

For some reason at that tense moment, David noticed how each of them was dressed and how telling it was of their personalities. Landon wore the same gray suit he had worn the day before, less the tie. Bruner was dressed in khaki slacks and a long-sleeve, white oxford shirt that had obviously been cleaned, pressed and packaged by his laundry service. Every fold could be neatly traced in the lightly starched fabric. David glanced at his own tan legs extending from his peach colored shorts, sock-less loafers and teal Polo golf shirt. The observation almost, but not quite, brought a smile to his face.

When he pulled himself back to the seriousness of the matter at hand, he noted that Landon had settled down a bit and now spoke in a more normal tone. "Some of the legal terms you used are not exactly correct, David, but your assessment relative to Cycla-Corp is valid and something we will have to address. But enough on that topic for now. There's another matter that I believe is more pressing at the moment.

"The homosexual issue is not, I repeat, *not* to become a factor in our dealings with Alex. Under no circumstances are either of you to mention this at any time in the future. Any appearance of discrimination toward someone in a protected group would damage the corporation's image and invite a deluge of trumped-up suits by ex-employees. I don't know how either of you feels about this matter, and I really don't care. Just don't let your prejudices enter into this investigation, now or later."

"I don't intend to make an issue of the homosexual thing," David replied after a thoughtful moment. "However, we may not be able to ignore it altogether. Cliff Hawkins and his secretary reportedly accompanied Alex and Maggie on various trips, including, as I understand, their wedding anniversary celebrated in St. Thomas. On other trips, Cliff and Alex went alone. The trips could be more of a factor than we might think and make for some embarrassing headlines in the press."

Landon's reply was cold and final. "If we have no alternative but to deal with the matter at some point in the future, *I'll* be the judge of when and how best to handle it *at that time*." With that, he stood and gestured to David that he could open the door. "It will take a miracle to resolve this debacle without the company's reputation taking a major hit," Landon said more to himself than to the others. "At the rate this thing is snowballing, I expect it will be an avalanche before it's over. Let's take a short break before discussing a strategy for our meeting with Alex on Monday."

CHAPTER 10

Thirty minutes later, the meeting resumed. The three men sat in a secluded office on a sunny, Saturday morning, pondering issues that could imperil the reputation of a multibillion-dollar international company. The outcome could send some to jail and destroy the careers of others—some of whom could be enjoying a leisurely round of golf at that very moment, oblivious to the tidal wave of allegations heading toward them.

"Okay," David said, "where do we go from here? Alex is going to be back to work on Monday, and we had better be ready for the worst."

"It's virtually certain he knows that something's up," Bruner said. "There have been too many closed door meetings on the fourth floor. Too many clandestine activities. Too many people in the loop. You can bet somebody's told him that we've been asking questions, and he's feeling the heat."

Landon seemed to ignore Bruner's comments as he addressed David. "What do *you* think were Peter's motives during his exit interview? Why did he pick *that* time to disclose this information about Alex?"

The question caught David off guard. Why would Landon ask something with such an obvious answer? In order to respond truthfully, David would be forced to bring up his boss' friendship with Alex. Was the attorney trying to establish a ploy by Peter and him to exonerate themselves by taking down Alex, while at the same ime torpedoing Landon's career? After all, it could be a major boost to his own career if Landon's friendship with Alex proved to a factor in this scandal.

"I'm not sure why he waited, but my opinion remains the same as it was last Friday when we first discussed this matter. And as you well know, I have an opinion about everything." Receiving no response from Landon and only the hint of a smile from Bruner, he continued. "I can tell you this for a fact. Peter hates Alex. At first, I couldn't understand why, but I think I do now. Peter was aware of Alex's unethical involvement with SSI and of his relationship with Cliff. Having to report to someone like Alex was just too much. At first, I think he was embarrassed being associated with Alex, and as the realization of Alex's depravity festered, it produced both anger and resentment. Finally, he simply rebelled against everything Alex stood for. Given Peter's intelligence and privileged background, I think he could no longer work for someone he considered a degenerate."

"Do you think Alex was aware of Peter's intention to do him in?" Landon asked.

"That's a strong possibility. Peter made the mistake of telling too many people that he was going to get Alex."

"And how did Alex feel toward Peter?"

David cleared his throat and looked at Bruner before responding. "I was told by Leroy Hansen on Thursday that Alex made a comment two weeks ago, something to the effect that if Peter ratted on him, he would, and I quote, 'make him regret the day he was born.' I think it's safe to say that these guys hate each other."

"That's interesting. I've worked with Alex for years and have never seen any sign of aggression, nor heard him make a threatening remark about anyone," Landon said calmly, glancing first at David, then at Bruner.

Once again, David felt the battle lines of opinion being drawn between them. "Landon, several of the consultants that I contacted this week voiced concern that Alex would retaliate with violence. Several made identical statements about how he could be a most intimidating force, especially when he was drinking."

"He's never made me feel intimidated," Landon replied sarcastically, again looking to Bruner for concurrence.

"You're at the top of the food chain in this organization," David shot back. "You're not going to be intimidated by many people around here, much less someone like Alex." David braced himself for Landon's response, but there was none.

After a few moments of awkward silence, Landon spoke. "You said you had an opinion about why Peter didn't report the situation sooner."

"That's right, I do. As I said last Friday, I believe Peter withheld the information for fear of losing his job."

"You mean he thought you would have fired him?" Landon asked.

Being boxed into a corner, David had to answer the question he was trying to avoid. "No...that you would have. Everyone in the office knows you and Alex are friends, and that he is a friend to a lot of influential senior managers in our division. Peter was afraid that you and Alex would turn the tables on him for blowing the whistle."

"That's ridiculous," Landon replied with a smile. "It's just possible he didn't turn Alex in because he had something to hide!"

"Not in my opinion," David said. "I understand exactly how he felt. I can say from personal experience—and you're not going to like hearing this, but I'll say it anyway—your friendship with Alex has at times clouded your judgment regarding his behavior."

David read Landon's steely stare as a death wish. Although he felt justified in making such a comment, he knew immediately it shouldn't have been said with Bruner present. He could well imagine the damage this meeting could have on everyone involved when Bruner replayed it for the boys back in Houston. For the first time he saw just how vulnerable they all were. It would have been much more prudent to privately discuss with Bruner the negative effect that Landon's and Alex's friendship had on the organization, but to have done so seemed to him disloyal. Now the deed was done and his comment could not be retrieved. For a moment, the three just sat in an uncomfortable silence. David could sense Bruner's gaze going back and forth between Landon and him.

Hoping to do some damage control and move the meeting to a conclusion, David finally said, "When Alex arrives at work on

Monday, I suggest Bruner and I meet him at the door and escort him straight to one of the first floor meeting rooms. I've seen Alex freak out before, and it's not something we would want to see happen on the fourth floor."

"Describe it," Bruner injected. "When he freaked out, I mean."

"If I hadn't seen it with my own eyes, I wouldn't believe it myself. He had been insubordinate to me in a meeting one morning, and it just so happened to be time for his performance review. I asked him to come into my office to discuss the matter. As I began explaining to him that his behavior had been unacceptable, he began to get visibly rigid; I mean he stiffened up like a marble statue. His eyes became wild and bulging, his fists clinched, and his face grew more flushed by the second. Then he started shaking. I mean he was trembling so hard I swear I thought he was having a seizure; maybe he was, for all I know. He was obviously in some sort of trance and apparently oblivious to everything I was saying. I stopped talking after I realized he wasn't with me."

"And what happened?" Bruner asked eagerly, scribbling on his notepad.

"For a couple of minutes we just sat there. I don't know where he was, but he wasn't with me. He never said a word, didn't blink, just sat there staring straight ahead into space. I'll admit I didn't know what to do. After a bit, he starting coming out of it. I could see him begin to relax and his color return to normal. He looked at me like a man who was coming out of a...well, I don't know what to call it. He was clearly disoriented."

"So, what did you say to him?" Bruner asked.

"I asked if he was okay, and his answer was something like 'why wouldn't I be.' I thought it best to act as if nothing unusual had happened. I suggested that, in the future, he speak with me in private if he had a problem with a position I was taking because insubordination would not be tolerated. As far as his little spell went, I'm sure he knew something had happened but was too shook up to ask any questions. He wanted out of my office as fast as possible."

"When was that again?" Bruner asked as he continued to make notes.

"Three or four years ago. I discussed what happened with our director of human resources and then with Landon. Since that time, up until the incident we had a few months ago when he verbally attacked Peter in front of the other project managers, he has controlled his temper pretty well."

"I'm sorry to dispute you, David," Landon said, "but I don't recall you ever mentioning anything about that incident before. I'm sure if you had, I would have taken action to get to the bottom of it."

"Well, I'm sure I told you. In fact, I put a written reprimand in his personnel file and, as I recall, sent you a copy. I can check my file if you'd like."

For a while the room was again silent. Then Landon said, "I don't want you in the meeting with Alex on Monday. Bruner and I will handle it."

David sensed that the tables had turned. Landon's tone was different, more detached and businesslike, as though a thought had occurred to him that made David's involvement irrelevant.

"But—"

"No, he'll take it better coming from me," Landon said. "Besides, being as I'm accountable for the environmental program, it's something I should handle personally."

"That's fine with me," David replied in as nonchalant a tone as possible. "I don't want to over dramatize the matter, but all hell could break loose when you confront Alex with this. I'm told that he carries a rifle in his Blazer and, all things considered, I think we should proceed on the assumption that he'd be willing to use it."

"Is there anything other than *your opinion* that suggests he would respond violently?" Landon asked.

David's first impulse was to laugh. Landon's naiveté was beyond his comprehension. How could anyone so brilliant in so many ways be so blind to obvious flaws in human nature, as well as to the concerns expressed by others? Fighting to resist the impulse to respond sarcastically, David slowly restated his concerns and those that had been voiced by others.

"If that isn't enough," David concluded, "we've all read how disgruntled employees have retaliated by blowing away their coworkers. Workplace violence occurs every day. It's reached epidemic proportions. In my opinion, Alex is a prime candidate for such violence."

After glaring at David for a moment, Landon responded in a placating, soothing tone. "I understand your concern, believe me I do, but I think you're getting somewhat carried away. Bruner and I will talk with Alex, and I will inform him that he's on a paid leave of absence until our investigation has been completed." He took a deep breath before continuing. "I want you and Leah to take some time off at company expense and leave town. Go down to the Keys for a week or wherever you like, but get away for a while. It will do you both good, and by the time you get back, we'll have finalized the severance agreement with Alex. I'm sure if we offer him an attractive settlement, pick up his medical benefits for, say, six months, and offer assistance in helping him find a new job, everything will work out just fine. Don't you agree, Bruner?"

"It's worked pretty well in the past," Bruner responded, "but there's one other thing we could do. We could also put surveillance on him to monitor his activities for a few days."

"That sounds good to me," David responded, encouraged that at least one person in the room appreciated his concern. "I want to know what he's doing, whether he's headed for Peter's house in the middle of the night or parked outside my place. Landon, I realize that you don't appreciate my concerns about Alex, but I trust my instincts completely. Alex will crack. It's just a question of when. As you know, my home is pretty isolated. Leaving town doesn't solve anything. I want to know if he's after me. I can't hide from him the rest of my life."

"Now, David, you're going off the deep end, just like you have accused Alex of doing," Landon said in a condescending manner. "How long would you expect us to keep a tail on him? Two days? Three? A week? Do you know how much it would cost to have private detectives doing around-the-clock surveillance?"

"I don't care what it costs," David snapped back angrily. "You're more than ready to offer a sweet package to Alex, but you can't afford to provide proper protection to Leah and me, not to mention Peter Everett."

"As I said," Landon replied, "you're free to take some time off, but I'll not approve surveillance. I don't think it would speak well of our division if we had to stake out one of our managers."

The room was silent again.

"If that's the best the company can do, then so be it. I'll come into work Monday as usual. Besides, how do you think I'd feel if I'm lying on the beach next week when Alex comes in and starts blowing away my staff? Don't forget, Landon, the group president sits only six offices down from your office. You'd better wake up, pal, and smell the roses. They've got thorns."

"I don't give a damn what you do," Landon exploded, "just shut the hell up! I'll handle Alex, or rather Bruner and I both will."

Ignoring Landon's angry response, David turned to Bruner and asked, "You'll be carrying a gun, won't you?"

Bruner did not respond immediately, obviously caught off guard and somewhat flustered by the pointed question on the heels of the angry exchanges that had occurred. David continued, "You know, he could just walk out to his Blazer, get his gun, and come in blasting away."

"None of my people are permitted to carry a gun, including me," Bruner responded apologetically. "I'm told that to do so would significantly increase our insurance costs."

"You mean to tell me you guys carry those briefcases around and there's no gun?"

"No sir, only handcuffs, a cell phone, and a laptop."

"Oh, boy," David sighed. "Alex could walk into this office on Monday and start shooting, and all you could do would be to dial nine, one, one."

"That's not *all* we could do, but it is a fact that we could not shoot back. Each member of my special security team is highly trained in martial arts, and that has proven adequate to handle any problems we've encountered to date."

"If that were to happen," David said, turning to face Landon, "we would be buried in law suits. We wouldn't have a defense in the world for failing to take appropriate precautions to provide a safe work environment for our employees, especially given these circumstances and my legitimate concerns."

"So far," Landon said with a look of pompous satisfaction, "the courts have consistently ruled that providing a safe office environment does not warrant an armed guard. I might also add that we're self-insured up to two million dollars. Our insurance carrier would pay all claims between two million and two hundred and fifty million, if that were necessary. I believe we could settle out of court for well below two hundred and fifty million dollars."

David stared at him in disbelief. With that he stood up, walked to the door, and said, "That's enough for me. I'll see you guys on Monday."

Landon replied, "Suppose I pick you up, just in case something changes in the meantime. Make it six-thirty."

David simply nodded in agreement and left without another word. He figured they still had things they would not discuss with him present, given his potential involvement. He also knew that no matter what happened, his attitude toward the company would never again be the same. As he headed toward his office, he realized that his anger had been replaced by a sense of betrayal.

CHAPTER 11

Saturday afternoon, July 13

When David got home, he found Leah sitting in the Florida room, knitting a baby blanket for a friend. She was wearing one of his favorite sundresses, a buttercup yellow cotton, slightly oversized and short enough to reveal her long, graceful legs. He particularly liked this dress because he'd picked it out and because of the way it hung loosely from her tan, sculptured shoulders by two thin spaghetti straps.

She wrapped her arms around his neck. "My husband is out of town, in case you're interested," she whispered

"I am." And he was.

An hour later he headed downstairs, leaving her to her nap adorned only by a satin sheet. Knowing that she would be resting for a while, he grabbed his fishing gear from the garage and headed for the river. Next to golf, fishing was his favorite pastime and a proven therapy for stress. When he returned some three hours later, he got his pipe, poured himself a glass of Merlot, and retreated to the porch. The air was still and warm, but pleasant. Leah soon appeared, smiling contentedly.

"May I get you a glass?" he asked, hoping she would indulge with him.

"No…but thank you. This tea is fine…and I don't feel comfortable with you drinking so much," she replied in a soft, caring tone.

Since the kids had moved out, he'd gradually adopted the routine of having a glass each night before dinner. He never drank hard liquor, but he knew she worried that his drinking could get out of control, particularly with the stress of his job at Expressway and the fact that his father had once been a heavy drinker. She also knew his inclination to do things in excess.

"One glass isn't going to hurt me," he said, making no attempt to hide his amusement. "From everything I've read, a glass or two of red wine every day is good for you. Improves your circulation and whatever." He grinned at her.

"Justify it however you choose, but I think there are better ways to improve your circulation than drinking," she replied with a smile.

They sat side by side in the wicker swing, holding hands and enjoying the beauty of the evening. The afternoon showers had skirted their area, and the sun peeked out from behind the clouds just in time for a spectacular sunset. The aroma of magnolias hung heavily in the air.

"Catch anything?"

"A few, but I let them go so I wouldn't have to clean them. Our freezer's already full." They exchanged smiles. "No trophies this afternoon, but one of these days I'm going to have a bass this big hanging on the wall in my office." He extended his hands far apart. "Seen the 'gator lately?"

"Not in a few days, but apparently it got the Zambino's dog the other night. They heard him barking around midnight and haven't seen him since." She paused. "How'd your meeting go?"

"Do you really want to talk about it?" He turned and looked at her, his eyebrows raised. "Seems like what's going on at the office has been our main topic of conversation for the last week."

"Yes, Dave, I *do* want to talk about it. I want to know everything that affects you and us."

He felt the serenity of the evening slipping away and sighed. "Okay, but you asked for it. It was interesting, to say the least. Looks like it could get a bit tense before it's over. When Alex comes in on Monday, Landon and Bruner are going to meet with him, and he'll probably be terminated."

"He'll be fired on Monday?"

"It doesn't work quite like that anymore. Nowadays, a person being terminated—we no longer say fired—has the opportunity to respond to all alleged deficiencies in performance. Management then goes through the charade of considering the responses, even when they already know the person is guilty as sin. This delaying tactic gives management a chance to see if the person intends to get a lawyer and challenge the termination. Within a couple of weeks, a certified letter is sent to his or her home, officially giving notice of the termination. I guess it's safer to inform a person by mail than to break the news at the office. The policy originated at Expressway a few years before I was hired, after a man was let go. He went to his car in our parking lot, got a gun out of the glove compartment, and blew his brains out right there on the pavement."

Leah shuddered. "Do you think Alex would do something like that?"

"I doubt it. He'll be offered a severance deal that will look pretty sweet. By the time the money runs out, he'll be working somewhere else and thinking how lucky he is to be with his new employer."

"You mean the company will pay him to leave?"

"Yep. Companies have found that a payoff, in some cases up to a year's salary, is better than having to go to court and defend the termination before a judge. Judges typically rule in favor of the poor, mistreated employee who is being harmed by the big, bad company. To receive the severance payment, the terminated person must sign an agreement never to bring a lawsuit against the company or its employees. And, of course, there's a confidentiality clause. It's really weird."

"Times have changed."

"Not for the better, I'm afraid."

"So much for employee loyalty…and job security."

"Exactly. Anybody wanting to climb the corporate ladder—or even make their working career at one company—used to be committed to that company, and they worked their tails off. Not any more."

"Why the change?"

"A lot of reasons, I guess." He stopped to pack his pipe, then gave her a questioning look. "Do you mind if I smoke?" A frown crossed her face, and he laid the pipe down on the table. "One of them is the downsizing, or restructuring, as they prefer to call it now. Experienced managers are given incentive packages to retire early in order to reduce overhead. They are replaced with younger men, who are bright enough, but with not enough time in the trenches. Landon's a good example of this. In other cases, after a person retires, the position simply isn't filled. Instead, the work is reassigned to those left behind or outsourced or a combination of both. Employees end up working longer hours for about the same pay. After a while, people just get worn out and decide to heck with it.

"Used to be when someone's position was eliminated, the person was reassigned and, if necessary, retrained, regardless of age. Now, if the lawyers feel company actions can be defended, they're terminated or given early retirement. Sort of a thank you and goodbye mentality. The company no longer commits to those who have given it the best years of their lives. So employees have no reason to feel loyal to the company. They're expendable, and they know it."

She shook her head. "I don't think I like what's happening."

"Neither do I, but that doesn't change it. Twenty years ago, the company's stock was owned by people who believed in its long-term viability and cared about its future. Nowadays, many big institutions that care only about the bottom line own most of the shares. In Expressway's case, that's about 85%. If a company doesn't keep increasing earnings every year, the institutions simply sell off a few million shares, the price of the stock dives, and heads start to roll." He took a drink and offered the glass to her, but she declined.

"Why don't those who understand what's happening just quit and go to work somewhere else?" She pushed the swing back and kicked her feet out like a little girl, causing it to pivot about his feet that were still firmly planted on the floor.

"I get the message." He grinned and joined her in pushing the swing, letting it sway back and forth a few times. "This isn't as much fun as our old tire swing, is it?" Without waiting for a response, he continued. "I'll tell you why they don't just move on. There's no assurance they'd be better off with the new employer. It used to be different. Not anymore. If we were to merge with another company and my position eliminated, or if the company decided to outsource my responsibilities, there's nothing I could do about it. I'm at the age where the federal discrimination laws may provide some protection, but I'm not in one of the main groups covered by that law, you know, a female, minority, or so on."

"What's really sad," Leah said, "is that so many wives and mothers have to work just to make ends meet. And then there's the single mom who has no choice but to find a job outside the home...and still try to meet all her children's emotional needs, not just shelter, food, and clothing. Honey, I'm so grateful that I was able to be home with our children while they were small." She reached over and kissed him on the cheek. "Where do you think it will all end?"

He didn't answer immediately. The sunset glowed red, with golden fingers fading into a blue backdrop. A slight breeze moved the draping filaments of Spanish moss in rhythmic waves. A bull-frog began its evening ritual, soon followed by others that apparently were lined up along the riverbank.

"How could such a small thing have such a big voice?" she said under her breath. Soon the chorus was almost deafening.

He put his arm around her and hugged her tightly. "I love you so much," he said, "and I'm so thankful for you. But I don't know where all this stuff at Expressway's going to end. It's really pretty depressing when you think about it. I used to think sex was the driving force that made men corrupt, but I was wrong. Perhaps it is for a season in a man's life, but ultimately the problem for most is the quest for money and power."

"Materialism," she agreed. "No matter what a person has, it's never enough. Something huge will have to happen before people start caring more about each other again than about things."

"I agree. But I also think the answer, at least in part, lies in how a person or a society defines success. You and I may believe that love is the greatest power on earth, but we're in the minority. When I hang it up for the last time at my job, I hope that I will leave behind a staff that really cares about and supports one another. That

90

would go a long way toward defining my success as a manager. Success as a person is a bit harder to measure."

"Speaking of success, do you think the Colemans are too materialistic? You know, you and me?"

"Let's talk about something else," he said with a wry smile. "I'd rather discuss society in general."

"No, I want you to answer me. Are we too materialistic?"

"You tell me. Are we?"

"I asked you first," she laughed. He lifted her hand to his lips and gently kissed it. "I love you, too, David, but you aren't getting off the hook that easy."

"Okay, you asked for it. Yes, I think we could live in a smaller home, own a cheaper car, and use more of our income to help those in need. I think we could volunteer more of our time doing worthwhile things, you know, getting out of our comfort zone. I think it would be great to move to a little town, find a way to provide for the necessities, and escape the rat race."

"Then why don't we just do it, now, while we still have our lives in front of us?" she asked. "I'm serious. Why don't we? We could sell this big house, move someplace where the cost of living is low, and redefine ourselves, 'smell the roses' as you like to say."

After a moment of wishing he had never broached the subject in the first place, he answered, "In my case it's fear. Fear of failure. Fear of not being in control of our destiny. Society dictates that my responsibility is to provide for the needs of my family. After the nightmare we went through with the bankruptcy and all, how could I not feel this way? In my own eyes, I would be derelict in my role as a husband and father if I did less than that. At least my income from Expressway provides for our needs. Believe me, I'd do it in a heartbeat, if I knew for certain that all our financial needs could be met."

"Where is your faith, Hon?" Leah responded, patting him on the knee. "If you really mean what you just said, I think that you should resign from Expressway and find a job that you truly enjoy doing. We can sell the house, and with both of us working, I'm sure we'd do just fine. The thought of a simpler life style feels pretty good to me."

"Would you *really* be willing to do that, if that was what I believed we should do?"

Leah met his stare. Tears began to trickle down her cheeks. "Of course, I would. I don't need *things*. My life is you, and every moment we can be together. I want you to be happy and free to follow your dreams. If you can't, then we're trapped by the same system that's trapped our society. Wherever you go, I'll follow. I don't mind the unknown as long as I'm there with you."

"Let me think about it," he said lightly.

"That's a cop-out and you know it. If you really believe that's what's best for us, then let's do it. You know I mean every word I'm saying."

The sun hovered just above the horizon, a magnificent golden glow illuminating a large cumulous cloud to the west. To the east, darkness made its way toward them. They sat there, she staring at him as he stared into the distance. He struggled with the thought of losing the security they had only recently begun to regain and all the ramifications that would impact their lives. No, he could never voluntarily subject her to the unknown.

"We'll see," he said with a sigh. "I'll be honest with you...it's very tempting. You're right about everything you've said. Unfortunately, it would take a lot of courage, more than I have right now. It would take a lot of faith, too, definitely more than I have right now. But I appreciate more than words can express the fact that you'd willingly give all this up to follow me *wherever*, if that's what I wanted to do. There's not one wife in a million like you, Leah. No man, least of all me, deserves to share his life with such a woman."

"You wouldn't be alone in making that decision, you know. Regardless of the outcome, it would always be *our* decision."

"I don't think it's possible to love you more than I do at this moment," he said as he put his arm around her.

"Maybe so," she said playfully, "but I still love you the most." After getting him another glass of wine, and a small one for herself, she turned on the lamp and was about to rejoin him on the swing when the phone rang. "I'll get it," she said heading for the kitchen. After a few moments she returned with the handset. "It's your son. He wants to talk with 'Dad.'"

"Hi, Son, what's up?"

"Dad, I just had to tell you about something that happened this afternoon. I was there and I still don't believe it. I mean, man, it was so funny. The State Fair is at the fairgrounds this week and I've been manning the radio station's booth after classes. They let me work about whenever I want to." After relating the incident and getting no response, he asked, "Dad, don't you think that's funny?"

"Yeah, it is, Son."

"You know everywhere I go now people tell me they've caught my program and love it. Makes me feel like a celebrity or something. Maybe the guy I was telling you about was right to be staring at me, huh…me being a celebrity and all?"

Again, no response.

"Dad, is something wrong? You haven't called me in over a week and I can tell you're not with me. What's up?"

"I'm sorry, Son. It's just that there are some issues going on at the office and we may have to fire one of my men. You know, one of those unpleasant things a manager has to do sometimes."

"Okay, Dad, if you say so. Hey, I've gotta go. I've got a date with this babe from Atlanta."

"Love you, Son."

"And I love you, too," Leah chimed in.

"Hi, Mom. Didn't know you'd picked up. But I do have to go. I'll call ya'll later. Okay?"

"Bye, Son," they said together.

Returning to the porch, she asked, "What was he telling you before I picked up?"

"Oh, I don't know. Just some funny things that happened at the fair. Boy, I needed that call and a few laughs for a change."

She frowned. He hadn't laughed. "David, are you sure you're coping with this pressure okay?" she asked, sitting back down beside him. The worry lines creasing her forehead extended down between her brows. She'd continually monitored his stress level since the difficult period they'd gone through before.

"Yeah, I'm doing fine, but I'm not going to lie to you. The heat's on high over this Alex affair and it's no fun being in the kitchen."

"Is there anything I can do to take some of the pressure off, I mean like I did this afternoon?"

"No, but you're sweet to offer." He gave her a reassuring grin. "I promise you, I'm doing fine."

"Okay, if you say so, but I'm not sure I believe you. I thought we might just have a salad for dinner. Is that alright?"

"That sounds great. Whatever you want is fine with me."

She reached over and wrapped both arms around his neck, pushing the swing again with her feet. As if by accident, one of the spaghetti straps slid off her shoulder, but her coy little smile suggested it was no accident.

"And what about after dinner? What are we going to do?" she asked.

"How about a dip in the pool?"

"Are you up for skinny-dipping?"

"Are you serious?"

"Have you ever known me to bluff about such a thing? Or was I too much for you this afternoon?"

He laughed and shook his head. "Leah, I don't think I could get enough of you tonight. I love you so much."

"But I still love you the most," she said with a grin.

"Prove it!"

"You dirty old man," she scolded as she gave him a quick kiss on the cheek and removed the other strap from her shoulder.

"Honey, I'm sorry I've been so detached lately," he said, trying to ignore the now-strapless dress. She laughed out loud, as though reading his mind. "I know I've been preoccupied and not much fun."

"That's okay," she said, laughing. "I won't hold it against you."

"Sorry to hear that," he said. "I was in hopes you would."

"You really are a dirty old man, you know!"

He kissed her eyes, her lips, and then her neck.

"That's far enough, mister. Just who do you think you are?" Her eyes twinkled.

"I don't know what I would do without you," he said, as he pulled her up and stood to embrace her.

94

"You don't need to worry about that. You'll never be without me. Unless things change, women outlive men by at least ten years."

Ha!" he said as he reached around and unzipped her dress, allowing it to drop to the floor. "Now we'll see who's all talk and no action."

She pulled free and darted out the door for the pool.

CHAPTER 12

Sunday, July 14

Departure time for Delta's flight 1632 to Boston was scheduled for 6:10 p.m., with a stopover in Atlanta. It was 5:45 when the two men met at gate D-32. The waiting area was packed with tourists returning home from a week in the sun and businessmen beginning another week on the road. Rather than taking separate seats in the lobby, they decided to await the boarding process in the main corridor near the check-in counter. It had been a very eventful week, and the interview scheduled for eight o'clock in Atlanta promised to provide some crucial information.

On Wednesday, Bruner had learned that someone named Billy Ray Harris had first hand experience with SSI's activities and was willing to talk. In fact, when Bruner talked to him by phone on Friday, he seemed eager to discuss 'the sleazy practices at SSI.' After leaving SSI in March, he had moved to Atlanta and joined Alpha Environmental as a senior project manager. That night was the only time he could arrange to meet with them, and the information they hoped to obtain could potentially alter the outcome of the meeting with Alex scheduled for the next morning.

"Where are we meeting?" Landon asked, as he surveyed the faces of those waiting to board.

"I've arranged for a room in one of Delta's executive clubs next to gate A-17," Bruner replied. "He'll be waiting for us at the door, since he's not a member."

"Are you sure he's willing to talk?" Landon asked.

"Oh, he'll want to be assured that we won't prosecute him for his involvement, but if we can satisfy him on that point, my guess is he'll spill his guts. He feels he got screwed by SSI and wants to return the favor."

"We can't make any promises to him," Landon replied. "If criminal acts have been committed, he'll have to take his chances. If he doesn't talk now, he may be talking to the FBI down the road. However, if he hasn't personally broken any laws, he has nothing to lose by talking with us."

"You might have to offer him something in return for his information, you know, quid pro quo. Of all the people David and I have turned up this week, he's the only one with firsthand information willing to break ranks with Cliff Hawkins and his pals. The rest were only hearsay, which, as you pointed out, is not admissible if this thing goes to court."

"Is he bringing a lawyer?" Landon asked.

"When we last talked, he didn't plan to. Of course, he could change his mind. If I were him, I'd bring my lawyer for sure!"

"I've met Billy Ray before, you know," Landon responded. "He was involved in several property deals we were looking into, and I think he trusts our relationship, at least up to a point."

"We're now ready for boarding flight sixteen thirty-two to Atlanta and continuing on to Boston," a feminine voice announced loudly over the speaker. "Anyone needing extra time or assistance may now board, along with anyone holding a boarding pass in our first-class section."

With that, the two men headed for the gate. First-class travel was one of the perks Expressway provided for senior executives. When offered drinks by the stewardess, both declined. At six-fifteen, the plane was pushed back from the gate.

"How do you want to handle this?" Bruner asked, once they were airborne.

"I'll play it by ear," Landon replied. "I would prefer to ask the questions, while you note any issues needing follow-up. When I've finished my line of questioning, I'll look to you for any further questions. I intend to record the interview if Billy Ray doesn't object."

"Sounds fine to me," Bruner replied with a slight smile of satisfaction. He was wired to record the meeting whether Billy Ray approved or not. After all, Landon's friendship with Alex could eventually lead him down a trail that led to Landon's own office.

"Bruner, did Billy Ray mention anything in your conversation to suggest that David might be involved?"

"His name didn't come up, and I didn't indicate that he was under any more or less scrutiny than anyone else. Billy Ray made it clear he has damaging information, and that there is no love lost between him and Cliff Hawkins," Bruner continued. "I think he sees this as his pay-back time. Billy Ray is *the* guy we've been looking for."

One hour and fifteen minutes later the wheels touched down gently in Atlanta. Since neither had eaten dinner, they stopped briefly in the food corridor before heading for their meeting. As they approached the Crown Room Club, Landon and Billy Ray's eyes met at the same instant. He was leaning against the wall next to the entrance. Billy Ray, in his early thirties, wore jeans and an Atlanta Braves T-shirt. His most distinguishing feature, besides his receding hairline, was his bushy blond mustache.

"Hello, Landon. Man, it's good to see you again," he said, grinning broadly.

Bruner had been told that he was an open, easy-going person who was exactly what he appeared to be, with no hidden agendas. From all reports, he was well liked by those who knew him. He had joined SSI in 1986, shortly after the company was formed. He spent the next eight years moving up the ladder before being abruptly ejected. His last position there, national sales manager, made him responsible for developing new accounts and resolving relational issues with their larger clients, like Expressway.

After introducing Bruner to Billy Ray, Landon inserted his membership card into the card reader. The lock clicked, and the three entered the ornately decorated foyer where an attractive young hostess seated behind a desk greeted them.

"Welcome to Atlanta, gentlemen, and to Delta's world famous Crown Room," she said in a drawl that was pure magnolias and mint juleps. "Is there anything we can do to assist ya'll with your connecting flights?"

"No, but thank you for offering," Landon responded solemnly. "Our flights have been taken care of."

"Miss," Bruner said flashing his friendliest smile, "I believe you have a conference room reserved under the name of B. J. Bruner."

"Yes, sir, we sure do," she replied without checking her logbook, "and I'll just bet you must be our Mr. Bruner."

"Yes, ma'am, the one and only."

"Will there be anyone else joining ya'll here at the club?"

"No, it's just the three of us."

"Gentlemen, you will be meeting in the Pecan Room, second door on the right," she said, pointing across the lounge. "If you need anything else, just let us know, okay?"

The Crown Room Club was a large open area furnished with plush leather couches and chairs in tan and peach. Around the corner to the left of the hostess was a counter with coffee service, water, and fruit juice pitchers set up at the far end. Beyond it was a magazine rack neatly stocked. Bowls of peanuts, popcorn, and pretzels were placed on tables throughout the lounge. Opposite the entrance was an area raised two steps above the main floor. The lower level was set-up for casual conversations and for reading, while the platform area was furnished with small library tables for those needing more space. Above the chair-rail the walls were tastefully decorated with a pastel mural featuring golden airplanes and hot air balloons sailing away into a welcoming blue sky. Brass lamps were placed about the lounge, lending an air of coziness to the large room.

"Man, this is really nice," Billy Ray said with another broad grin, much like a kid on his first trip to a restaurant. "Guess I need to fly Delta more often. If I'd known airports had a lounge this nice, I would have scheduled longer layovers."

"Miss, would you please arrange to have coffee delivered?" Landon asked the hostess after they had taken a few steps.

"That's already been taken care of, sir."

"Thank you very much," Landon replied. "Would you inter-rupt us at 10:15 if we haven't finished by then?"

"I'll be happy to."

Crossing the sparsely occupied lounge, the three entered the Pecan Room and closed the door. A dark oak conference table was located in the center of the room, surrounded by eight leather-trimmed oak chairs. Against the wall to the left of the door was a smaller table stocked with two thermos bottles, one containing regular cof-fee and the other decaffeinated. In the opposite corner sat a small table, straight-back chair, and telephone.

"Make yourself comfortable, Billy Ray," Landon said, smil-ing for the first time since greeting Bruner at the airport. "Our flight is at eleven o'clock. What are your time constraints?"

"None, my time is your time. I live about thirty minutes from here, and my wife learned a long time ago to expect me when she sees me pulling into the driveway."

Landon and Bruner removed their coats and hung them on the back of their chairs. After Bruner poured coffee for everyone, Landon gestured for them to be seated. Although Billy Ray appeared to be relaxed, he was obviously startled when Landon removed the small recorder from his briefcase and placed it on the table.

"Since our time is somewhat limited, I'd like to skip the chit chat and get right to the business we are here to discuss." Without waiting for Billy Ray's consent, he continued. "Mr. Bruner is with Pyramid, Expressway's parent company located in Houston. As you know, Billy Ray, we want to discuss certain allegations that have been made regarding SSI's business conduct. Since I do not take notes very well, I would like to record this meeting...if you don't object, that is. It will save time for all of us."

"I guess its okay with me," Billy Ray answered, obviously disconcerted by Landon's formality and the presence of the small, black tape recorder.

Without further comment, Landon started the recorder. He then stated the time, place, and purpose of the meeting, along with the names of those present. Before proceeding further, he checked to see that the recorder was working properly. Once that was confirmed, he proceeded.

"Billy Ray, I understand that you last worked for SSI as their national accounts manager. In that capacity, you may have obtained certain information regarding the relationship between SSI and Expressway that could relate to allegations we're investigating—allegations of impropriety between managers of both companies. I would like to explore several different areas to determine whether your knowledge may be pertinent to our investigation. Do you understand the purpose for this meeting?"

"Yes, sir," Billy Ray replied. "Ask anything you want to, and I'll do my best to answer it."

"Why don't you start by telling us about SSI, how they've operated with Expressway, and what, if anything, they may have done differently from what might be considered within the industry to be proper business conduct."

After hesitating for a moment, Billy Ray cleared his throat and began. "To put it bluntly, Landon, SSI is rotten to the core, especially Cliff Hawkins. I mean, he will lie, cheat, and steal to make a dollar. There is nothing sacred to those guys. I didn't know anything about the company when I was hired. SSI had been in business about a year then, and I was fresh out of college. It sure looked like a good opportunity to get in on the ground floor. Everybody I met seemed nice enough, you know, friendly and all that, but, man, let me tell you, they are low-life. By the time I figured out their game plan for doing business, I was making too much money to quit. Man, I hated it. I hated myself for being involved.

"Don't get me wrong; I mean, I'm no saint, man, but I still have a conscience. The things that go on at SSI are terrible. I'm glad to be out of it. My salary now is about half what it was with them, but I wouldn't go back for twice what I was making. Before I got fired, and that's all you can call it, I could hardly look at myself in the mirror without cringing. They'll do anything to make money, without even thinking twice about it. They find a customer's weak spot and then capitalize on it. I never could figure out why Expressway, a big company with a good reputation, would do business with

SSI." He was speaking directly to Landon as though they were the only two men in the room. Landon stared back without expression.

"There's something else that's different about that company. I don't know how you feel about gays and all that, but SSI has its share. I mean I guess that's something everybody has to decide for himself, but it made me uncomfortable. Anyway, Cliff and Alex are like this," Billy Ray said with a wink, holding up two fingers twisted together, "in more ways than one. They're like lovers, you know. There's nothing Cliff wouldn't do for Alex. Alex has made SSI. They wouldn't be in business today without him, that's for sure."

"Just for the record," Landon interrupted, "the personal relationship you describe between Alex and Cliff Hawkins is not a consideration in this matter and of no consequence in our investigation. According to the U.S. Supreme Court, sexual preference can no longer be considered in evaluating a person's job performance. I would prefer to avoid any further reference to it. Is that clear?"

"Whatever you say. I was just trying to paint the whole picture for you."

After a brief pause, Landon continued. "What can you tell me about gifts made to Alex Carter or anyone else on our payroll?"

"Alex has been on the take since day one. I know for a fact that Cliff has given him a ton of stuff, I mean a boat, truck, guns, trips, women, and men, too, for that matter. You wouldn't believe the things those guys have done. Oops, sorry. I didn't mean anything sexual by that."

"Can you be more specific about the gifts? Did you see kickbacks or payoffs being made in return for business favors?"

"Man, I not only—" Billy Ray suddenly stopped, looking first at Landon and then Bruner. "Wait a minute. You're asking me to incriminate myself, aren't you? I may be telling you something that will be used against me, something that could get me in serious trouble."

"I'm not asking you to incriminate yourself, and I'll turn off the recorder if you like," Landon answered reassuringly. "I just want to know any facts you feel free to share with us. We already have enough hearsay evidence to know what's been going on, but we haven't talked with anyone who was actually present when certain things happened."

The worried look didn't leave Billy Ray's face. He began again, this time more somber and deliberate. "I've got a wife and kids to support. I mean, I want to help you guys out, but I'm no lawyer. I don't know how involved I already am, and I can't afford to incriminate myself. You can understand that, Landon."

Landon reached over and turned off the recorder. "Okay, this will be off the record. Unless you have actually broken the law, the information you give here will not be used against you. If you have broken the law, your involvement will come out sooner or later, and you won't be talking to us. You'll be talking to the FBI and lawyers representing various states."

For a few moments Billy Ray appeared to ponder his alternatives. Tears welled up in his eyes, and he blinked repeatedly in an attempt to fight them back. Finally losing the battle, he took out his handkerchief, wiped his eyes, and blew his nose. After regaining his composure, he continued.

"Sorry, fellows, I really do want to get this off my conscience. I've been living with it too long, and I'm tired of feeling dirty. Maybe by confessing, I can get some peace. I hate feeling guilty. I wasn't raised like that; I had good parents and a good upbringing. I just want to provide for my family and be happy about myself. I want to close the door on this mess and go on with my life. I don't want you to think I'm a bad person or something."

Landon looked at his watch. It provided the nudge Billy Ray needed to move on.

"When we first started doing business with Expressway, I was told to buy as many people at your company as I could."

"And what did you do?" Landon asked.

"I wined and dined your people like they were kings. We routinely went out to bars and strip joints. I even lined up women if your guys wanted them."

"Who did you entertain like that?

"Alex, of course. He was always involved. And Jeff Timmons, Charlie Lyons, Dick what's his name, and Peter Everett. You know, I'd say most of the key guys on Alex's staff."

"What about David Coleman?" Bruner asked, more as an afterthought than a pointed question.

"Never. David isn't someone we ever considered approaching. We'd heard about the high standards he holds himself to and knew he wouldn't get involved in that stuff. I used to be like that, too, but you'd never know it now, I'm ashamed to say."

"Do you think David ever suspected what was going on between SSI and his staff?" Landon asked, searching for the slightest chink in David Coleman's armor.

"I don't know, but I seriously doubt it. My guess is that he would have put a stop to it." Billy Ray hesitated and then continued. "I'm pretty sure he didn't know."

"Did you ask for favors from the men you entertained?"

"Not directly. Cliff's philosophy was that by giving someone special treatment, they'll automatically reciprocate, and he's right about that. I've seen it work more times than I care to admit. He liked to say that it was human nature to repay favors with favors. I think his father must have been a politician. Either way, his methods are just like those used by lobbyists in buying influence in Congress."

"Were you ever present when one of the Expressway people promised to do something in return for favors?"

"No, I don't recall hearing anything like that."

"What about the gifts made to Expressway people?"

"Yeah, there were gifts. I even delivered a few myself."

"Such as?"

"I never gave Alex anything. Cliff handled him personally. I gave a set of Ping golf clubs to Charlie and a computer to Jeff. I also obtained tickets for Peter to attend a few PGA tournaments, and Cliff even arranged for him to go to the Master's one year."

"Was the computer a laptop unit?" Bruner asked.

"Yeah, it was. I don't remember the manufacturer, but it was definitely a laptop. I remember asking Jeff to call the distributor and place an order for whatever he wanted. It was delivered to SSI, and I took it to him at his home."

"Was anything ever given to David?"

"Yeah, we sent him a smoked turkey one Christmas."

"I know about that," Landon said impatiently. "He asked me if he should accept it, and I approved it since it was of nominal value and given as a Christmas gift. I also received one that same Christmas from SSI."

"To the best of my knowledge, that was the only thing he ever got from us. After that Christmas, he asked Cliff not to send him anything personally; but if we wanted to, it would be okay to send cookies or something like that for the office staff to share. He also suggested that we make a donation to some charity."

"What was given to Alex that you do have firsthand knowledge about?"

"I was in a management meeting on one occasion when Cliff told the others that Alex wanted a four-wheel drive recreational vehicle. There was a heated exchange that time between Walt and Cliff about the amount of stuff Cliff had already given him."

"Walt?" Bruner queried.

"Walt Whitmire was the money man, or money fairy, as we called him. He put up the cash and secured the credit to get SSI started. Other than that, Cliff ran the show. Walt told Cliff that Alex was getting pretty expensive to maintain, and Cliff replied that if it weren't for Alex, SSI wouldn't have a business. Walt exploded and told Cliff to give him one of the company's blankety blank vehicles, then find some way to back off with him."

"Did they discuss how the cost of the vehicle was to be handled?"

"Not exactly. Cliff just told Gus, SSI's controller, to cover it. I assumed he meant to bill it somehow to Expressway. I heard Alex paid Cliff one dollar just to make it legal."

"Do you know for a fact that the vehicle was billed to Expressway?"

"I didn't get involved in the bookkeeping for the major gifts like boats and stuff, but you can be sure of one thing, Expressway ended up paying for it one way or the other. They paid for everything."

"How was it invoiced?"

"Extraordinary expenses, as they were called, got billed to various projects either as equipment, rental, or labor charges. With the amount of work SSI does with Expressway, twenty thousand bucks can easily be passed through the system without a trace."

"Do you know for a fact that Alex funneled business to SSI in return for favors?"

"Does a cat have a tail?" Billy Ray asked with a smirk. "I was told by Cliff to always be competitive on our bids, even to bid work under cost from time to time. We would make it up and a lot more to boot in change orders, you know, additional work authorizations."

"Which Alex approved?" Bruner asked.

"Exactly."

"Do you think some of the falsified invoices were submitted on jobs that were reimbursed by the state of Florida?"

"No doubt about it, by Florida and a lot of other states, too. Most of Expressway's projects are reimbursable. Yeah, I don't think there's any doubt about that being the case."

For the next hour the three men discussed how fraudulent charges could be passed through without detection. Billy Ray detailed a variety of ways. It was easy since Alex was the one who authorized the invoices for David's approval.

The final issue Landon wanted to discuss was the allegation that Expressway managers had taken foreign trips at SSI's expense. "Do you have firsthand knowledge of such trips?" he asked.

"I was never present, if that's what you mean, but I can guarantee you that a number of such trips were taken by Alex and Cliff."

"What about other Expressway employees?" Bruner asked.

"Not as far as I know. Those trips were exclusively for Alex. Alex and Cliff would slip off to the Bahamas or someplace for a long weekend. Sometimes Alex would take Maggie. Other times, he would tell her he was going to a conference or something. Either she was too naïve to figure it out, or else she just didn't want to know what he was doing. And from what I hear, when those guys traveled, they went first class all the way."

"I find it hard to believe that David was oblivious to all this going on right under his nose for almost seven years. How certain are you that he wasn't involved, possibly accepting favors himself under the table?" Bruner asked.

"Man, I just can't believe that David was involved," Billy Ray replied. "Alex hated David, I mean, he bad-mouthed the man all the time. But I never heard Cliff say anything to indicate he had had any discussions with David, except when they met to negotiate annual rates. I think Cliff respected David too much to try anything with him. Besides, he didn't need David. Alex was the key person to have in his pocket, and he owns Alex, make no mistake about that."

It was ten o'clock.

"Do you mind telling me why you finally decided to leave SSI, or rather what happened that got you fired?" Landon asked.

Billy Ray gave a long look, first to Landon and then Bruner. His cheeks and throat began to flush. Finally, he took a deep breath and said in almost a whisper, "Okay, if you really want to know, I'll tell you. I could go along with getting girls for guys. I mean, it isn't right, but after all, it's human nature. One might not approve—I don't approve—but boys will be boys. But I couldn't go along with arranging homosexual orgies. I had to draw the line somewhere, and that was it. At first, Cliff only wanted me to make the arrangements, which I did much to my regret. Later on, he tried to make me participate. When I refused, he threatened to tell my wife a bunch of lies about me. I told that sleazebag to go to hell. He fired me on the spot. I've still got some pride, you know. Not much to be sure, but some."

"I want to thank you for agreeing to meet with us and for being candid in your answers," Landon said as the three stood to leave.

"Does it sound like I've broken any laws?"

"What you've done is certainly unethical, but probably not illegal enough to warrant prosecution," Landon answered. He put the recorder back in his jacket pocket. "One last question. Is there anyone at Expressway, other than those we've already discussed, who are involved inappropriately with SSI or with Cliff Hawkins?"

Billy Ray thought for a moment. "I don't know her name, but I believe Cliff is friends with a woman in your human resources department. Cliff and SSI's office manager, who's a lesbian by the way, occasionally have dinner with this woman. I think Alex has joined them at times; maybe the four of them even took a trip together. But I don't know her name."

"Thanks, Billy Ray, you've been a big help. At this point I don't expect to contact you again unless something else comes up where we would need your input," Landon said, reaching out to shake hands.

"Man, that's a relief," Billy Ray said, smiling from ear to ear. "I feel like the weight of the world has been lifted off my shoulders. I don't mind telling you, I hate Cliff Hawkins. I hope you put that slime-pit out of business."

On the flight back to Tampa the two men talked very little. Landon ordered a double scotch on the rocks and spent most of the trip with his head back and eyes closed.

"Do you know who was he talking about in our human resources group?" Bruner asked just before they landed.

"I'm not positive, but I have someone in mind. If it's who I think it is, it's a woman we already know about." After a moment's hesitation, Landon sighed. "It's an ugly world we live in, Bruner, and the older I get, the uglier it seems to become."

"Do you still think David may somehow be involved?"

Landon's concerns regarding Alex seemed to have been confirmed beyond a reasonable doubt. He hated the thought of being the one to destroy Alex's life because he was a friend. But the case against him was rapidly taking on a life of its own, and Bruner was documenting every detail. On the other hand, David's apparent lack of knowledge and involvement was an ironic twist that Landon was having a hard time admitting even to himself.

"It's looking doubtful, but who knows? I would never have believed that Alex could be involved, but that seems to be the case. So I'm not ready to rule out David yet. If we do determine with reasonable assurance that he had knowledge, any knowledge, of what's been going on, I will personally fire him."

Landon closed his eyes as though trying to sleep, but he knew there would be little sleep for him that night. He was saddened by Billy Ray's admissions and sickened by the whole sordid mess. A wave of nausea swept over him as he realized what the fiasco would do to his own career. With Bruner involved in every detail, there was no way Landon could avoid being blamed by the bigwigs in Houston, especially by those who didn't like him in the first place. The more he pondered his fate, the more resentment he felt towards both Alex and David—Alex for the betrayal of trust and David for not somehow knowing what was going on, and for making a big deal out of his friendship with Alex.

He had hoped that Billy Ray would provide something, even if only a reasonable doubt, regarding David's involvement. But that didn't happen. His last hope for implicating David would be Alex in the meeting the following morning. If it didn't happen then, David would be off the hook and he would be on it. It didn't take a genius to know that Jim Hargrove would sacrifice him without a second thought rather than jeopardize his own reputation.

The day of reckoning for Alex was at hand, and a verdict had been reached in the courtroom of Landon's mind, even though Alex had yet to take the stand. David's punishment would come later. Landon would somehow see to that.

Part 2

The Calm

CHAPTER 13

David Coleman

After finishing high school, John Coleman left Brooksville, Mississippi, hitchhiked his way to Birmingham, and went to work as a mill hand for U.S. Steel. He spent forty-two years there as a blue-collar worker. A quiet, hard-working man with a tender heart, he never realized his ambition to own and operate his own service station.

Alice Kyle Coleman graduated from Birmingham Southern College and became an elementary school teacher. Even though she was better educated than her husband, she never questioned John's role as head of the family. In those days, the husband was head of the household by definition, and the fact that he was eight years her senior served to further validate his role. Their marriage was in some ways dysfunctional, but no better or no worse than most marriages during the thirties, forties, and fifties. Family, church, and job defined life for Alice. For John, it was shift work, family, and, at times, coon hunting and a jug of moonshine.

In 1946 a son, David Riley, was born to John and Alice Coleman.

David's childhood could best be described as happy and uncomplicated. An exceptional athlete and an excellent student, he signed a football scholarship with the University of Alabama upon graduating from high school. His dream of playing four years for Coach Paul "Bear" Bryant ended abruptly when a knee injury at the beginning of his sophomore year sidelined him permanently. Later, he was elected president of the student body and at graduation was recognized as the outstanding senior in the College of Engineering.

Leah Ansley was born in Montgomery, Alabama, also to a middle class family. Her mother worked nights in a local cotton mill during World War II, while her father served in the Navy. After the war, they moved to Birmingham, where he worked in a foundry and her mother answered phones and filed records at a doctor's office.

Despite the inequalities imposed by racism, whatever animosities present were not evident in the tranquility that generally existed throughout the South. People in Alabama knew their neighbors for blocks around. Evenings were spent on family activities, from sitting on the porch talking or playing cards, to listening to the radio. On Saturday nights, families would often go to a movie, which on weekends was a double feature, one of which was invariably a western. Divorce was frowned upon and crime, virtually nonexistent. Homes were seldom locked, and children played outdoors day or night without concern for their safety. It was not Camelot, but it was a simpler time, and David and Leah were products of that culture. The values that permeated their childhoods shaped the adults that they became.

They met and fell in love as sophomores in high school. He was tall and handsome; she, a beautiful, brown-eyed Southern Belle. She led the cheers while he led the football team to the Alabama state high school championship. They married after David's freshman year at Alabama and a year later, became parents.

David's collegiate achievements caught the eye of a recruiter for Pyramid International. He was flattered by the company's interest in him and impressed by the quality of managers he met during his interview in Houston. After joining Pyramid, he and Leah were transferred from place to place every year or two, and with each move he climbed another rung up the corporate ladder.

In 1973, the Arab countries formed a cartel and imposed an oil embargo. Energy prices skyrocketed. Recognizing their vulnerability and the need to secure additional energy reserves, Pyramid immediately began buying the mineral rights on land containing oil, coal, and gas resources, particularly throughout the mountain states. David was put in charge of Pyramid's holdings in Colorado, and for the next several years the Colemans made Denver their home.

In 1979 an investment group approached David to head up a new company. The plan was to purchase and develop properties adjacent to existing and proposed ski slopes in anticipation of the inevitable growth that was taking place in Colorado. Before making a decision, David sought advice from his friends at Pyramid. The company had been good to them, and he felt obligated to seek their counsel and blessings. By cashing out their assets, the Colemans were able to raise their share of the investment needed to start Capital Enterprises of the Rockies. For the next few years, the company prospered beyond their wildest dreams.

The oil cartel collapsed in 1982 and with it, the prices for oil, coal, and natural gas produced within the United States. From Texas to Alaska, energy development skidded to a halt. Land investors throughout the region withdrew from the market, reversing the buying frenzy and propelling land values downward. The Colemans, who had used their share of the profits to buy out most of the other partners in the company, took a major hit as the country spiraled into a severe recession.

David tried to liquidate their land holdings to meet the balloon payments coming due on his loans. The debts, many of which he had personally guaranteed, were too large to resolve, and some of their lenders felt no compunction to negotiate settlements. Several million dollars in debt, the Colemans ignored their lawyer's advice to file for bankruptcy and determined to somehow work out settlements with their creditors in an honorable manner, no matter the sacrifice. Over the next three years, they watched their assets disappear. David successfully negotiated settlements on most of the properties by trading equity in some to service debts on others. Eventually the only asset left was their home.

In view of the dismal prospects for a turnaround in the near future and the likelihood they would eventually end up filing for bankruptcy anyway, they sold their home, packed up their belongings and moved to Florida.

Soon after arriving in West Palm Beach, he accepted a job as division manager with a construction company. Leah found a job as receptionist for a law firm. With both working, they were able to make ends meet but unable to make a dent in the outstanding debts left behind in Colorado. Hanging over their heads was the two-million-dollar note he had personally guaranteed for a townhouse project in Beaver Creek. Some banks had been willing to accept discounted payments for loans made during the boom years, but not Pacific Trust.

Pacific Trust refused to negotiate with the Colemans, instead hounding them for payment. Each month a registered letter came threatening legal action if payment against the note was not received, and reminding them that Pacific Trust was prepared to wait the statutory limit of twenty years, if necessary, to collect. Every six months the bank would demand a financial statement, and each time the Colemans responded, they would get a certified letter back challenging the accuracy of the information they had just provided.

The years and the demands took their toll, especially on David. Finally giving in to Leah's urgings, he agreed to file for bankruptcy.

Although the bankruptcy brought an end to the harassment by Pacific Trust, it also ruined the Coleman's credit rating, effectively ending his dream of once again owning his own business. Besides, starting over would also require energy—more energy than he had to give. He needed time to heal. Moving ahead was their only option because looking back was too painful.

Out of desperation, he contacted his old employer, Pyramid International, even though he knew it was Pyramid's policy not to rehire employees who had left the company. Two weeks after sending them his résumé, he received an invitation to interview for an environmental position with their marketing division, Expressway Inc., in Tampa. He hoped this would be the opportunity they needed to get them back on their feet.

When he entered Expressway's lobby, David was met by an attractive, middle-age woman who introduced herself as Mary Fisher, executive assistant to the division president.

116

"I understand from Mr. Snelling that you two are old friends," she said. "Since he was in town yesterday for a meeting, he decided to stay over and meet with you himself."

"Yes, ma'am, that's right. I knew Steve when I was with Pyramid back in the seventies. I left in 1979 to seek my fortune."

"And did you find it?" she asked with a smile.

"Yes, but unfortunately, I also lost it."

"From what I've heard, you still have many friends in Pyramid. I know Mr. Snelling's looking forward to seeing you. I suppose you know he's now President and Chairman of the Board for Pyramid International. With him on your side, I'd say your chances of coming back are pretty darn good."

David's hopes soared.

Mary ushered him to Jim Hargrove's lavishly decorated office, then stepped aside as soon as they entered. Steve Snelling was already heading toward him, hand extended and a broad grin filling his face.

"It's been a long time, David. Good to see you. You look great, really great."

"That just shows how deceiving looks can be, Steve. It's good to see you, too. It's hard to believe it's been almost ten years."

"David, I want you to meet Jim Hargrove, division president of Expressway, and Landon Walters, Jim's right-hand man. Landon is both an economist and attorney, which, as you can appreciate, is a hell of a combination in this business."

It occurred to him that Jim looked like a man who either had a drinking problem or had had one in the past. His large, yellow teeth gave testimony to many years as a smoker, and his physical appearance suggested he had not yet bought into a lifestyle featuring exercise and a low-fat diet. There was something about him, however, perhaps his big boyish grin, that told David this man had never met a stranger.

"Good to meet you, David," Jim said, pushing himself up from his chair. "Steve has told me all about you and your glory days with Pyramid. According to him, you were a rising star before going off on your own. How does it feel to be interviewing with the very

117

company where you started, some…what is it now, six or eight years ago?"

"It's been longer than that," David answered, reaching out to shake Jim's hand. "And to answer your question, it feels good. I'm grateful for the opportunity. Pyramid was always good to my family and me, and we owe the company a lot. Maybe their investment in me back then will pay off yet."

"Please sit down, fellas," Steve said, turning toward the door. "Mary, we'll need some coffee, and bring another cup for David." Once Mary had left, he turned his attention back to David. "Last I heard, you were buying up half of Colorado and taking options on the rest. What happened?"

Before responding, David leaned over to shake hands with Landon, who had remained seated on the couch. He appeared to be a tall, gaunt man, most likely in his mid to late thirties. "Don't bother to get up," David said with a grin, hoping to lighten the somewhat awkward moment. Landon responded with a polite smile and nod.

After taking a seat David answered, "As you well know, Steve, the bottom fell out of the energy business after the Arabs started cheating on each other in the early eighties. I didn't see it coming, and by the time I got up to speed, it was too late. But in the process, I learned a good…no, let me correct that…I learned an expensive lesson."

"And that was?" Steve asked grinning broadly, turning to wink at Jim Hargrove.

"That leveraging property may be a great strategy when the economy is on the upswing, but those balloon notes turn into barracudas when land values start falling. Leah and I did well for the first few years. In fact, another few years like those and we could've owned our own island somewhere, or at least a part of one. Unfortunately, that wasn't to be, and by the time we left Colorado, we were lucky to get out with the shirts on our backs."

"Sounds like you have a few regrets," Steve said, looking over the top of his glasses, which were sitting well down his nose.

"Yeah, a few I guess," David replied, glancing at the others in the room. "But if I had it to do all over again, I'd do about the same thing. I had an opportunity few men ever have—to build a business from scratch. If I hadn't taken it, I would have always regretted not doing it and spent the rest of my life wondering what might have been. I've learned a lot about people, most of all about myself. But that's history. I'm ready to move on, Steve, hopefully with the company."

"So what brought you to Florida?"

"Leah and I tried for several years to negotiate our way out of debt, but that wasn't to be either. You might as well know up front that we've recently filed for bankruptcy."

"Happens to the best, my boy," Steve replied without hesitation. "Mitchell Powers, the ex-senator and a good friend of mine, recently had to do the same thing for about the same reason. As they say, no guts, no glory. Speaking of Leah, how's she doing? I was always fond of that woman."

"Thanks for asking. She's fine...never complains."

"I'm sorry your business didn't work out," Steve said, "but we may have an opportunity here at Expressway that will be of interest."

David's heart skipped a beat as the cloud that had hung over him since the loss of his business began to lift. Only the lack of enthusiasm on the faces of the other two men dampened his spirits, but he dismissed it. Steve had enough for all three, and he was, after all, the *big* man.

"As I said earlier," Steve continued, "Jim's president of our marketing division. In Jim's division, we operate a chain of convenience stores selling under the Expressway sign. Our stores move close to 70 percent of the gasoline produced in our refineries. That guarantees a sales base for our products, leaving only 30 percent to sell on the open market."

"I understand that you're currently working in construction and hold a pretty responsible position," Jim interjected. "Raises a bit of a question in my mind as to why you contacted us." David detected the reserved tone that bordered on coldness.

"That's a good question, Jim, and I'm glad you asked it. I do have a responsible job that pays well, but money has never been my primary motivation. Although my job is plenty challenging, it's not what I want to do long term. I miss being part of a team, being associated with professionals like you, and I simply miss being a part of Pyramid, which was once like family. Construction is a tough, competitive, cutthroat business. For me, there has to be more purpose in my job than just trying to squeeze every dime out of every project. Bottom line—my confidence in the management team at Pyramid and the fact that I always loved working for the company. That's why I'm here."

David's answer was obviously as good as Steve could have hoped for, as he looked first to Jim and then to Landon with an 'I told you so' look on his face and a smile as big as Texas.

After acknowledging Steve's smile, Jim continued, this time with less edge in his voice than before. "Did personnel explain the position we have open?"

"To some extent. Manager of special projects, as I recall."

"That's right. The position reports to Landon, to whom I've recently given the responsibility for our new environmental program, in addition to those he as for our law department. Your experience in construction and land acquisition could also fit in nicely down the road, once we get past the compliance issues. How much do you know about environmental regulations?"

"Not much, I'm afraid, but I'm a fast learner. I've never had the luxury of prior experience going into any job I've held."

Steve interrupted, "Jim, take my word for it, David can handle the job. He's already proven to me what he can do. If he can't handle it, I don't know who can."

"I'm sure he can," Jim replied evenly. He turned to David. "As I said, you would be reporting to Landon. Our counselor here joined us right out of law school where he was top in his class at Ole Miss. You'd be working for the best," he said, obviously proud of his young attorney. David looked at Landon, expecting some type of a response. Landon returned his look with a blank stare.

Sensing that Jim had turned the discussion over to him, Landon handed David a thin pamphlet. "Here's a copy of the

Underground Storage Tank Regulations. We have to implement these rules over the next ten years. You'd be responsible for putting together a staff to manage the upgrading of our facilities and for cleaning up the locations where gasoline has leaked into the ground."

"How's that done?" David asked.

"The contaminated soil can be dug up and replaced, but it must be disposed of properly. As we speak, new technologies are being developed that leave the soil in place while selectively removing the gasoline. If the groundwater beneath the site is impacted, it has to be treated, too. In fact, it's the groundwater that is of primary concern since much of the country gets its drinking water from underground aquifers."

"I've managed a lot of projects over the years," David said with growing confidence, "and I'm sure if given a chance, I can handle this job. I promise you one thing, I'll certainly do my best."

For the next thirty minutes the men discussed how the department would be organized and some of the more urgent matters needing attention. As they were about to conclude the meeting, Landon brought up one last topic.

"We have someone in mind who, we feel, would be a great asset to you in managing the regulatory issues. His name is Alex Carter. He sent us his résumé about six weeks ago, and when he received our standard 'thanks but no thanks,' he drove down from Atlanta and waited in the parking lot one morning for Jim to arrive. Alex isn't a man who takes no for an answer. When Jim arrived, he introduced himself and said he wanted to work for Expressway.

"Jim was impressed and asked me to interview him, which I did. Alex convinced me that he should be on our team. He could be a key man in our new organization, especially in view of your lack of experience in this area. He has been working as manager of environmental compliance at a large hazardous waste plant near Atlanta. He has over ten years experience in the business, and I think he's someone you'll need."

"I'd like to meet him, and if he is as good as he sounds, I'm sure I'd be fortunate to have him on board," David said, "assuming, of course, that I'm offered and accept the job." David sensed that hiring Alex was a forgone conclusion to which he was expected to agree.

"You'll receive our official offer tomorrow, but take it from the horse's mouth, the job is yours if you want it," Steve replied with a big grin. "And I can assure you, salary will not be a problem."

"Gentlemen," David said, looking at each of them, "I appreciate being considered for this opportunity, but I want to make it very clear, if I haven't already, that I will be starting at ground zero in the environmental business."

Steve leaned forward and looked him squarely in the eye. "David, we can hire technical knowledge like this Alex fellow apparently has, and we realize you will need that type of support, at least for a while. What we can't go out and hire is someone with proven integrity. The person we want in this job must be someone who will protect the public trust we've spent so many years developing. One screw up could cost the company more than all of us combined will make in our lifetimes. I'm not speaking just for myself...although as chairman of the board, my opinion does carry a little weight around here. David, you have the confidence of Pyramid's senior management team. You've got other friends besides me in Houston who will be very disappointed if you don't take this job. We need you in this organization, and I won't take no for an answer. Have I made myself clear?"

Given Steve's vote of confidence and the opportunity the position represented, David felt both excited and relieved. He could go home and tell Leah that the end to their problems was in sight. They'd come full circle. Good times waited just around the corner.

CHAPTER 14

Three weeks after his interview at Expressway, David walked into the lobby as a new employee. On his second day, he met and interviewed Alex Carter, a meeting that had been arranged by Landon. Alex was friendly and outgoing, a handsome, dark-complexioned man in his early forties with a ready smile and a lively sense of humor. Below the surface, however, there was something about Alex that soon reminded David of a boss he once had. That man had had a king-size ego and enjoyed flexing his muscle with those he deemed to be beneath him. Fortunately, David had only worked with the man for a short period, but it was long enough to make a lasting impression. He dismissed that small red flag as unwarranted paranoia based on a single bad experience

David explained his inexperience with environmental laws and his need for a right-hand man to handle the regulatory matters and bring him up to speed. Alex assured him he was indeed the man for the job and would gladly accept whatever position was available, assuming the pay was right.

During the interview and later when the two met with Landon for lunch, Alex peppered the conversation with environmental jargon. David tried to temper his annoyance at the apparent jab at his own lack of expertise in that arena. Once more he gave Alex the benefit of the doubt. With such an enthusiastic endorsement by Jim and Landon, he didn't feel justified in questioning their judgment without something more substantial than a gut feeling. So after another review of the man's experience, David notified Carol Shanks in personnel to extend the employment offer. Two weeks later, Alex moved into the office next to David's.

On Thursday of David's second week at Expressway, he learned from his administrative assistant that Landon had not favored hiring him. She'd overheard Landon saying he would have preferred someone with extensive environmental experience and ideally an attorney, but under pressure from above had reluctantly agreed to go along with the decision to hire David. The red flags that had popped up during his interview and that had since resurfaced could no longer be ignored. David asked Landon for a meeting the following morning to discuss the matter.

Jim and Landon were already deep in conversation when he arrived. Jim was seated behind the desk and Landon in the chair directly across from him.

"David, have a seat," Jim said, motioning toward the couch instead of the chair next to Landon. "I understand you have a matter you wish to discuss with the two of us." His tone lacked any warmth, and his manner was strictly business.

"Yes I do, and I'll come right to the point," David replied just as firmly. "I've heard from a reliable source that Landon was not in favor of my being offered this job due to my lack of experience. If that's the case, I'm not sure it's in our best interests, either yours or mine, for me to continue here. I believe I made it very clear from the outset that I didn't have environmental experience. Since you still offered me the position, I assumed I would be given the opportunity to prove myself." He paused for a moment. "Of course, I could be misinformed about Landon's reservations, and if so, I apologize for this entire matter. But I believe we need to be up front with one another, and I want to start out on that basis."

Jim and Landon exchanged glances before Landon replied. "Originally, that was true. I did have reservations, but only because of your admitted lack of experience. In view of the complexity of the regulations and the liabilities, I felt someone with previous experience both in legal issues and in managing environmental programs would have been a better choice. I'll come back to this in a minute because it is an area that you need to fully appreciate.

"Although I expressed my concerns to the chairman, he was convinced that you had the proven leadership ability, not to mention the respect and confidence of other managers within Pyramid. I still have those concerns, but given the support of an experienced staff and the appropriate time to learn the regulations, I'm comfortable with the decision and with you.

"We believe," Landon continued, "that Alex will make up in environmental knowledge what you lack at this time. Actually, Alex wanted your job, but our assessment was that he may be somewhat weak in administrative skills, plus he's still an unknown quantity. You, on the other hand, have an impeccable track record with the company. We're not about to turn over a program of this magnitude to someone in whom we don't have total confidence."

The words sounded good, but the lack of friendliness in Landon's demeanor troubled David. This young attorney was impossible to read. Resigning himself to the fact that it was either a technique Landon had learned or that the man was simply lacking in personality, David responded after a few tense moments of silence.

"I understand your concern, but I assure you, I've gone into other jobs with little or no experience, and I've always handled them successfully. If given the support I need upfront, I'm sure I can manage this department. Management involves providing leadership and working with people to accomplish desired goals. I have years of experience doing just that, and I believe my interpersonal skills have been thoroughly tested and proven. I'll tell you what, Landon, if you aren't satisfied with the results in six months, I'll give you your money back and resign."

Jim let out a belly laugh. Landon did not appear to be amused.

"I must explain certain aspects of this position which you need to understand clearly," Landon continued without a trace of a smile. "There are major risks inherent for those of us who are responsible for enforcing the company's environmental policies and also risks to the company's reputation. I'll start with the company first. I'm sure you read about the incident in Bhopal, India, several years ago where a Union Carbide plant released toxic gas that resulted in the deaths of thousands of people. Since the Bhopal incident, the public has become sensitized to environmental issues.

"Farmers now know about the toxicity of insecticides because the EPA has taken many of them off the market. Housewives read labels on cleaning products, such as detergents, that list all the hazards related to their use. Kids in school learn about environmental responsibility. My little girl can tell you how many acres of the Amazon rain forest are being cut or burned every day. Politicians are being elected or rejected based, in part, on whether or not they are sympathetic to environmental issues. Preachers even speak out from their pulpits against pollution. Protecting the environment is one of the hottest social issues out there. It's not even open to debate. It's a given. Granted, much of it is hype being generated by the tree huggers and reported by the media."

Both David and Jim were nodding their agreement.

"We market gasoline in thirty or so states through our own retail operations. Every fill-up can potentially result in a spill. Fortunately, most are just small ones. A certain percentage of these spills occur when a customer is busy doing something else while his tank is filling and the automatic shut off valve fails to stop the flow when it should. The first time he may notice the problem is when gasoline is pouring out onto the pavement. One carelessly tossed cigarette could cause a life-threatening event. Since gasoline fumes are heavier than air, they can quickly find their way from the spill into a neighbor's basement next door. Under the right conditions, when their furnace or water heater kicks on, it could blow the place up and people along with it. I could go on and on, but the point is that there are many serious risks to the public and enormous exposure to the company from a public relations angle.

"The public will not tolerate mistakes where the environment is concerned. An embarrassing incident would result in bad publicity for Expressway, and bad publicity translates into lower gasoline sales. It's your job to ensure that Expressway is never exposed to an environmental incident that would offend the public or embarrass our stockholders."

At that point, Landon stopped talking and just stared at David as though expecting him to hoist a white handkerchief. Getting no response, he continued, elbows on his knees and leaning forward in

David's direction. "Congress, in its infinite wisdom, has included civil and criminal penalties for those who violate environmental laws. The EPA offers rewards to employees who report their employer for a concealed violation. This is referred to as the whistle-blower law. Federal sentencing guidelines have been proposed which stipulate how many months in jail a particular offense carries. Violations are given a numerical rating, and depending upon various factors, a minimum jail sentence is determined. If convicted, the responsible parties face a mandatory federal sentence. That means the convicted persons must, and I repeat *must*, serve the full time.

"What I'm getting at, David, is that in today's environmentally regulated society, managers either follow the laws to the letter or risk personal fines and jail time, or perhaps both. The enforcement arm of the EPA is being beefed up to catch violators. The federal judiciary system has been instructed to prosecute whenever a conviction is likely, especially if an injury occurred, or if the violation was willfully committed.

"You and I must see to it that no Expressway employee, and especially our senior management, is ever prosecuted for an environmental crime. Even if Expressway only gets named in an indictment and we later prove our innocence, the adverse publicity will generate dozens of frivolous lawsuits from people looking for an out-of-court settlement. Those who live next door to our operations will claim that we have somehow caused damage to their property, their health, or to their quality of life. Am I making myself clear?"

For the first time, David realized the time bomb he'd inherited. He felt at risk personally by the responsibilities of the job, liabilities he may not have accepted had he known them prior to his coming onboard. Glancing first at Jim and then to Landon, he replied, "Yes, you are. I understand your concern for hiring me in the first place. I wasn't aware that criminal prosecution was possible, and obviously that concerns me, as it would anyone. What happens if I or one of my staff is indicted for something about which we had no knowledge?"

"We will serve as your defense," Landon responded coldly, "unless it's an illegal act willfully committed. If that's the case, you're

127

on your own and personally responsible for your defense and for any fines. The law mandates that. This is why I would have preferred someone more versed in the regulations, but I also recognize and respect Steve's position. You have years of proven experience in managing projects and in handling sizable investments for Pyramid. Obviously, we need someone managing this program who, above all else, is honest, can manage people, and can administrate multiple projects."

Throughout Landon's comments, David had listened intently and tried to read between the lines. He'd never met anyone who was harder to connect with on a personal level. It was clear that Landon Walters was not as approachable as David would have preferred. In the past, he'd always become friends with his boss. That did not appear likely this time around.

"I appreciate your candor," David said. "I want to assure both you and Jim that I won't let you down. I'll do whatever it takes to manage this program responsibly while protecting the company's interests. I don't know what more I can do."

Jim rose and stuck out his hand. "That's good enough for me. I hope we understand one another now. What say we go to work and try to make this company some money?" With that, the meeting was adjourned. *I believe I could become friends with Jim,* David thought as he headed back toward his office, *but with Landon, it could be a different story.* He felt somewhat encouraged that they had talked and apparently made progress in getting a better feel for each other. The new job was not exactly what he'd bargained for, but it was a job with a company he respected, and at this point, he had no choice but to make a go of it.

Except for Alex and Landon, Expressway's organization had little or no experience with environmental law. Prior to the recently enacted Underground Storage Tank Regulations, the gasoline retail business had been virtually unregulated. The staff David inherited, for the most part, was made up of people who were expendable in their previous jobs within Expressway. Isaac Malone, a man in his mid-fifties, had been a one-man environmental department for the past ten years, but had no experience with the new regulations. He'd spent most of his time in recent years obtaining the various permits needed to open or operate stores in the various states.

Although David liked Isaac immediately, it took only a couple of weeks for him to realize that the man was administratively incompetent. The white-haired, pipe-smoking grandfather was as affable as he could be, but he had apparently managed to survive by making friends with the bureaucrats in the various regulatory agencies. By the end of his first month, David knew Isaac was in way over his head and decided to voice his concerns to Landon.

"If you have a few minutes, I'd like to speak privately with you about Isaac," David said as he stepped through the open doorway of Landon's office.

The attorney looked up without comment and nodded for him to close the door. Following the rather volatile meeting he had had with Jim Hargrove and Landon a few weeks before, it had seemed to David that Landon had gone out of his way to avoid him. Since that meeting the two had only met briefly a few times to discuss programs that Landon felt important. On each of those occasions, the conversation had been strictly business, with Landon showing no interest in getting to know David or anything about his personal life.

David began by explaining the areas of concern he had with Isaac's performance, while praising him for his strengths, especially his relationships with the state regulators. After describing in detail Isaac's administrative weaknesses, he suggested that Isaac's job be redefined to take advantage of his business relationships, while at the same time relieving him of his administrative duties.

As David continued to talk, he could see Landon's displeasure growing by the set of his jaw and his labored breathing. By the time he had finished, he wondered if Landon had accepted anything he'd said.

"No, you're not touching Isaac or his job," Landon responded emphatically. "He is this department. He's spent his entire career with Expressway, and he taught me a lot about the environmental business. He's also managed to get us out of some tight spots over the years." Landon's flushed face matched his bulging eyes.

"My guess," David replied in an even tone, "is that most of those tight spots were ones he had gotten us into in the first place."

Landon's eyes widened further, his lips tightened, and his jaw muscles throbbed noticeably. With the exception of Jim Hargrove, no one ever challenged his opinions and certainly not someone who reported to him. Refusing to be denied, David continued.

"This guy is going to get us into real trouble if we don't move him out of that job. I don't think Isaac has kept half the documents we're required to have on hand, and if the EPA were to audit us, I doubt he could find many of the ones we do have."

Landon's face had grown quite red with veins protruding noticeably on his neck. "I said no! I will *not* hurt that man. He and I sail together, we fish together, he even stayed with me at the hospital the night my daughter was born. Demoting him is out of the question! Do you understand?"

David realized he should have stopped at that point, but he didn't. "No, I don't understand, and it needn't be called a demotion. It's my responsibility, as I understand it, to manage this department and to keep this company in compliance with environmental laws. I've inherited someone who probably never should have been in his job in the first place. Before the new regulations, things might have been different, but all of that has changed now, and we're regulated to the hilt. My recommendation, and I'll put this in writing if need be, is to reassign Isaac and place him under an experienced administrator. I won't be responsible for the violations resulting from his incompetence."

Landon abruptly stood and began moving around the desk toward David. "I think you've said enough. In fact, you've said too much! You've got a job to do, so get out there and do it. You're the first person who has ever said one negative thing about Isaac," he said through clenched teeth. His face and ears were now aflame. "You've been here for one month, and all of a sudden you're ready to pass judgment on Isaac, accusing him of incompetence. He's not incompetent in my opinion, and I'll not listen to anymore of this, do you understand?" By then Landon was standing directly in front of him, his face only inches from David's.

David backed away a step and this time chose not to dispute Landon's statement. The two men glared hotly at each other, almost

130

as if daring the other to blink. It was clear Landon was unable to separate his personal feelings for Isaac from the facts, which, in David's judgment, should have been obvious to anyone. He suspected that Landon's apparent dislike for him, for reasons he had not yet figured out, could also be affecting his judgment. He knew from past experience that drawing against the Lone Ranger was not smart, and Landon's gun fired silver bullets. That had been made clear the day they had met in Jim's office. David had no choice but to cut his losses for the time being and defer the matter until later. Perhaps after he had developed a better relationship with his boss, he would bring it up again. One thing was certain—Landon was an impulsive hothead, not a quality any company should tolerate in a manager at his level.

"Okay, you're the boss, but I'm going to write a letter for the file, noting that you rejected my recommendation about Isaac. I'm sorry this has turned into an argument. I had hoped to receive an impartial hearing in this matter." With that, David turned to leave, shaken by what had transpired. Although the door had been closed, he figured others had heard their raised voices.

"I don't care what you put in the file," Landon exploded as David reached for the door. "Just remember, you're not the only one who can write a letter to file."

Unfortunately, that confrontation was only the first of many the two men had over the next few years. Virtually every recommendation David made thereafter was summarily rejected, many of which Landon was later forced to adopt. Landon never acknowledged errors in his judgment, nor did he in this matter, even after being forced by circumstances to terminate Isaac two years later. In 1992, the EPA's Region IV office in Atlanta requested certain compliance records for the 1989 to 1990 period. Just as David had suspected, the documents were nowhere to be found.

The EPA investigation also discovered that Isaac had secretly authorized certain activities prohibited by the new regulations. Between legal fees, fines, and the rework necessary in the field, damages to Expressway reached well over two million dollars, not to mention a certain amount of negative publicity for the company.

A senior executive in Houston demanded that the responsible parties be terminated. Since Landon could not protect Isaac without admitting his own involvement, he personally handled the matter. In view of the man's thirty-seven years of service with the company, he was allowed to take early retirement. David always wondered to what extent Landon might have implicated him, but he never knew for sure.

CHAPTER 15

Alex Carter

Times were hard during the depression, and nowhere much harder than on the Carter farm outside Carrolton, Georgia. Alex's grandfather, Russell Carter, spent his mornings as a rural mail carrier before heading for the fields to work his crops. The day for him and his wife, Sarah, started before sunrise and ended when they were both too exhausted to do another thing. On Sundays they rested, like most folks did in the Bible belt. Alex's father, Joe, was the youngest of the Carter children.

Their two-story clapboard house sat at the southeast corner of the 160-acre farm that had been in the family since before the Civil War. Union forces had once camped in the pasture just west of the house and before moving on into Alabama had set fire to the barns. Somehow that long ago act seemed to provide added determination to their battle for survival.

By the time Joe finished high school, he had long since decided to leave the farm and find a paying job in the big city of Atlanta. Five years later he met Emily Glover, and soon afterwards they were married by a justice of the peace. He had established himself as one of the up-and-coming salesmen for the Liberty of Georgia Insurance Company. One day after they celebrated their first anniversary, Sue was born, followed four years later by Alex and two years after that by Bob.

What began as a happy marriage began to deteriorate during their third year. Although Emily loved Joe and tried hard to measure up to his expectations, he soon began to lose interest in her. She suspected that he was seeing other women, but she never confronted him with her suspicions. She just worked all the harder to please him. As his affection for Emily waned, his devotion for Sue increased. By the time Alex came along, Sue had become Joe's pride and joy—the most important person in his life. Joe would teasingly say to Emily, "I've got my little girl, and now you have yourself a boy." Emily knew Joe no longer cared for her the way he had at first; however, she was careful never to complain. It was better to have a dissatisfied man than no man at all.

Shortly after Alex was born, Joe was fired for drinking on the job and for womanizing, and he was unable to find another company willing to hire a salesman of questionable character. His only other skills were those learned as a boy on the farm, where for years he had helped his father repair their farming equipment. Eventually, he landed a job as a mechanic near their duplex apartment.

Emily's mother, a widow, worked evenings as a switchboard operator at Marietta's Good Samaritan Hospital. Knowing that her daughter's marriage was in trouble, she offered to loan them five hundred dollars for a down payment on a home. Emily hoped that owning a home would renew Joe's sense of family and hold their shaky marriage together. The small, two-bedroom house was only a few blocks from her mother's and about twenty minutes from Joe's garage. Emily never seriously considered taking a job outside the home, but, like many women of her generation, stayed home to raise the children. She helped some by taking in sewing and ironing from their neighbors.

Joe, on the other hand, grew more miserable with each passing year. He felt trapped by a wife he did not love, kids he could not afford, and a job that offered no hope for advancement. He viewed his future much like a prisoner who was doing life without parole. By the age of thirty-one, he had become a bona fide alcoholic. They were trapped, he by the responsibility to put food on the table and she by the family's dependence on him for financial survival. Joe made no effort to hide his affection for Sue and his total disinterest in his sons.

Emily developed mixed feelings toward her daughter. Maternal love on one hand gave way to resentment and jealousy on the other. Partly to punish Joe and partly to fill her arms with someone to love, Emily transferred her affections to Alex. He was a beautiful little boy with mischievous brown eyes and a ready smile exposing perfect little teeth. His personality captivated everyone.

The couple's bondage came to an abrupt end early one Sunday morning. The coroner's report stated that Joe was intoxicated at the time of the accident and had apparently fallen asleep at the wheel. The car crashed into a bridge abutment, instantly killing him and his two hunting buddies. The only survivors were the two blue-tick hounds locked in the trunk. Although he had once been one of the top insurance salesmen in the state, his own policy totaled a mere two thousand dollars. After paying the funeral expenses, Emily was left with four hundred dollars, three kids to raise, and a monthly house payment...and with neither marketable job skills nor work experience.

Through the efforts of Joe's friends at the insurance company, she was offered a clerical job in the same office where he had once worked. At first she only filed, but she soon taught herself to type and within a year was helping to process claims. After two years she was promoted to claims administrator, a job she held for the rest of her working career. With her mother's daily assistance, she managed to provide a relatively stable life for the children.

At the time of Joe's death, the relationships between Emily and the children were firmly established. Alex was always her favorite, with Bob a distant second. Although she tried to embrace Sue and fill the void left by Joe's death, mother and daughter never connected.

She worked hard at the office, often not taking a break for lunch. After work, she rushed home, arriving just in time for her mother to dash off for her evening shift at the hospital. Supper needed fixing, and there were dishes to wash, clothes to clean, ironing to do, and kids to bathe. Weekends brought house cleaning and grass cutting chores.

During the months following Joe's death, men occasionally asked her out for dinner or to go to the movies, but few came back a second time after seeing her needy brood. She didn't want to be clingy, but she couldn't help herself. She had no life of her own and no immediate prospects for improvement.

A year after Joe's accident, Emily began drinking for the first time in her life. It started innocently. One night while cleaning the last of Joe's belongings out of a closet, she found a bottle of whiskey hidden in a shoebox. Recalling the giddiness she'd felt as a teenager after her first and only experience with alcohol, she fixed herself a whiskey and 7-Up™ highball. It helped her relax and seemed to free her from the depression that wrapped her in a black cloud. At first she drank to relax; later, to escape; eventually, because she couldn't help herself. Typically, she indulged in a highball while preparing supper. Following a stressful day at work or on those nights when she was more depressed than usual, she treated herself to a nightcap after putting the kids to bed. Just two drinks per evening…that was her self-imposed limit.

The summer of '62 was one of the hottest on record in Georgia, setting a new high almost daily. Sue, age fourteen, had complained for months about wanting more privacy. She and her mother shared one bed, with the boys each having a twin bed in the other bedroom. To accommodate Sue's pleadings—or perhaps to shush her endless complaining—Emily agreed for her to change places with Alex. The kids were getting old enough to need their own privacy, but she hoped to buy a little time before having to purchase a larger home. In the meantime she planned to add a room divider between the twin beds to give Sue more privacy.

It happened on a sweltering night that August. Emily arrived home one evening more depressed than usual. Just before quiting time, she'd had an argument with her boss and been raked over the coals. Then she came home to squabbling kids and an empty refrigerator. The house had no air conditioner, just a window fan for moving air through. The thermometer on the porch read ninety degrees and the humidity hung in the air like a wet blanket. It was definitely a two-highball night. After putting the kids down, she sat out on the porch swinging until about ten o'clock. Before running a bath, she broke her own rule and fixed another drink.

136

As she lay in the tub sipping her drink, her thoughts turned, as they did from time to time, to the first night she spent with Joe. Never before or since had she felt such desire or felt more desired. Savoring every detail, she played the scene over and over in her mind.

After drying off, she wrapped herself in a towel and staggered toward the bedroom. By the time she knew she'd had too much to drink, it was too late. Closing the door, she let the towel drop to the floor and stood in front of the mirror above the dressing table, turning first one way, then another, not remembering that her son rather than her daughter now shared her room.

"You shtill look pritty good fer havin' three kids," she slurred, patting her bare belly. "Jus' a li'l bulge." She sucked it in. Turning, she looked over her shoulder and ran her hands over her smooth backside. "Thish should make a man 'appy." She frowned. "Sho where's the 'appy man?"

The sound of her voice had awakened Alex, who was now watching her every move. As she reached for the lamp on the dressing table, her eyes met his stare, riveted on her reflection in the mirror.

"Do ya like what ya see, li'l man? Is ya mama shtill pritty?"

She switched off the lamp and fell into bed beside him. He didn't move and didn't know what to think, but he was acutely aware of his beating heart and quickening breath. He knew what happened next shouldn't have…but it did.

Before turning over and falling asleep, she kissed him on the lips. "I love ya the mos', l'il man. Yer m'fav'ritc…but ya know that already, don' ya?" As he lay motionless, she gently stroked his flushed face.

The warmth of her still-damp skin, the pungent odor of the whiskey on her hot breath, and her soft, lingering kiss were branded into his memory. And he would spend the rest of his life trying to forget.

The next day, Alex went back into the room with Bob, and Sue rejoined her mother. Two years later, the family moved into a larger house, where Sue and the boys were given their own bedrooms.

Emily did her best to make amends for her drunken indiscretion that hot summer night, while trying to assure herself of Alex's love and respect. But the more affection she bestowed upon him, the more he shied away.

By the time Alex was fourteen, he was on his way to earning the Eagle Scout badge he wanted so much. His troop leader, an avid outdoorsman like Alex understood his dad had been, took a special interest in the slightly built boy who longed for a father figure. Alex thrived on his friendship and craved his approval. During that summer the troop leader took his scouts to a camp in North Carolina. When it was time for the boys to bathe, he stood guard at the door as each took a turn in the shower. He said with a laugh that he was watching to be sure everybody washed under his arms.

After the traditional round of storytelling ended and the boys had fallen asleep, Alex was awakened by someone fondling him. His eyes popped open as he rolled away from the offending hand. Before he could protest, the troop leader whispered for him to keep quiet, saying that he only wanted to show him how much he loved him. The boy's mind flashed back to that night years before when his mother had stood in front of the mirror, the night just before his eleventh birthday, when she'd said she loved him the most and kissed him.

By the time he returned home, Alex had lost his mentor, his interest in scouting, and his desire for the coveted Eagle's badge. He'd also lost what was left of his innocence.

From his earliest recollection, Alex was the smallest boy in his class, but he could not remember when he was first called Skippy. He hated the nickname.

He may have been diminutive in size, but he had good looks, an outgoing personality, and a great sense of humor going for him. In spite of these assets, he felt an enormous need for acceptance. Rather than defining his self-esteem in his own terms, he became a chameleon—whatever his friends expected him to be—in most cases, the class jokester.

Since he wasn't physical enough to compete in contact sports, he devoted himself to track. What he lacked in size, he made up for in speed. For the first time in his life, he experienced success as an athlete. Running became his passion, followed later by tennis. He never became an outstanding student, but in truth, he never tried. Abstract concepts didn't interest him.

Shortly after he graduated from high school, his mother remarried. Bill Dexter, a lighting fixture salesman, immediately sold his home and moved in with Emily and her two boys. Sue had left home several years before with a man twice her age, and had not been heard from since.

Soon Bill openly demonstrated his dislike of Alex, brought on more times than not by Emily's smothering affection for the boy. He berated Alex at every opportunity, referring to him as Little Skippy, and badgering him to get out on his own and act like a man. Emily was caught in the middle. After six months of verbal and emotional abuse, Alex accepted a job at Chemtrac Industries just south of Atlanta, and moved into an apartment shared by two guys his age from the plant. By that time, Alex's hatred for Bill knew no bounds.

Alex's roommates equated manhood with beer, girls, pickup trucks, and hunting. He quickly bought into their lifestyle and started doing all the things they did. For some inexplicable reason, he emerged as their leader. With this new role came a sense of power he'd never known. Finally free of the despised nickname, he'd come into his own.

Four years after leaving home, Alex met Maggie on a blind date. She worked as a nurse at Saint Mary's Hospital in Atlanta and was three years his senior. They dated only six months before deciding to marry. She supplied the security he had previously found in his mother, and he satisfied her need to care for somebody. She was the more intelligent of the two, but encouraged him to be the leader in their relationship, as her father had been in their family. Two years later, they had a son whom they named after his brother, Bob. Three years after that, Julie came along.

Alex intended to be a good husband and to provide a better situation for his family than he had endured growing up. He adored

139

his children, and they, him. But from the beginning the marriage was dysfunctional. He sought Maggie's approval on almost every decision, then bullied her to get his way.

He did care for her, a lot, in fact—but every time he wanted her, the vision of his mother in the mirror haunted him. He remembered her hot whiskey breath on his face and her kiss—and a part of him felt guilty for his desire. Every time he reburied the recurring image and made love to his wife, he struggled with the realization that both he and Maggie were being cheated in their relationship. He could never fully give of himself, nor share with her his most personal feelings, certainly not the traumas of his childhood.

As their relationship deteriorated both emotionally and physically, Alex became increasingly addicted to the sleazy thrill of pornography. And although he would flirt with other women and fantasize about his sexual prowess, he was too insecure to become physically involved.

Using the savings Maggie had set aside for a down payment, they purchased a home soon after Bob was born. Maggie paid the bills and managed their business affairs. With her encouragement, Alex enrolled in night school and eight years later, received a bachelor's degree in history. During those years, the management at Chemtrac was impressed with his 'I-can-do-it' attitude and his popularity with his co-workers. Upon receiving his degree, he was moved from operations to an office job in the environmental department. In the years that followed, he made steady progress. His affable personality and aptitude for memorizing regulations made a winning combination.

At age thirty-five, he was promoted to manager of environmental services. His knowledge of plant operations, coupled with his rapport with union representatives, weighed heavily in the decision. After the promotion, his ego soared. For the first time in his life, he was truly in a position of authority. When an important environmental issue had to be addressed, he was the one everyone consulted. His knowledge of environmental regulations was clearly superior to that of anyone else on the staff, and he was generally recognized as an authority in his field, a reputation he promoted at every opportunity.

Maggie continued working as a nurse, as well as fulfilling her roles of wife, mother, and decision maker. Although she was proud of her husband's success, she became increasingly concerned with the emotional instability she observed in his behavior. The added responsibilities at the plant pitted him daily against managers having superior intellect and education. Sensing his inadequacies in competing with his peers, he, like his father, found refuge in the bottle. As his drinking increased, the combative relationships both at work and at home worsened. During his nightly tirades, he screamed criticisms and ridicule about the other managers, bragging about how much smarter he was than the engineers and complaining that he wasn't getting the recognition he deserved.

Word of the changes in his behavior eventually came to the attention of his supervisor, as did the rumors about his drinking. With increasing regularity, his boss counseled him regarding his stubbornness and cautioned him about his verbal abuse of fellow workers. He also expressed concerned about Alex's tendency to take credit for accomplishments rightfully due others. As time passed, Alex found it increasingly difficult to distinguish between fact and fantasy.

When challenged on environmental issues where he felt his expertise was being questioned, he responded angrily. Engineers particularly infuriated him with their rigidity and what he interpreted as arrogance. When confronted with an issue he did not fully understand, he became hostile and put the other person on the defense. Typically, they backed off or resolved the matter by going around him to his supervisor. The more abusive he was in those encounters, the more respect he felt he received. Eventually, he became known as a person one did not want to cross. Anybody who did made an enemy for life.

Communications with Maggie continued to disintegrate, as did all other aspects of their life together. Arguments and alienation prevailed. The unhappier he became, the more he blamed others for his misfortune.

With growing problems in both his marriage and his professional life, he spent more time either hunting or shooting at a nearby target range. Having mastered the use of a rifle, he took up hunting with a black-powder musket. When that, too, lost its challenge, bow hunting became his passion. He found in it the ultimate test of skill, and determined to become a recognized marksman. In his own eyes, this made him a man's man as nothing else ever had. He hungered for the recognition, respect, and adulation of others, and his hunting exploits seemed to him to satisfy these needs.

Several years after his promotion to environmental manager, a large conglomerate acquired Chemtrac. The new owners rectified what they recognized as weaknesses in the organization, and Alex was demoted to environmental shift supervisor. Incensed that he had been so unfairly treated and convinced that the individual who was promoted into his old position had stabbed him in the back, he convinced himself that the new executives of Chemtrac had united against him.

He began sending out résumés to prospective employers. Much of the information reflected his exaggerated perception of himself. For education, he listed numerous post-graduate environmental classes that had never been completed. His responsibilities were likewise overstated and accomplishments listed in which he had no direct involvement. The document portrayed a seasoned manager uniquely equipped with impressive environmental qualifications. Because prior employers are reluctant to release negative information about an ex-employee's performance, he knew that such subtle misrepresentations would not likely be uncovered. He made it clear in his cover letter that his current employer could only be contacted after obtaining his personal approval. When eventually contacted by his new employer, he knew Chemtrac would follow company policy and provide only the most basic information. He would finesse the demotion if it became an issue by attributing it to dirty politics, but he convinced himself that would not happen.

Through his network of business contacts, he learned that Expressway was looking for environmentalists to staff a new department being formed to manage their underground storage tank program. He already knew the essence of the regulations, as well as the jargon, if not the underlying rationale. When he received a form letter stating that his résumé would be kept on file for six months, he decided to go to Tampa and personally offer his services to the president of the company. It worked. He knew from the responses he received from Jim Hargrove and Landon Walters that they saw in him what his previous employer was too blind to see. If given the chance, he would not disappoint them.

By the time Expressway's offer came, Alex had convinced Maggie that it would be the opportunity of a lifetime. For her, the choice was either to quit her secure job at the hospital and go with him to Tampa or stay behind and seek a divorce, an option that violated her convictions. Although their marriage had always been difficult, she was not yet ready to end it. She needed time alone to work through that decision. She also wanted to give him the opportunity to prove himself at Expressway, so she persuaded him to go on without her while she stayed behind to sell their house. After delaying her decision to relocate for several months, she finally joined Alex in Tampa and determined to do what she could to salvage the marriage. She still believed that time, effort, and circumstances, coupled with her love for him, would allow him to become the kind of man she felt he had the potential to be, the kind of man she thought he wanted to be.

CHAPTER 16

Carol Shanks had not exaggerated when she described the Tennis Exchange Apartments to Alex. As advertised, the complex had been designed primarily for serious tennis players. The upstairs unit Expressway kept under contract was located next to a canal that flowed into the bay a mile to the south.

The gray two-story units were almost hidden by oaks, bottlebrush trees, schefflera, bougainvillea, and a variety of other shrubs. The complex was built in clusters, with each cluster containing six units that housed eight apartments. The center courtyard for each cluster featured a stand of trees and undergrowth left undisturbed by the developer to preserve the natural setting. Eight lighted tennis courts were located just north of the buildings. Picnic tables and grills had been placed along the winding sidewalks connecting the units. A dock, complete with slips and boatlifts, was available for residents owning boats. Two pools, an exercise facility, lounge, and restaurant combined to give the Exchange a resort-like atmosphere.

Residents at the Exchange were for the most part young, attractive, and by necessity in the upper-income bracket. They were fun loving adults who seemed to be enjoying the good life, and more importantly, able to afford it. The Exchange offered the lifestyle Alex had only dreamed about, and to be mixing with such beautiful people was simply too good to be true. His apartment was a world removed from his modest little home in Atlanta.

Within a few days he'd made several new friends and was invited to play in a standing doubles match first thing every morning.

His playing partner, Tim Bradford, was a young stockbroker who'd knocked on his door the day he arrived. Although Tim appeared a bit effeminate, he certainly was not so on the tennis court. He could hold serve with anyone Alex had seen in the amateur ranks.

The screened lanai on Alex's unit overlooked the canal and provided a perfect view of the sunset. His unit featured a living room with fireplace, breakfast area, dining room, kitchen, washer and dryer, walk-in closets, and two king size bedrooms. The expensive furnishings, pictures, and other decorations were owned by Expressway, or so the complex superintendent had told him. He then proceeded to name various Expressway managers who had stayed there in the past and with whom he remained personal friends.

It never occurred to Alex that his position did not warrant such accommodations. Only later would he learn that Carol had bent the rules as a favor to Cliff Hawkins, a personal friend and president of SSI.

On Friday of that week, Tim invited Alex to join him and a business colleague for dinner. Reservations had been made at Benny's Steak House, a premier restaurant specializing in homegrown, aged beef. Tim's friend turned out to be Cliff Hawkins. Cliff was not at all what Alex had expected the president of an environmental consulting company to be. He was in his mid-thirties, slight of build, and reflected the grooming that typically one could only acquire from having been raised among the privileged. Alex had expected the stereotypical executive, hard-driving, assertive, middle aged male. Not only was Cliff's appearance a pleasant surprise, but he seemed to be both unassuming and genuine, with an air of New England refinement. From their initial handshake, he knew that they were destined to become good friends.

Upon learning that Tim also handled Cliff's personal investments, Alex assured him that once he sold his large home in Georgia, he would look to him to handle some of his investments as well. Alex loved being wined and dined...and the feeling derived from associating with important and successful people like his two new friends.

Sitting in the opulent surroundings of Benny's dining room, Alex wished that the guys at Chemtrac could see him now. His ego reveled in those almost godlike feelings. He had never felt more important than he did at that moment, knowing he held the keys to Expressway's coffers. Alex drank heavily and before the evening was over, was boasting about his new position, his responsibilities, and the influence he could exert in the right places.

Alex's suit was obviously inexpensive, as were his black, well-worn loafers. To even a casual observer, it was apparent that he was enamored with his newfound prestige and eager to prove he could back up his claims. Ambitious but oblivious to his own limitations, he displayed the characteristics of a man who could be bought by the highest bidder.

Cliff encouraged Alex to do most of the talking. Only when his comments became repetitious did Cliff politely suggest they head back to the Exchange. Alex was only vaguely aware of Tim's invitation to Cliff that he stay at his apartment rather than driving back to his home in Orlando. Although the thought briefly flashed through Alex's foggy mind that they might be gay, it was of no concern to him. All that mattered was that he was on his way to really being *somebody*. There would be no stopping him now.

On the following Monday, when Alex arrived at Expressway for his first day on the job, he was met at the receptionist's desk by Carol Shanks. She was responsible for the recruitment logistics for all managerial positions. She wore no make-up on her tanned face, and her blond hair was cut short, not much longer than his. Her coordinated ensemble of tone on tone slacks, blouse, and blazer, was well tailored and expensive. From their very first meeting, she seemed to take a special interest in him and went out of her way to make him feel important. She looked to be in top physical condition, perhaps into bodybuilding.

After a brief get-acquainted chat in the lobby, Carol escorted him to her office on the ground floor. He thanked her profusely for her assistance in making his move to Tampa as painless as possible and assured her that his accommodations could not be nicer. He noticed that there were no pictures or personal items in her office to answer his curiosity about her marital status. He couldn't decide

146

whether the ring she wore on her left hand was a friendship ring or a wedding band. In spite of their numerous conversations over the past few weeks, she had never once volunteered any information about herself. He elected not to ask. Chemtrac had ingrained in all their managers not to ask questions pertaining to a candidate's personal situation during job interviews for fear such information could lead to a discrimination claim.

The first step in the process that morning was to complete a stack of forms dealing with Alex's choice of health care, thrift plan, credit union membership, Christmas club savings, and investment savings. He had opted to go through the medical exam required by Expressway before turning in his notice at Chemtrac, just in case there might have been an unexpected problem. After completing the forms, Carol escorted him to the security department, where he was photographed and issued his own personally coded identification card. The lady in security explained that the card would allow him to enter the building twenty-four hours a day simply by inserting it into one of the card readers located at each entry. For the executives who traveled, being able to come and go at their convenience was essential. Although guards manned the desk in the main lobby and patrolled the building around the clock, company policy prohibited them from authorizing entry based upon visual recognition.

"Well, Alex, what do you think of Tampa so far?" Carol asked.

"Are you kidding? I could live the rest of my life at the Exchange and never look back."

"I was sure you'd like it," she said with a smile. "We have two of the units rented year around. They come in handy for executives who are relocating here. When they're not in use, our VIPs from Houston stay there instead of a hotel."

"Only two?" Alex asked jokingly.

"Only two at the Exchange. We have other units around town, but knowing your interest in tennis, I thought you would want to stay there. Have you had a chance to meet any of your neighbors yet?"

"I sure have. I can't believe how friendly everyone is...it even beats Georgia hospitality. I met a stockbroker that I like very much. We have a standing tennis match every morning."

Carol nodded her approval. "Now that the paperwork is done, are you ready to go to work?"

"You bet I am." He stood and turned toward the doorway. "Are you going up with me?"

"But of course," she said with a laugh. "Alex, I just know that you will enjoy working with the company. I've been here for ten years, and I hate to think I would ever have to work for anyone else."

"Thanks for all you've done. I really appreciate it. Maybe we could have a few drinks sometime."

"It was my pleasure to do what little I did," she said, ignoring his invitation. "You're a very important person to us, and the Exchange is the least we can do to make your relocation a bit easier."

After stopping to chat with several people on the way to the fourth floor, they arrived at his office, which turned out to be somewhat larger than he had expected. The light oak desk was clean and polished, as were the empty bookshelves. His chair, covered with a burnt orange fabric to complement the tan carpeting, looked comfortable and inviting. The other furnishings consisted of a credenza, computer, file cabinets, two armchairs, and a coffee table, all in matching oak. The wall opposite the doorway was full-width glass overlooking the main entrance to the building, with mini-blinds to block out the morning sun.

"Not bad, not bad at all. I think this will do for now," he said, flashing a boyish grin as he walked toward the window. "I left my books and stuff in the car. I guess I'll bring them in later, when lugging them in won't be so obvious."

Within moments, David Coleman came around the corner with an extended hand and a welcoming smile. After greetings were exchanged, Carol excused herself and left the men to get better acquainted. For the next two hours they talked about their backgrounds and families. David laid out a four-week orientation schedule that would introduce Alex to many of his peers while exposing him to different departments within the company. Since David had only been with Expressway for a short time himself, Alex assumed it was the same orientation David had been given. He later learned that the indoctrination arranged for David by Landon had lasted less than one week.

For lunch, other managers whom David had invited joined them in the executive section of the dining room. David pointed out the cafeteria's various serving areas and apologized that the process seemed so chaotic. People hurriedly crisscrossed the serving area carrying their trays and making their selections. "Rather than fight the chaos," David said, "I thought it might be more comfortable to order off the menu, which we can do in the executive section."

"Sounds good to me. I always did enjoy being waited on," Alex responded with a grin. "And I like table cloths," taking note of the more formal setting before them.

Alex made the most of the opportunity to charm his coworkers and by the end of lunch was well on his way to winning them over. The group had spent the last hour laughing and joking together like old friends. Even David seemed to enjoy sitting back and allowing Alex to take the lead. And Alex wasted no time in establishing himself as a leader. He was on his way to the top.

CHAPTER 17

By the time Alex completed his orientation, he was eager to take charge of the remediation program. He had heard through the grapevine of the heated exchange between Landon and David the week before. Although no one knew exactly what the argument had been about, rumor had it that it was quite a blow-up. Realizing that a rift had developed between the two, Alex set his sights on David's job. He began laying the groundwork for a coup.

For the next few months, David and Alex enjoyed something of a honeymoon. Each was preoccupied with getting the department organized and in assuming his new responsibilities. One of Alex's first priorities was to hire an experienced project manager to share in the workload. Additional staff would later be needed.

"David," Alex said as he fell heavily into an armchair in his boss's office, "I thought I'd better touch base with you before going any further in hiring a project manager. It's becoming clear, even as good as we both know that I am, that I need some help."

David laughed and looked with amusement at his personable associate. Everyone liked Alex and had gone out of the way to tell David so. The man made friends easily and had already demonstrated his people skills. David's natural reserve coupled with Alex's friendly and outgoing personality should make them a great team. And his background with the company and managerial experience complemented Alex's knowledge of environmental regulations.

"In view of the technical requirements needed for designing our remediation systems and for reviewing the designs by our consultants, I suggest that our first project manager be a chemical engineer. Would you agree with that?" David asked.

Pausing only a moment, Alex replied. "No, I'd rather hire a geologist, and if I can't get out of it, maybe bring in an engineer later. I want someone with good skills in dealing with consultants and, nothing personal, David," he said flashing a big grin, "but I've never had much success in communicating with engineers."

"Well, I would agree that some engineers may be lacking a bit in that arena, but most should be qualified to evaluate system designs, and we will be spending millions on those systems."

"I hear what you're saying," Alex replied, his smile now replaced by a look of consternation, "but you're forgetting the fact that on many of our sites the groundwater is contaminated, and it takes a geologist to evaluate that part of the problem. Besides, I just don't like working with engineers. My experience has never been good where they're concerned."

"Alex, engineers are no different than doctors or any other group of professionals. Some doctors have a great bedside manner, and others have none at all. I'm sure we can find an engineer with the ability to handle the technical questions and with the personality needed to get along with consultants. Being an engineer myself, I can relate with the species. My experience has been that engineers typically are more disciplined than geologists and, because of their analytical aptitude, do a better job managing the details of a project. I've worked with a lot of engineers in construction."

"There's a huge difference between environmental projects and construction," Alex retorted, his face set for combat. Leaning forward in what David perceived as attack readiness, he continued. "You're always bringing up your construction experience, but you don't really understand environmental work."

David got up and walked slowly around his desk, stopping to sit down on the corner directly in front of Alex. He had already begun to see that Alex was insecure, and his inability to discuss a difference in opinion was simply confirmation of that point.

"I would beg to differ on that point, my friend," David countered a little louder, his temper beginning to surface. "Managing projects is a logical process of planning, scheduling, coordinating, and supervising the work in the field. Granted, environmental projects involve geology, but that's an expertise the consultants will provide. No matter what the size or the nature of a project, and I have managed my fair share over the years, all of them go through pretty much the same steps." David paused to allow Alex to respond, but instead he sat staring past David out the window, his expression defiant.

"I'll say one more thing," David said. "If you have a problem working with engineers, I suggest that at least part of that problem lies with you, Alex. Not liking to work with engineers is not a satisfactory reason for choosing a geologist. On the other hand, I do admit we'll need a good geologist at some point on your staff. If you find the right one before you find an engineer, I'll go along with hiring a geologist first."

Both men were silent now, Alex's gaze still fixed somewhere in the distance. David's was fixed on Alex.

"Is that all?" Alex finally asked, still refusing to look at David.

"What do you mean, is that all?"

"I mean, can I get out of here and get back to work. I need to start looking for an engineer or a geologist, and I can tell you right now, finding a geologist is going to be a lot easier than finding the right engineer."

"Alex," David began, but before he could finish, the man was up and out of the office, leaving his boss to stare after him as he tried to process what had just transpired. If this episode was any indication of the way Alex dealt with differing opinions, he clearly was going to be a challenge to manage. Rather than overrule him as he could have, David decided to concede the matter since other project managers would be added in the months ahead and some would be engineers, whether Alex liked the idea or not.

In spite of issues on which the two seemed to be at cross-purposes, they developed a strained but workable relationship. David grew increasingly concerned about Alex's need to be in control. Everything he observed in Alex's behavior indicated that he was even more insecure than David had earlier feared. Before long other problems began to develop within the department, and Alex was always involved, directly or indirectly.

David's concerns heightened even more when he later became aware of derogatory comments about him that seemed to always point back to Alex, but none of which he could prove. Collectively, such comments, if they could be proven, would have been grounds for termination. Taken individually however, David dismissed them as Alex's attempts to feed his ego at someone else's expense. He hoped that given time, encouragement, and friendship, he would be able to earn Alex's cooperation and respect.

In the ensuing months, Alex and Landon began spending more and more time together, both on and off the job. David knew of their developing friendship and was concerned because his own relationship with both men was growing more difficult. Alex frequently could be seen sitting in Landon's office. Landon occasionally assigned special projects directly to Alex without observing the chain of command by going through David, who was unsure how to respond in view of his strained relationships with both men. When he did allude to a concern regarding some aspect of Alex's performance, Landon would either rally to Alex's defense or simply cut him off, making it clear he was not interested in discussing the matter. In spite of David's repeated attempts to reconcile the three-way relationship, the situation progressed from bad to worse.

Off the job, Landon and Alex shared a common interest in hunting. Alex's skill could not be denied, and he knew Landon was eager to learn from him. It wasn't long before the two were spending weekends together, hunting wild boars in the groves around Lake Okeechobee. In spite of their social and economic differences, the days they spent together testing their archery skills against the dangerous boars resulted in a friendship forged out of mutual reliance.

During those trips, Alex subtly planted seeds of doubt about David. He would acknowledge certain strengths in David's management style while implying that David was fundamentally lacking in other areas. At times it would be a tone inflection, other times a facial expression. He was also adept at asking a rhetorical question deliberately aimed at undermining his boss. In time, Alex persuaded Landon that it was he who deserved credit for the overall accomplishments of the environmental group and that David was being carried along for the ride.

David's management style regularly drew Alex's veiled criticism. David empowered his staff and allowed each to operate within broadly defined guidelines. He established controls in order to monitor progress and evaluate performance. Alex interpreted David's empowerment of the staff as evidence of incompetence and used the trust bestowed in him as a license to betray.

David had little in common with most of the managers within Expressway since most had worked their way up through the ranks in sales or marketing. Lacking such experience and typically surrounded by sales oriented supervisors, David appeared to others to exercise a certain reserve in management meetings unless the topic being discussed dealt specifically with environmental issues. At every opportunity, Alex hinted that this evidenced his boss's aloofness, insensitivity, and self-centered attitude. David's initial inexperience with environmental regulations was portrayed as ignorance, his delegation as weakness, and his occasional assertiveness as dictatorship. From the beginning, Alex found ways to use both David's strengths and weaknesses against him. With the patience and precision of an artist painting a canvass, he utilized slander and partial truths to create the image of David he wanted others to see.

Alex's network of friends allowed him to develop considerable influence, both official and unofficial, throughout the company. He used those opportunities to discredit David, always, of course, under the guise of humor. He was cunning enough, however, to know with whom not to criticize David.

A number of Expressway employees lived in Alex's neighborhood. Tim Davis, one of the administrative assistants to Jim Hargrove, lived only a few blocks away, and the two alternated weeks in driving to work together. Every afternoon, while downing a couple of beers on the drive home, Alex would bash David and the events of the day. Tim was one with whom Alex could speak openly, since he had determined early on that David posed an obstacle to his own career. Tim delighted in participating in office gossip, especially when he knew he could pass along the information without reprisal. Anything that might enhance his career was eagerly seized upon. Alex knew that Tim would not only promote rumors about David, but embellish them. He also knew that Tim would influence Jim Hargrove's opinion, as well.

Alex found another anti-David sympathizer in a young paralegal who reported to Landon. Kathy Rogers had joined Expressway shortly after Alex, and, like him, she was an excellent tennis player. Kathy was both naïve and ambitious. She joined Expressway while still dealing with the trauma of losing both parents in a tragic boating accident. Alex befriended her at a time she needed a sympathetic ear.

During the period Alex was living alone in Tampa, the two would play tennis several times a week. Afterwards, they would go for a few beers at the Sportspage, where they would discuss the latest goings-on at the office. Alex knew that being taken under his wing would make Kathy feel important and foster a commitment to him that went beyond a purely business relationship. Kathy's job was to monitor and interpret regulations and keep senior management apprised of key issues that could impact the company. In time, what Kathy lacked in official power she compensated for in how she elected to withhold or disclose critical information to others.

It was easy for Alex to persuade Kathy that he, rather than David, should be running the department. It was also Alex who planted the idea that if she chose to bypass David with key information, it would hasten exposure of David's incompetence. Kathy soon sought opportunities with Landon to expound on Alex's strengths and David's weaknesses. Through Kathy, Alex had found another pipeline to Landon, and, this time, it was one of Landon's own people.

Andy Hicks, director of engineering at Expressway, was an avid runner. He and Alex ran together regularly during their lunch hour as well as in marathons. During those times, Alex did most of the talking. Another recruit, Robert Mathews, coordinator of new acquisitions, traveled extensively to evaluate properties that were being purchased. Since environmental contamination was a major consideration in most transactions, Alex frequently accompanied him for days at a time. He too was a great listener and a dyed-in-the-wool rumormonger. Alex's ability to discreetly recruit soldiers into his privately declared war against David was uncanny and extremely effective.

David's greatest vulnerability grew out of his absence from the corporate mainstream during his years in private business. He did not appreciate the polarization that had developed in the workplace, arising from the feminist movement, nor the zealousness with which some corporate women viewed the cause. He'd always had fun teasing his own daughters and enjoyed teasing some of the younger women in his department.

Alex suggested to one young feminist that she keep a file documenting comments David made, telling her that David was a chauvinist who considered women to be inferior. As suggested, she began keeping a diary of David's sayings that could be later used to prove discrimination or harassment. Such records would serve her well, should David try to fire her, and she might even be able to sue the company for sexual discrimination if she were ever passed over for a promotion.

Leaving no stone unturned in his strategy to remove his boss from power, he defined David for the others—coldly, deliberately, maliciously, day by day, year after year. To Alex, everyone else seemed stupid and pliable. He felt almost godlike in his ability to maneuver people like pawns on a chessboard, making all the moves necessary to produce a checkmate.

In time, Alex became a power broker at Expressway. It was common knowledge that if someone wanted to know anything, he was the man in the know. Everyone, from the janitor to the president, liked him. His influence grew until it permeated every corridor and office in Expressway. As his popularity increased, confidence in David waned.

David's department performed well, in fact, outstandingly in most areas. Morale was never harmonious, but even with Alex stirring things up, it was no worse than many other staff groups. To most, David seemed likable enough, although he did tend to isolate himself. The pictures and wall hangings in his office reflected the peacefulness of his nature, yet only a few people really felt positive about him. They liked him, but…He seemed sharp enough, but… His performance was good, but…David was a victim of prejudice and only Alex knew for sure from whence it came.

David felt the increasing coolness toward him around the office and concluded that his problems were, at least in part, the direct result of Alex and his inner circle of friends. Unfortunately, he could think of no way to counter the growing bias against him. Lacking a mentor to turn to within Expressway, he knew he had to be careful. It could prove to be a career-ending mistake to risk going around Landon and Jim Hargrove and taking his case to Steve Snelling. Besides, he had no tangible proof of any conspiracy. His reputation and everything he stood for was being desecrated, yet his attacker remained unseen. Frustrated by his inability to gain control over Alex, he felt constantly threatened by Landon's obvious favoritism toward the man. He prayed for strength to overcome the prejudice and for a change in the hearts of those who, for reasons he did not fully understand, seemed to dislike him no matter what he did.

Through it all, David learned from daily experience how hurtful it is to be slandered. He also found out that the only defense one has is to persevere with good actions. In his mind, Tryon Edwards stated the matter well with these words:

"The slanderer and the assassin differ only in the weapon they use; with one it is the dagger, with the other the tongue. —The former is worse than the latter, for the last only kills the body, while the other murders the reputation and peace."

Since David could find no way to right the situation, he decided to bide his time. If he pushed for a showdown prematurely, it would most likely be him and not Alex who would be filing for unemployment. For his own peace of mind, he decided to focus his energies on others within his department who were loyal to him, and allow Alex to play out the strategy to which he was committed…and, hopefully, hang himself with his own rope.

157

Part 3

The Whirlwind

CHAPTER 18

Week Two Resumes - Monday, July 15, 1996

Bruner and David were both watching for Alex's Blazer as he turned off Eisenhower Boulevard and pulled into the parking lot. Bruner stood between two intense, well-built men in dark gray business suits. Employees arriving that morning nodded or spoke in passing, assuming them to be corporate executives or visitors there for an early morning meeting. A closer inspection might have created doubts, since there was something coarse about the trio that was atypical of most Expressway executives. Some managers recognized Bruner but none stopped to chat with him about the purpose for his visit. He was simply a presence wherever Pyramid's most senior managers were to be found. Although Alex and Bruner had met at various corporate functions, Bruner was not one to mix business with friendship. He took his responsibilities far too seriously to let his guard down and allow familiarity, even with those who had been on his staff for years.

What creatures of habit we are, David thought, as Alex selected the same parking space he always chose, even though others were available closer to the building. After removing his bag and briefcase, he carefully surveyed the lot before locking the door. His stride that morning was not that of a finely conditioned runner, which he was, but cautious, as a man about to hear a medical diagnosis that would forever change his life. He trudged slowly, as though aware that a terrible fate awaited him upon reaching his destination. After watching him cross the parking lot and disappear through the revolving door, David breathed a sigh of relief, thankful Landon had chosen to exclude him from the meeting. At least Alex was now in the hands of experts.

In one hand Alex carried his briefcase, in the other a duffel bag used for his running gear. As long as his hands were occupied, Bruner knew that he could be prevented from suddenly placing anyone at risk. Alex showed no surprise as he walked through the revolving door and was immediately confronted by the waiting trio.

"Morning, Alex," Bruner said.

"Hi, what's up?"

"Landon wants to meet to discuss a situation that may involve you."

As if rehearsed, both men spoke in the same hushed manner.

"What kind of situation?"

"I'll let Landon answer that. We're meeting in one of the small conference rooms." He nodded toward the far corner of the lobby. With that, each deputy took hold of Alex as if assisting an elderly person across a busy intersection and escorted him toward the conference room.

After a few steps Alex jerked free. "Get your damn hands off me. Who the hell do you think you're dealing with?"

"It's okay, fellas," Bruner said in a firm voice. "Alex isn't going to need any help."

The conference room was one of several such rooms used for staff meetings and for meetings with salesmen who were not authorized to go to the upper floors. As they entered the room, Bruner suggested that Alex leave his briefcase and bag with the deputies. Before he could reply, both items were pried from his grip. One of the deputies closed the door behind them, leaving Alex, Bruner, and Landon staring at each other in awkward silence.

Landon was even more pale and somber than usual. Alex's demeanor betrayed his attempt to appear unconcerned.

"How's it going, Alex? How was the vacation?" Landon's monotone offered no hint of familiarity, no evidence of friendship.

162

He was about to interrogate a man he had grown to like very much and someone he had trusted implicitly. All weekend he had rehearsed the scene in his mind. He wanted to clearly send the message to Bruner that he and Alex were not the close friends David had made them out to be. In truth, he had never had a better friend than Alex, and to be the one to destroy him was painfully difficult.

Without waiting for a reply, Landon continued. "Please take a seat, Alex. Bruner and I want to discuss certain allegations of a rather serious nature that have been brought to our attention. Since I can't take notes very well and talk at the same time, I would like your permission to use this tape recorder," he said, gesturing toward a small recorder that was just then being placed on the table by Bruner. Landon was sitting directly across from Alex, with Bruner sitting at the end of the table, thus giving him a clear view at all times of Alex's hands.

After a moment Alex nodded. "I guess it's okay to start with, but I reserve the right to change my mind," he said with a wry grin.

"My name is Landon Walters. I am meeting with Alex Carter and B. J. Bruner in Conference Room One of the Expressway office building in Tampa, Florida. The date is July 15, 1994. The time is seven thirty-five a.m. I have been given verbal authorization by Mr. Carter to record this meeting. We're meeting to discuss allegations of possible wrongdoing about which he may have knowledge. Alex, do you have any questions or comments before we proceed?"

"No."

"The allegations we're here to discuss are potentially very serious in nature. If they're found to be factual, disciplinary actions up to and including termination of your employment with Expressway may be taken. I have asked David not to be present at this meeting in order for you to have complete freedom in providing any information you may wish to give. If others, including David, are involved, I expect a full disclosure of that information. Is that clear?"

"Yes."

"Should our discussions lead to areas of possible criminal violations, I will do my best to advise you accordingly. Are there any questions on this issue?"

Alex shook his head.

"If you don't mind, I would ask that all your answers be verbal," Landon said. "Are there any questions regarding your understanding of criminal violations and your potential involvement?"

Alex considered the question carefully before responding. "Can this tape be used as evidence against me in court, should it come to that?"

"That would be for the judge to decide. We would attempt to have it entered as evidence. You have the right to remain silent should you elect not to answer any of my questions."

"No, I have no questions," Alex replied.

Landon continued, "Since this is not a formal deposition, you are not required to answer the questions that will be asked, and I will not ask you to take an oath regarding the truth of your answers. I would encourage you, however, to be truthful and precise in providing whatever information you may choose to give. Are there any other questions before we begin?"

"No, let's get this over with," Alex answered caustically.

"There are four areas I want to discuss, and I expect this will take most of the morning. Feel free to make yourself comfortable. If you need a break, just say so. I have coffee ordered that should be here shortly.

"The first area has to do with gifts. Have you, or has anyone on David's staff, accepted gifts from a consultant for items that were more than of nominal value and which are not typically available to other employees?"

"Could you explain what you mean by nominal value?"

"I'm referring to gifts in excess of fifty dollars given to a particular employee."

"I can't recall anything of that sort," Alex replied. "Consultants typically send something at Christmas but not anything expensive, things like cookies, a smoked ham, potted plant, or something like that."

"Have you ever received gifts from a consultant which may include cash or items such as a boat, truck, racing bike, or hunting equipment?"

Alex removed a pencil from his pocket and began passing it back and forth between his fingers. "Where did you hear that?"

164

"A few days ago we received information from someone outside the company that gifts had been given to you by one or more of our consultants. The firm most often mentioned happens to be Scientific Solutions, Inc., to whom you have awarded over 40 percent of our projects. Considering we work with twenty or so consultants around the country, it's somewhat unusual that a relatively small firm such as this would be given such a high percentage of our business. In the past, when David and I have brought this matter to your attention, you have always been able to demonstrate that they had earned the work on a fair and competitive basis. In light of certain allegations which we will discuss in detail this morning, this disproportionate assignment of work becomes somewhat suspect."

Alex stared intently at Landon but gave no response.

"When we first became aware of the allegations, I asked David and Bruner to look into the matter as discreetly as possible without mentioning anyone by name. They have spoken with a number of our employees and with several of our consultants. The answers they have received suggest strongly that you have been given gifts from SSI over the years, some of which were of substantial value."

"That's a damn lie!"

"Are you saying you have not received such gifts from SSI?" Landon asked.

"What I'm saying is I may have exchanged gifts with a friend who works for SSI, but they were strictly personal and not business related. There's nothing wrong with friends exchanging gifts. I believe this is still a free country, isn't it?"

"Would you mind listing for us the specific gifts you have received from your friend at SSI?"

Alex looked first at Landon and then Bruner before shifting his gaze to the pencil. He then took a deep breath before returning his gaze to Landon. "As I recall, I received a bicycle for my birthday one year and a 30-06 rifle for my birthday another time, but I really don't see that this is any of your business."

"What would have been the approximate value of the bicycle and the rifle?"

"I don't know, but they weren't what I considered to be expensive. I suppose the bike might have cost a couple hundred dollars and the rifle, about the same."

"Do you recall the manufacturer of the bicycle? We've been told that it was a French racing bike, possibly valued at more than two thousand dollars."

"That's absolutely untrue," Alex said with his first relaxed grin of the morning, "unless Sears is a French company. I believe it was bought at Sears. I don't know where the gun was bought. You don't normally ask someone where they purchased your birthday present."

"And the make of the rifle?" Landon asked.

"I really can't recall. I'll be glad to get back to you on this, if you really need to know."

"Did you receive a Blazer from your friend at SSI?"

"I purchased, I repeat, purchased the vehicle at fair market value from SSI. It had been used extensively and because it had high mileage, I got a good deal on it."

"Do you remember what you paid?"

"No, but I remember that it was somewhere between whole-sale and average retail, closer to wholesale, I think."

"Do you have a bill of sale for the vehicle showing what you paid?"

"I'm not sure, but I can ask Maggie if she knows where it is. I may have one, I just don't remember. In this state, all you need is a title showing the vehicle was sold to you. The taxes are taken straight from the county's tax schedules."

"Can you produce a canceled check or proof of a loan taken out to purchase the Blazer?"

"I paid cash for it. I always pay cash for anything I buy. I don't like to use checks."

"You paid cash for a vehicle and can't remember how much you paid for it?" Landon responded in astonishment.

"I think it was thirteen thousand dollars, but I'm not positive. I remember that I paid with hundred dollar bills, and the envelope was stuffed. Cliff laughed when he opened it and saw the wad of cash inside. I just did it to make the point that I felt he was cheating me on the price, seeing as how it was not in the best condition."

"So payment was made to Cliff Hawkins?"

"Yeah, that's right."

"What about the thirteen thousand dollars? Is there a bank statement or other record showing the source of the cash?"

"I'm afraid not. My brother loaned me the money, and I doubt that he would be willing to produce records of that sort."

More questions followed concerning the alleged gifts, but it was obvious Alex was not going to acknowledge any wrongdoing. The thought occurred to Landon that Alex's responses were well thought out, possibly even rehearsed. He flatly denied that a boat had been given to him, sticking to his account that he had bought it. It, too, had been paid for in cash. After another thirty minutes of fruitless questioning, Landon suggested that they take a break. Alex seemed more relaxed at that point, apparently confident he could weather the storm. It was 9:00 a.m. and a serving cart had been placed outside the door. Bruner opened the door and motioned to one of the deputies that it could be rolled into the meeting room.

"I gotta take a leak," Alex said, smiling. "Do I need to be escorted to the john?"

"That's not a problem," Bruner replied before Landon could answer. "I'm going that way myself." With that, the two left Landon alone to prepare for the next round of questioning.

CHAPTER 19

At nine twenty-three the questioning resumed. "I now want to discuss certain trips which you may have taken at the expense of SSI or your friend at SSI," Landon said. "First, I would like to clear up one point. Is the friend with whom you have occasionally exchanged gifts, Cliff Hawkins, president and principal owner of SSI?"

"He's one of my friends. I don't know whether he's the principal owner of SSI or not, and I really don't care one way or the other. He and I have exchanged gifts on special occasions, and I offer no apologies for doing so."

"Have you made trips that were paid for by SSI or by Mr. Hawkins that would involve air travel?"

"I've made several trips with Cliff as friends, but I've always paid my own way. I feel certain the money he spent was his own and not corporate funds. It wasn't any of my business, so I never asked."

"Do you recall the destination of those trips, who accompanied you, how long you were gone, and the name of the establishment where you stayed?"

"I remember a trip to Acapulco and one to Saint Thomas. My wife, Maggie, Cliff and Miss Street, Cliff's secretary, were also present. I think we stayed three or four days, maybe a week. No, it was three nights and four days, I'm sure. I believe we did stay a week in Acapulco but only four days in Saint Thomas. I don't remember the names of the condos. They all look alike to me."

"When were these trips made?"

"I believe we went to Acapulco in ninety, maybe ninety-one, but I'm sure we were in Saint Thomas last spring."

"Was there a trip to Cancun that may have been taken?"

"Oh yeah, I forgot that one. It was no big deal. We went over a long weekend, Easter, I think. The airline was running a weekend excursion. I believe the package went for four hundred dollars per person."

"Do you remember where you stayed in Cancun?"

"Not really, just some hotel downtown, maybe the Empress or something like that. Can't remember for sure."

"Did you arrange for any of the trips through a travel agency, and if so, which one?"

"I was never involved in the details. Cliff made all the arrangements. He travels a lot and likes to handle things himself."

"Could you produce records of payment or receipts for your portion of any of these trips?"

"No, as I told you earlier, I always pay with cash. I don't like checks or credit cards, and I don't keep receipts."

Getting nowhere with that line of questioning, Landon moved on to the next issue. Both men knew that without the use of checks, credit cards or receipts, it would be virtually impossible to determine whether Alex had in actuality, paid his share of the expenses.

"Alex, we understand that you may have been present during some rather extravagant entertainment...shall we call them outings? Do any such outings come to mind?"

"Not that I can think of. Consultants expect to wine and dine their customers. That's part of their business. They all do it, SSI no more and no less than anyone else."

"Does the name 'The Palace' mean anything to you? I understand it's a night club in New Orleans."

"I've been there a few times. I attend a trade show and technical conference every year that's held in New Orleans. One of the consulting firms invites me to go along since they know it's one of my favorite spots."

"Who do you usually go with, and who picks up the tab?"

"Just different guys in the environmental business, you know, other managers like me and the same bunch of consultants who all know each other. The consultants pick up the tab, and I believe they split the cost."

169

"What would an evening at The Palace for a group of ten men typically cost?"

"I don't know for sure, maybe five or six thousand dollars."

Landon's mouth dropped open. "Five or six thousand dollars! How could ten men spend five thousand dollars in one evening? Was there prostitution involved?"

"Absolutely not! Girls, dancers, they always join us for drinks. They dance with you, and for an extra twenty bucks, you get to feel the merchandise. You can spend money pretty fast in a joint like that. You know, the drinks are watered down to start with, and you can drink all night without getting too drunk. The girls are there to run up the liquor tab, and you can bet your sweet ass their drinks are mostly water. It's no big deal. You're having fun and that's just the way it works. It's customary to leave a pretty good tip too, so the girls will remember you."

For several moments Landon sat motionless, staring at Alex with his cultivated stare. When Alex didn't divulge any additional information during the silence, he continued.

"Who else from Expressway accompanied you to The Palace?"

"No one in particular, just whoever happened to be along on the trip. Typically, it would be Peter and Charlie, and occasionally Jeff."

"Were these evenings requested by an Expressway employee or was it the consultant's idea?"

"We never asked them to spring for it. They looked forward to it just as much as we did. Taking us along allowed them to write it off as a business expense. It's an imperfect world, Landon, I'm sorry to say."

"Did Cliff or other SSI senior managers go along on these outings?"

"Yeah, some of them were usually there."

"Did they usually pick up the tab?"

"I'm sure they paid their share. I'm not sure about who paid what. Usually by the time we left, we were doing good to find the door." With that comment Alex grinned and then seemed annoyed when neither Landon nor Bruner reciprocated. "What's wrong? Are you guys prudes or something?"

Landon ignored the question. Alex's contemptuous expression didn't go unnoticed, but he was careful not to react to it.

"I want to return to the topic of gifts and trips for a moment. I'm curious about how you could afford to make such expensive trips and also how you were able to exchange rather valuable gifts with Cliff."

"Well, I'm not exactly a pauper. You know what I make, and my wife makes another thirty thousand or so as a nurse. I'm not going to get into the details of how we manage our budget. That's none of your business!"

As much as the response irritated Landon, he was not about to let Alex bait him into losing his composure. It also occurred to him that Alex was probably performing a bit for Bruner's benefit. When he smiled, Landon saw that he was apparently pleased with his answer.

For the next few moments, both men stared at each other across the table. Although the situation was difficult, Landon felt no genuine animosity. They had been close friends, and he was saddened by the effect this matter would have on their relationship.

"There's only one remaining area that we need to discuss at this time." Landon had purposely saved the most serious allegation until last. Until now, every issue had focused on Expressway's code of business conduct, a set of policy statements that all managers at Expressway had agreed to respect.

"Were any of the expenses incurred for the gifts, trips, or entertainment ever billed to Expressway as a remediation expenditure?"

Alex hesitated. "Has anyone said they were?"

"I'm not making an accusation. I'm simply asking you the question," Landon replied. He hoped that Alex would say no, for a yes would surely result in a firestorm of investigations that could only end with many Expressway employees, and the company itself, getting involved in a major debacle.

After a short pause, as though he were pondering the question intently, Alex replied, "Not to my knowledge. What difference would it make if they had been?"

"It could make a significant difference if non-business related expenses have been billed to Expressway, which we in turn, have submitted to a state for reimbursement. If such expenses have been included as legitimate remediation expenditures in an application for reimbursement, it would constitute mail fraud, a violation of federal law."

"How so?" Alex asked, the haughtiness draining from his tone.

"It would be a federal crime if we have used the United States mail service for the purpose of submitting fraudulent claims. If that's been done, we'll have no alternative but to call in the FBI, and they'll conduct a criminal investigation. I need to make it clear that if this has occurred, you and anyone else who conspired in such a manner could be criminally prosecuted."

For the first time Alex's face registered shock as the weight of Landon's words began to sink in. It was obvious Alex had been caught off guard and, for once, was at a loss for words. The pencil he was holding began trembling noticeably.

Up until that moment, every issue Landon had posed had been anticipated and discussed the previous Saturday when Alex had met with Cliff. They had rehearsed exactly what his response would be for each question Landon had raised, including some issues he apparently was not aware of. But mail fraud had never been considered because the topic of reimbursements had not been discussed.

"Alex, do I need to repeat the question?"

"No, damn it! You don't need to repeat it! As far as I know, I have never approved an invoice for anything other than legitimate work performed on our projects."

"Have you ever approved a change order submitted after the authorized work had already been completed?"

"Definitely not! I always approve change orders, at least verbally, before the work is initiated. Sometimes I don't issue written approval until I receive the invoice, but it's always limited to the scope of work I have previously authorized."

"Do you operate any differently regarding change orders with SSI than you do with other consultants?"

"No, why would I?" Alex replied.

"Has SSI ever suggested to you that they would like to recover their miscellaneous expenses by sending through an inflated invoice?"

"Absolutely not!"

The questions were being fired at a staccato pace. "How do you suppose they generate the funds for expenditures such as a night at The Palace?"

"I suppose they just eat it. With the exorbitant prices they charge, they should be able to afford it."

"Did you ever suggest to a consultant that damages to a vehicle which had occurred on a hunting trip could be billed as legitimate reimbursement costs?"

Alex didn't immediately respond, but instead gave Landon a perplexed look. Then, as though the incident had been too unimportant to remember, he laughed softly.

"Oh, I know what you're referring to now—the damaged Jeep last winter in Texas. Look, I was drunker than a skunk and may have suggested sending us the bill, but I was only joking."

"Did you suggest it on more than one occasion over the weekend in question?" Landon continued.

"I might have. You know how I get after a few beers. I was only cutting up. Hell, Landon, it was just a joke. If they had actually tried to bill us for it, I would have flatly denied payment. I never thought anyone would take me seriously."

"Did you suggest specifically that the charges could be passed through as equipment rental expense?" Landon asked.

"I don't know. I might have said something like that, but I didn't really mean anything by it. Everyone there knew I was joking. I wouldn't have said it for everyone to hear if I had been serious, now would I?"

"Have you ever knowingly approved inflated invoices which were submitted to a state for reimbursement."

"You don't have to keep asking the same question," Alex snapped. "As far as I know, I have never approved an invoice for anything other than for legitimate work performed on our projects. Is that clear enough, or do I need to repeat it *again*?"

173

"Do you know of any Expressway employees, past or present, including David, who may have authorized payment for inflated or falsified invoices?"

"I'm not sure about this, but I was told after the fact that Peter Everett may have done that a few times on some small charges, and as I recall, I personally made David aware of it."

"Can you recall any details, such as on which job it might have occurred, or can you recall the approximate time frame when it occurred?"

The color began returning to Alex's cheeks. By involving Peter and David, this last line of questioning gave him the opening he had been waiting for.

"I believe it happened several times. It has occurred to me and probably to you, Landon, that David has a very expensive home and seems to be living well above his means. If I'm not mistaken, his place is in *your* neighborhood, isn't it?" Having made his point, he paused for emphasis, and then continued.

"In Peter's case, his family has money, and I doubt that he needs to milk the system, not that he wouldn't hesitate to stab me in the back if given the chance, mind you. He was one of David's favorites, and that has really made it hard for me to supervise him, what with him being able to go around me all the time. But if I were you, I would focus on David; after all, he gives final approval to every invoice before it gets paid. David is also the one who negotiates the contracts with our consultants. Even a one percent kickback would amount to a lot of money when you consider he's responsible for spending tens of millions a year."

"Do you have any suggestions where we might look to obtain evidence of wrongdoing by David or Peter?"

"I suppose you could obtain a sworn statement from every consultant with whom we do business. I doubt they would lie under oath, and with the power David has over their livelihood, none of them are going to volunteer such information, especially when it could incriminate them.

"I'm not saying I believe David has done anything wrong, and I want to make myself clear on that," Alex continued. "You asked me a question, and I'm telling it like it is. That's all I'll say on the matter."

"Tell me about your relationship with David."

Relieved by the question and the opportunity to discuss a different, non-threatening issue, Alex began to relax. "As you know, he hired me to provide the expertise he lacked in the area of environmental regulations. At first he didn't even know how to spell environment, much less how to manage such a complex program, and for a while, we got along just fine. He allowed me to make all the decisions, for which he took most of the credit, I might add. I'm not saying this derogatorily; it's just a fact. Everyone knew he was riding on my shirttail.

"After a year or so he started questioning many of my decisions and wanting to issue procedures that I felt were not in the best interest of the company. When I balked, he accused me of insubordination. I was afraid he would have me fired. After that, I cooperated, as he would say, and more or less went along with whatever he said to do, within reason. For the last two or three years we've gotten along pretty well. My performance ratings will bear that out."

"Did you ever tell anyone or suggest to anyone that David was not competent in managing his department?" Landon asked.

"I might have mentioned it. I call 'em like I see 'em."

"Can you name someone with whom you had such a conversation regarding David?"

Alex realized that Landon was seeking credibility for his comments. It also occurred to him that, after all the years he'd spent planting seeds of doubt regarding David's ability to fulfill the responsibilities of his job, harvest time had finally come.

"Andy Hicks for one. Andy and I run together, and we play tennis in the same league. I told him on a few occasions that David was out in left field on certain issues, and that if it weren't for me, our department would be in deep trouble. I felt like someone within the company should know."

* * * * *

175

Although Landon knew Alex's comments were self-serving if not outright lies, he was groping for anything that could be used as justification for replacing David.

In spite of the problems Alex had caused for the company, Landon still couldn't keep from liking him. In fact, he found himself wishing it were David sitting across the table rather than his hunting buddy. Unfortunately, the situation had gone too far for him to allow friendship to be a consideration, or for him to risk his career trying to salvage the man.

Alex was history. So was their friendship.

CHAPTER 20

After the three made another trip to the men's room and Landon had checked with his assistant for messages, the questioning resumed around 11 am. Landon and Alex sat down opposite each other as they had been all morning, with Bruner electing to stand next to the closed door. Based upon Alex's passive body language and non-threatening responses, Bruner no longer was concerned that he posed an imminent threat.

"Alex, what has been your relationship with David over the past twelve months," Landon asked, grasping for anything.

"You know the past year has been hell for me," Alex said. "Last fall Maggie and I reached an impasse and mutually agreed I should move out for a few months. After many years of marriage, we'd reached a point where we just couldn't communicate. I moved into an apartment. After a while, we started seeing a marriage counselor, separately at first but later on together...that is, before I got frustrated and quit going. Dr. Jacobs was someone that Carol Shanks recommended. Actually, Expressway picked up the cost for our sessions."

"If you don't mind my asking, were you drinking during that time?"

"Maggie made a big deal out of it. Sure, I would have a couple of beers now and then, but I was never an alcoholic. You should know that from the times we've been together at various business functions where alcohol was being served."

Landon wished that remark had not been made, but he sensed no reaction from Bruner.

"I did agree to attend Alcoholics Anonymous just to pacify her, but no, I never thought it was really a problem." Alex stared at Landon for a moment before continuing. Landon returned his stare without expression. "After a while, the separation began getting to me. I wanted to be back in my own home with my family. Living alone was driving me crazy. Maybe I was depressed or something. Anyway, around the holidays, it got pretty bad."

"When was it that David called you into his office to discuss problems between you and some of his staff?" Landon asked.

For the first time since the meeting began, Landon's tone sounded more like that of a caring friend than a prosecuting attorney. Alex's attitude had also changed. The man was no longer sarcastic or defensive in his responses. He spoke softly, almost in a whisper, staring down at the table.

"I believe it was in February. He accused me of being uncooperative and unproductive, being overly critical of my co-workers. He even said he had gotten complaints from people outside the company."

"People like whom?"

"You know, consultants and a couple of property owners where we were doing remediation work."

"Was he having private conversations with Maggie during that period?"

"I don't know. He said Maggie had called him a few times and told him I was an alcoholic."

"Do you think they ever met to discuss you?"

"Who knows? She seems to think pretty highly of him, I'll say that much."

"What happened then?"

"As I'm sure you already know, to pacify him I agreed to engage in a three-hundred-and-sixty-degree analysis and counseling. I think I even asked you to complete one of the questionnaires used by Dr. Brown to evaluate me." He turned to Bruner. "Dr. Brown is the psychologist Expressway uses."

"When you met with Dr. Brown, what did he say regarding the feedback from your peers?"

"Something about me being narcissistic or some such crap. He said I viewed myself somewhat better than others did, but I figure everybody feels that way about themself. That's just human nature, isn't it? He also said that I might be carrying around some baggage from my childhood. He said delving into my personal issues was outside his charter or something like that, and I should hire my own therapist to work through those issues. You know, Landon, I can't help it if people don't always understand me." After a pause and a glance at Bruner, he continued. "A few weeks later Maggie and I began going out on a few dates. It was kind of fun. After a month or so of that, she agreed to take me back if I would promise to behave," he said with a grin.

"And did she?"

"Yeah, we got back together in April, just three months ago."

"Was David supportive of you during that period?"

"Sure, to my face he was, but who really knows? He always says the right things, but I don't trust him and never have. I know he's talked behind my back, and I can't trust anyone who does that. When we talked back in April, he actually hugged me and said he loved me. Imagine that if you can."

"Don't you think he has your best interest at heart?" Landon asked.

"Sure he does, and if you buy that one..." Alex replied with a smirk, his voice trailing off. "That's why he reorganized the department in May and now has my project managers reporting directly to him. With friends like that, who needs enemies?"

Landon realized he had obtained all the useful information about David he was going to get. To allow Alex to continue bashing David could cause Bruner to side with David. As bad as he hated doing it, it was time to drop the ax. Pausing to gather himself, he continued.

"I need a few days to think over what we've discussed here today before making a final decision. I want you to take some time off with pay until we conclude our investigation."

"How's it look to you at this point?" Alex asked.

"I'll be honest with you; we're leaning toward termination. These are serious allegations, and there has been sufficient evidence uncovered to indicate at least some wrongdoing on your part, and possibly others in the environmental group. If we decide to go that route, we'll help you make the transition to other endeavors."

"What does that mean?" Alex asked.

"First, it would be my recommendation that you be given a severance payment equivalent to three-months at your regular salary. Second, we would continue your family medical plan at no cost to you for a period of six months. And third, we would pay up to five thousand dollars to an outplacement firm to assist you in finding new employment. In return, we would expect you to sign a full release conceding any rights you may have to initiate legal action against the company or any employees of the company, both past and present."

Alex's face turned ashen. The pencil he had been holding flew out of his grasp and rolled across the table, coming to rest against the tape recorder. Cliff had telephoned him at his brother's house on Thursday to alert him that an investigation was in progress. Alex had then called a few of his closest consultants to find out if they had been contacted. He learned from them that David had been asking questions about gifts, trips, and entertainment. Cliff had warned him during their meeting that termination was a definite possibility. Alex had even suggested to Maggie before coming into work this morning that something like this could happen. But actually hearing it from Landon knocked the props out from under him.

He sat there in a daze, motionless. He was in his forties. Finding another job wouldn't be easy.

Financially, he and Maggie were strapped. They were always broke. She claimed it was because he liked to portray himself as a big spender, but he knew the real reason was she'd gotten careless with budgeting. And she spent way too much on clothes and things for the house.

Although they were back together, he no longer loved her and hadn't for years. He had stayed for the kids' sakes…no, to be

180

truthful, he'd stayed with her because she provided him security. Without her, he couldn't cope with all the decisions and complexities of life. He'd found that out during their separation.

If word got out that he'd been fired for taking kickbacks, his reputation would be ruined, much like his father's had been. Finding a comparable job would be difficult under the best of circumstances. And this was *not* the best of circumstances. The environmental community was like a big family where everybody knew everything about everyone else in the industry. There would be no way to keep this a secret.

The power Alex had wielded through his position with Expressway allowed him to have his way with most of the consultants. Without that power, he knew his friends with those firms would desert him. If the FBI got involved, he could be arrested and tried in court as a common criminal. For the first time it dawned on him that he could go to jail.

His world crashed down around him. He couldn't breathe. Drops of sweat beaded up on his forehead. He felt dizzy, nauseated, like he might throw-up. He had been in jams before, but never anything like this. How could he face Maggie and his kids. What would he tell his friends? Interlocking his fingers to steady his trembling hands, he rested them on the table. His tongue stuck to the roof of his dry mouth. He'd never experienced such a sense of desperation. Leaning forward to rest his head on the edge of the table, he felt completely alone and out of control, like a wounded bird plummeting to the ground.

"Alex, are you all right?" Landon asked. "Is there anything we can do?"

Bruner noticed drops of sweat, or maybe tears, dripping from Alex's chin into a puddle on the tiled floor, and gestured to Landon what was happening. No one moved. Landon and Bruner exchanged glances, and Bruner moved from his position by the door to stand behind Alex. For what seemed like an eternity, Landon stared without expression at the man who had betrayed him. Bruner stood ready to take whatever action was necessary, although the man bent over the table seemed more of a threat to himself than to anyone else. He had long since lost the capacity to feel pity for his fellow man; however, seeing a grown man broken like this made him uncomfortable.

Finally, Alex straightened up, wiped his face with his handkerchief, and said, "I'm sorry, guys. Sorry for losing it there for a minute."

For the first time in many years, Bruner felt the impulse to reach out to a soul in pain. "Here's a glass of water," he said, doing the only thing he could think of to help. Landon continued his expressionless stare.

Alex took the glass and gulped it down and turned to face Bruner with a look of childlike meekness. "Can I call Maggie?"

"Sure you can," Bruner replied with unaccustomed gentleness. "Let's step out into the lobby. You can call from one of the booths out there."

As Alex stood up, his knees buckled, and he quickly sat back down. After waiting for a moment, he tried again. "I think I'm okay now." That time he stood and walked unsteadily toward the door.

"Alex, I'm really sorry about this," Landon said, his voice lacking the genuineness conveyed by Bruner. "I've asked Bruner to drive you home. One of his men will follow and bring him back to the office. We'll make our decision and get back in touch with you by Friday. Until then, the official word will be that you have decided to take another week of vacation."

Alex made no reply. Landon consoled himself with the thought that Alex had brought the pain on himself.

As Bruner opened the door, the two security men snapped to attention from their positions at either side of the doorway, each bracing for whatever might happen next.

Bruner, Alex, and the two security men walked to the telephone booth as Landon strode briskly past them toward the elevators, tape recorder in hand. He had done what had to be done, and he now wanted to put Alex behind him once and for all. Bruner placed a quarter in the slot, handed Alex the telephone, and closed the door. All three watched Alex start to dial as though struggling to recall the number he had dialed so often. After the third ring, Maggie answered.

182

"Hello," she answered in a voice barely audible.

"Maggie, it's me. It happened just like I said it might. I'm on my way home."

Since the lobby would soon be filled with hungry workers headed for lunch in the cafeteria, Bruner suggested they leave as quickly as possible. The deputies were dispatched to retrieve Alex's briefcase and duffel bag, and the four men were soon on their way to the parking lot.

Bruner, back to his old self, instructed Alex to unlock the Blazer and get in on the passenger's side. Alex followed his orders without comment. One of the deputies placed the briefcase and duffel bag in the back seat. After giving whispered instructions to his deputies, Bruner got in and started the engine. Just as they had heard, Alex did have a 30-06 lever-action saddle gun attached to the back of the front seat.

There wasn't anything Bruner could say to lessen the difficulty of the situation or to change the tragic ending of Alex's career with Expressway. Although it was unspoken, both men knew the worst was yet to come. Bruner was occupied with negotiating the traffic, but every few seconds he would glance in the rearview mirror to reassure himself that the white sedan was still following. He had been in the business long enough to know that even those guilty of gross atrocities could demonstrate remorse one moment and lash out in violence the next.

From time to time, Bruner could see Alex wiping his eyes. He was also sniffling and blowing his nose a lot. Bruner hardened himself. He could only feel contempt for a man who would cry like a woman. If Bruner had ever cried, he couldn't remember it. The very thought was totally foreign to him. Alex kept his face turned away toward the side window. For the next twenty minutes, neither man spoke.

When they were about a block from Alex's house, Bruner pulled over to the curb, got out, and asked Alex if he could take it from there.

Once Alex had slipped behind the steering wheel, Bruner said, "Good luck, fella," and slammed the door.

183

Without acknowledging the comment or even looking in his direction, Alex pulled away. Bruner got into the sedan and the three watched Alex turn into his driveway. The overhead door rose and he disappeared into the garage.

"Okay, guys, that's that. Let's go grab a bite for lunch. I'm famished. I hope that's the last we'll see of Mr. Cry Baby." Back in control of whatever crazy emotions he may have succumbed to earlier, Bruner barked out the words like a drill sergeant.

Landon went straight to his office, speaking to no one along the way. When his secretary asked how it had gone, he brushed her off without bothering to explain. Closing the door, he removed a piece of paper from his billfold and began dialing the numbers written there.

"Person you wish to call, please?"

"Jim Hargrove."

Within a few minutes, the operator said, "Your party is on the line. Go ahead please."

"Jim, are you there?"

"Landon, it's me. How did it go?"

Landon proceeded over the next fifteen minutes to recap what had happened over the past few days and the meeting that morning with Alex

"What about David? Have you been able to link him to anything?"

"So far, not much. I'm still looking into the matter. Alex indicated David has knowledge about some of what's been going on in his department, but I don't think we can put much stock in his comments. Of course I'll continue my investigation into his involvement."

"Listen good to what I'm going to say," Jim said, his voice taking on a tone Landon recognized and had learned to dread. "I've been thinking about the implications of this matter for you and me. Corporate is going to ask a lot of questions, questions that will be embarrassing, if you know what I mean. I don't think for a minute that firing Alex is going to satisfy them. It's essential that we hang something on David and better yet, if we can involve others on the environmental staff, you know, so it looks like the whole barrel is rotten. Houston needs to get the message loud and clear that we uncovered this mess and acted swiftly and decisively to correct it. Our board is going to have to be satisfied that we've totally cleaned house. Keep planting doubts about David in Bruner's mind and don't miss any opportunity to involve the others. Find out who knew what was going on and failed to report it as they should've done. Bruner's report will go a long way in convincing Steve Snelling that your investigation has been properly handled."

"I understand fully what you're saying but at this moment, we have nothing tangible on David. I'm sure we can at least discredit him, by circumstantial evidence if nothing else. We already have sufficient grounds to fire four of the project managers, which will help." Getting no response, he decided to end the conversation before Jim could request something that he might not be able to deliver. "When will you be back in the country?"

"Sunday night about nine. I'll see you early on Monday."

Before Landon could reply, he heard the disconnect on the other end. He cradled the telephone and looked wistfully at the picture of FDR staring down at him from across the room.

At David's request, the guard on lobby duty had called as soon as Alex left the building. David knew Landon wouldn't bother to fill him in on the details. All morning he'd been routinely glancing out into the hallway, not wanting to be caught off guard should Alex suddenly appear in his doorway. At the very moment Landon was receiving instructions from Jim, David had stepped into an empty office to call Leah and put her mind at ease that all had apparently been dealt with peacefully.

CHAPTER 21

The Carter's home was located in Temple Terrace, an older suburb northeast of the business section. A golf course had been constructed in the mid-twenties, with houses gradually added over the years. Huge spreading oaks graced with long strands of Spanish moss lined the emerald-green fairways. It was a pleasant contrast to the newer developments that featured clusters of palm trees planted by the developer. The neighborhood had reminded them of the wooded hills in Georgia where they'd been raised. Neither Alex nor Maggie were golfers, although he had played a few times as a teenager. When he was unable to quickly master the game, he developed a dislike for it. From that time on, he ridiculed anyone who did play.

Although many of the houses were quite expensive, theirs was not. The Carters had found an older three-bedroom house located a block off number fourteen fairway and two blocks west of the Hillsborough River, which defined the eastern boundary of the community. Alex had a nodding acquaintance with the neighbors, but had never developed a close friendship with any of the men, most of whom were avid golfers. Because of her schedule at the hospital, Maggie had been slow to make friends, also, but the ones she made loved her.

Parking in the garage, Alex pressed the door closer and watched in the rearview mirror as the garage door slowly descended, shutting out the sunlight and leaving him alone in the darkness. For several minutes, he sat there trying to decide what he would say to

Maggie. All the way home, he had dreaded the moment he would have to face her. How he wished he could suddenly wake up and find that this was just another nightmare. Nightmares were familiar. They'd been a part of his life for as far back as he could remember. But this was far worse than any dream he'd ever had.

He told himself that somehow everything would work out, but his cramping stomach kept reminding him that the situation was real, an unfathomable disaster. With each passing moment, his hatred for David and Peter Everett grew. *Peter's to blame, that two-faced little punk,* he thought. *And David just can't stand having someone under him who's smarter. Everybody knows it, everybody. He's trying to get rid of me because Landon and I are friends. Everybody knows Landon hates David's guts. If I get fired over this trumped-up crap, I'll make that hypocrite wish...*

Finally, the heat in the garage became unbearable. Like a child who had disappointed his mother, Alex got out and headed inside, knowing he must once again deal with guilt and humiliation. Maggie had become more like a mother than a wife. It had nothing to do with her appearance, because Alex had always thought she was quite attractive. It was because he had become dependent on her for the same things his mother had always done, like buying his clothes, paying bills, and making day-to-day decisions for the family. When they communicated, she treated him more like one of the children than like an adult. In recent years, that behavior pattern had become the norm.

As he made his way toward the kitchen door, he wiped the sweat from his face. The proceedings that morning had left him exhausted. Opening the kitchen door, he caught sight of Maggie sitting at the kitchen table. Although she was not crying, he could tell from her red, puffy eyes that she had been. She glanced in his direction and then returned her gaze to her hands, which were folded in front of her on the table. At first, he thought he had interrupted her in prayer and for an instant, felt the urge to rush to her and beg her forgiveness. But it wasn't in him to humble himself to anyone, not even now. Without saying a word, he slowly crossed the room to the sink and filled a glass from the faucet.

Staring out the window in anticipation of the accusations he knew were sure to come, he could feel her stare burning into him. Finally, he turned and sat down at the oak table across from her. The table had been one of their first purchases as newlyweds. It hadn't been bought for its future value as an antique, but because it was cheap and in need of repairs which Alex could easily make. Over the years, they had raised their children around that table, and it stood as a solemn witness to arguments too hurtful to remember and too numerous to count. Somehow it seemed fitting that yet another painful episode was to unfold with the table between them.

He waited for her to say something, anything, because he realized he had nothing to say. It had all been said many times before, and nothing ever really changed. He would offer a token apology and promise never again to misbehave, or to betray her trust, or any number of other such vows he knew he would never keep.

Until today, she thought she'd heard them all. Since his telephone call, she'd been sitting at the table in a state of grief. In some ways, her emotions were comparable to how she had felt upon learning of her mother's sudden death a few years before, only this time she couldn't even find consolation in the belief that this was somehow God's will. At the moment He seemed very far removed from their situation.

Maggie had tried to feel compassion for Alex, knowing that this latest crisis would be devastating to his distorted sense of self-esteem. But all she could think of were the struggles they had endured over the years, trying to make a good marriage out of a bad one. She'd spent what should have been the best years of her life married to a man incapable of relating to her needs, a man who had destroyed every single dream she'd once cherished.

She had long before come to terms with the realization that Alex was emotionally ill and, worse yet, morally bankrupt. He seemed to lack both conscience and the ability to connect cause and effect. This had been proven two years earlier when he arranged an abortion for their son's teenage girlfriend. Maggie had been devastated that her husband and son had been accomplices in taking an innocent human life. Alex's involvement in that act had destroyed what little respect and hope she had left for him.

In retrospect, she regretted her decisions through the years to stick with him until the kids were grown. She used to worry about what toll a separation or divorce would exact on the children, but too late she had come to realize that keeping the family together had been a very costly price for them to pay. Now her son's complicity in support of terminating his girlfriend's pregnancy spoke volumes about the influence Alex had exerted upon the boy, and which she would never be able to reverse. Like father, like son...the tears surfaced again.

Eventually, Julie, too, would move out and make a better life for herself. But the years of emotional damage could remain forever, as would the amoral attitude that her son had already displayed.

Maggie also knew that Alex's destructive influence on her could never be undone. She would forever bear the effects of his sins, like ugly scars upon her conscience and soul. She had indeed been in prayer when he had arrived. For the past few years, it had been her only source of strength to face another day.

She suspected that Alex had violated Expressway's code of conduct somehow, but did not know what he had actually done. She'd been there when Cliff Hawkins telephoned Alex at his brother's the previous week. She suspected at the time that he was lying when he told her a problem had developed on one of his projects, requiring them to cut short their vacation. Her suspicions were confirmed when he didn't go into the office upon their return.

On Saturday he had gone to Orlando to meet with Cliff. When he returned later in the day, he had suggested that they go out for dinner that evening. Somehow she knew that something bad was going to happen. Over dinner, he explained to her that while they were on vacation, David and Peter had conspired to frame him.

Although she found his story impossible to believe, she hoped for their sakes that he wasn't guilty of any serious violations. Alex told her that he would likely have to meet with David or Landon on Monday and that, although the trumped-up charges were without merit, anything could happen. She couldn't remember exactly what

189

he'd said after that, something about how this would backfire on David and could turn out to be the opportunity Landon needed to give him David's job.

When Alex had called her from Expressway that morning, she knew from his voice that her worst fears had come true. Whatever he had done must have been something major. She recalled how he had often bragged to their friends that in his line of work, potential criminal violations went along with the job. Exposure to criminal prosecution and interaction with Expressway's attorneys had always fed his ego. After his call, she'd sent Julie to her room, explaining that Alex had a problem at work and it would be best if she weren't around when he got home.

As she had sat at the table awaiting his arrival, she broke into anguished sobs. The fragile emotional props that had supported her so often before had finally collapsed. She had intended, as in the past, to be bravely supportive so Alex could draw strength from her, but she'd cried as though her heart would break…and in truth, it did. Her sobs brought Julie out to see what was going on, but when she saw her mother with her face buried in her arms, she had silently slipped out of the room.

By the time Alex arrived, Maggie had regained some of her composure. He would need her to help him cope with this latest crisis. But with renewed resolve, she promised herself that once his situation was manageable, she would file for divorce and this time go through with it.

Now they sat on opposite sides of the table in awkward silence, the only sound coming from the rhythmic dripping of the faucet Alex had never gotten around to fixing. It no longer mattered. Lost in thought she struggled to deal with her emotions.

A sense of foreboding welled up within her. No, it was more than that; it was unadulterated fear. She knew her husband was capable of violence and feared that his repressed anger might now explode, placing her and others in grave danger. On different occasions, she had seen a demonic nature come over him, bearing witness to the instability she had long suspected.

* * * * *

190

Finally realizing his world was on the brink of collapse, Alex broke into tears and wailed as only a man who has been deeply wounded can. He bent over, assuming the same position he had taken just a short time before in his meeting with Landon. And once again his tears splashed onto the floor.

As the periods between his sobbing lengthened, he whispered, "What am I going to do now? What are we going to do?" And finally, raising his head to look at Maggie, he asked, "Does Julie know?"

"Yes. I talked with her after you called," Maggie said.

"What did you say?"

"I told her you were being sent home and may be leaving the company."

"And?" Alex asked.

"Of course she wanted to know why. I told her I wasn't sure of the details, but it had something to do with a decision you made which had not worked out as you had expected. I didn't know what else to tell her. I suggested she stay in her room until we had a chance to talk things over." After pausing a moment, she continued. "Alex, what really happened? I know David well enough to know he didn't try to frame you. There has to be more to it than that."

Alex hesitated, desperately trying to posture himself in the best light possible. "It all has to do with some favors Cliff did for me. The company is making it into something a lot worse than it really is."

"What kind of favors?"

"Cliff paid for a few trips, some of which were more for pleasure than for business. You went with me on two of them. You know, our trips to Saint Thomas and Cancun. Kathy said Peter told David that Cliff gave me the Blazer. They're even saying it was improper for him to give me birthday presents."

"But I thought your brother loaned us the money for the Blazer and is carrying us on a note until we can start paying him back."

"Bob did loan me the money, but Cliff gave me a better deal than he would have given just anybody. After all, it was high mileage and all that, not to mention that I'm probably his best friend."

"What right do they have questioning birthday presents?" she asked. "Why is that any of their business?"

"The gifts are just an excuse to get rid of me," he said. "Everybody accepts gifts in this business, everybody. David has always wanted to dump me, and Peter gave him his golden opportunity. David has always been out to get me. I'm a threat to him, because I know more about this business than he'll ever know. Besides that, he's jealous of Landon and me. He's afraid I'll eventually get his job, and I would have, too. Landon has all but said so. I ought to kill David for what he's trying to do to me."

Maggie didn't respond. She had listened to Alex blame David for his troubles many times before. This time was no different.

"I hear what you're saying, and I certainly don't know any of the details, but isn't it possible the problem is not with David, but with you? Alex, when are you ever going to admit that you have a problem? In fact, you're your own worst enemy. I may never know what this is all about, but I suspect there's more to it than you've told me."

He jumped up with such force that his chair flew backwards against the wall. "To hell with you, Maggie! You don't know a damn thing! You've *never* known anything. I knew you'd side with them. You don't give a damn about me."

He stormed out of the room, leaving her stunned by the viciousness of his remarks. It wasn't the first time he had spoken to her so cruelly, but with all the other times, he had at least been drinking. His words cut deeply, but she knew he didn't really mean all the hurtful things he had said. When backed into a corner, he always lashed out.

Within minutes, he returned wearing his shorts and running shoes. "I'm going to run," he said as he hurried past her, slamming the door in his wake.

For a long while Maggie sat slumped in the chair, too numbed by the magnitude of the calamity to even move, much less feel. Any hope for happiness, which she had clung to in the past, had been yanked away, and she didn't even know why. Finally, she rose and made her way across the kitchen, surprised by the weariness she felt. She picked up the phone and started dialing.

After telling Expressway's operator the person she was calling, he answered on the second ring.

"David Coleman."

"David, this is Maggie Carter."

After a pause, he said, "Hi, Maggie, how's Alex doing?"

"Not good. We had an ugly argument, and he's gone to run. That's his answer for all problems, you know, that and guzzling his beer."

"I don't know what to say. He left us no alternative."

"I know," she sighed. "I'm sure you did what you felt you had to."

"Did he give you the details?"

"He gave me his version of the story, for whatever that's worth. In his mind, he hasn't done anything wrong. He's never to blame. He says you and Peter framed him. That you've always been against him." He could hear that she was crying.

After waiting for a few moments, he asked, "Is there anything, anything at all, that I can do?"

"No, at least not now. I may have to call on you later, but for now we can only try and work through this somehow. I do ask for your prayers."

"Both Leah and I will be keeping you in our thoughts, Maggie. Please call if you need me, whatever the time, day or night. I'd still like to be supportive to Alex if he'll let me, but—"

"I know. You've always been good to him, as good as anyone could've been. I know that, but I don't think he ever will. He's not capable of understanding certain things."

After giving Maggie his pager number and reassuring her again he was there should she need him, they hung up. Maggie dried her eyes and headed for Julie's room.

Julie was lying on the bed listening to the radio that had been turned up loud enough to drown out what was being said in the kitchen. Maggie turned the volume down and lay down beside her.

"Where's Dad?"

"He's gone for a run. He's pretty upset, as you can imagine."

"Did they fire him?"

"Not yet, but it looks like that may happen soon. It's going to be pretty difficult around here for a while. I think it might be best for everyone if you went to Sarah's house for a few days."

They'd never had a really close mother-daughter relationship and had become more at odds in recent years. In all family disputes, Julie took sides with her father. He was the one to blow up over something Julie had or had not done, or some rule infraction, but it was always Maggie who provided the necessary discipline. Julie worshiped her father, as he did her, but they were too much alike for compatibility. Julie got up, removed a backpack from the closet, and began packing.

"Mom, why does Dad have so many problems?"

"I don't know, Hon, it's just the way he is. He only sees things from his point of view and just can't seem to see them any other way. He's going to need our...." She stopped short of saying the word love, then continued, "...support for a while. We'll just have to take this one day at a time, and it's not going to be easy. But I'm sure somehow we can get through it together." With that Julie broke down. "It will be less awkward for your father if you aren't here right now. He's very embarrassed over the whole situation."

"Poor Dad. This is going to kill him. He was so proud of his job."

"I know. Finish packing now. I'll run you over to Sarah's before he gets back. I'll let you know when it's okay to come home."

"Tell him I love him." Tears streamed down her face.

Maggie, who had been sitting on the bed watching Julie put her things in her pack, rose, and they embraced for the first time in months.

CHAPTER 22

While Alex was out, Maggie called the hospital and obtained her supervisor's permission to take the rest of the week off. At first, her request was denied, but after explaining she had a family emergency that was too personal to discuss, her leave of absence was approved. She was one of the most respected nurses on her floor and had never before requested a leave on such short notice.

After a couple of hours, Alex returned home exhausted. The run had given him time to think, and to some extent, helped him regain his equilibrium. Although he really needed someone to whom he could confide, Maggie was not the one. As had always been the case, he could not bring himself to discuss his innermost feelings with his wife.

For supper she prepared a pot of vegetable soup, leaving it on the stove for him to eat at his convenience. She spent the rest of the afternoon in the yard, staying busy in the flowerbeds and trying to put aside her fears for the family's future.

Finding her in the yard and the house empty, Alex went to the bedroom. He closed and locked the door. Picking up the receiver, he started dialing a number he had dialed hundreds of times over the years.

"Good afternoon, Scientific Solutions, Inc."

"This is Alex. Is Cliff in?"

After a moment, Cliff's voice came on the line. "Hi, Alex, how did it go this morning?"

"I met with Landon instead of David and a guy from Pyramid's security department in Houston."

"And…?"

"It went about as bad as it possibly could've."

"I figured as much," Cliff replied. "Things around here are a bit tense right now, too. Expressway's auditors came in unannounced this afternoon and started going over our books. They're digging for anything they can find."

"We need to get together, tonight if possible."

"How about Pal's, say around seven?"

Alex hung up the phone, encouraged that he had a friend like Cliff to whom he could turn. He quickly showered, dressed, and without so much as a word to Maggie, headed for Orlando.

Pal's was a bar where they had met many times and could talk privately. During football season, Monday nights would be standing room only but, during the summer, business was slow. After chatting briefly at the entrance, they headed for a booth in the corner.

They talked and drank until about 11:30. After rehearsing the agreed upon story line until every possible detail had been covered, Cliff suggested that it would be best if they didn't meet for a while, at least until the investigation was completed. Reluctantly, Alex agreed. Cliff assured him of his continued support and of his intention to help him find another job. Alex knew Maggie would not agree to move again, given the present circumstances. For the short term, they could stay afloat on her income alone, but not for an extended period. After leaving the bar, the two argued briefly in the parking lot about whether Alex was sober enough to drive back to Tampa and, as usual, Cliff gave in to Alex's stubbornness.

When he arrived home, Maggie appeared to be asleep. It didn't matter one way or the other. Although they still shared the same bed, they hadn't shared themselves in months. Within minutes, he was fast asleep.

* * * * *

The next morning Alex called Cliff's lawyer, Joe Morgan. As promised, Cliff had already relayed to Joe what had occurred the day before, and Joe was prepared to rearrange his schedule in order to meet with Alex. The fact that Joe was someone Cliff trusted implicitly was all the recommendation Alex needed, but it also helped knowing Cliff was picking up the tab for Joe's assistance.

Alex and Maggie arrived around noon as previously agreed. It was decided that Joe would contact Expressway on Alex's behalf that afternoon and get back to him by phone as soon as he had anything to report. He would inform Expressway that his client was obviously the victim of a trumped up charge. Furthermore, in addition to the possibility of an unlawful discharge, representatives of Expressway had already slandered his client's reputation by the manner in which the investigation had been handled. He would then propose a one-year continuation of salary, with benefits, along with a letter of recommendation for his victimized client. Although the settlement Landon had mentioned was much less than this, Joe felt confident that Expressway had not made their best offer and would sweeten the deal to avoid publicity. All things considered, he felt they would agree to a settlement somewhere in between.

Only once did Maggie enter into the discussion. She impressed upon Joe the importance of getting as much severance as possible since they were already living from paycheck to paycheck. She also asked if Expressway could be required to treat all details relative to Alex's termination in confidence. Joe assured her that confidentiality was in everyone's best interest, and he would make that a key point in any severance agreement.

After the meeting, Alex was almost giddy. With a year's severance pay in hand and a new job, he already felt back in the driver's seat. He also felt good knowing Joe would negotiate with Expressway on his behalf. Before heading back to Tampa, he asked Maggie if she would mind if they drove by Peter's new home, just to see if it was everything he had been told. To avoid argument, Maggie agreed. He was talking a mile a minute about how everything was going to work out better than they could have dreamed.

Following the directions he had received from Cliff, he turned right off Orange Boulevard into the Grove Park Estates. His first thought was that he had somehow made the wrong turn. The houses were enormous, and the lawns manicured to perfection.

"What's the address?" Maggie asked as she stared incredulously at the affluent neighborhood in which they now found themselves.

197

"Sixteen-forty, Parkway Drive, but this can't be right." One block off Orange, they came to the intersection with Parkway Drive. Turning left, they had only gone a short distance when there on the left was a large, red brick house bearing the address Sixteen Forty on the mailbox, along with the name Everett. Stopping the car, Alex sat gaping at what to him was a mansion.

Finally, Maggie couldn't resist asking the obvious, "How could Peter afford a house like that?"

"I heard it was a wedding gift from his father-in-law."

He then drove past the house several times, becoming angrier by the moment. On the drive home, he seemed lost in thought, unaware that there was anyone traveling with him. His only conversation was with himself as he cursed under his breath and mumbled about the injustice of it all. Once home, he sat by the phone until well past six o'clock awaiting word from Joe.

It was the next morning before Joe called to report that Expressway would only agree to four months severance, and that they had implied that if their offer was not accepted immediately, it would be withdrawn. He had, however, been able to negotiate a one-time, lump-sum payment without any of the standard payroll deductions. Alex went berserk and began cursing Landon for trying to screw him. At the first opportunity, Joe calmly assured him that, given the information he had received, the settlement seemed reasonable. Landon had stated emphatically that Alex was in no position to be dictating terms to anyone. According to Joe's calculations, Expressway's offer was equivalent to about six months of normal take-home pay, after benefits were deducted. The lawyer did his best to convince Alex that things would work out just fine, given his impressive experience, Cliff's help, and the services to be provided by the outplacement agency. Alex spent the afternoon running off his anger and after dinner, fishing at a nearby lake.

Since the ugly scene on Monday, he had been trying in his own way to make up with Maggie, but as usual, he had not been able to verbalize his apology. That would require admission of fault, something he could not bring himself to do.

On Friday, he received a certified letter from Expressway. After discussing the terms thoroughly with Joe, he decided it was in his best interest to accept Expressway's offer. After signing the agreement and forging signatures for two fictitious witnesses, he drove to the post office just to be sure the letter would be delivered at Expressway the following Monday. It was a relief knowing he would soon receive a rather large payoff. Later that afternoon, Bruner called to suggest that he come out the next morning to remove his personal belongings.

Alex arrived at the office at exactly nine o'clock as had been suggested. Bruner was waiting out front. Neither man had much to say and proceeded directly to Alex's office. David had prepared a list of items that Alex would be allowed to remove.

The only item in question was the Rolodex file containing business cards. After conferring with David by telephone and receiving his agreement, Bruner told Alex to take the cards. As David had pointed out, the cards could assist him in networking to find another job, and it was to everyone's advantage for him to get rehired as soon as possible.

Once his personal belongings had been packed, Bruner collected his credit cards, identification badge, and other company property. After helping to load his boxes into the Blazer, the two proceeded to the exercise room to empty his locker. By ten-fifteen everything had been loaded, and he left Bruner without saying another word.

Arriving home, Alex found that Julie had returned from her friend's house and was sitting in the family room watching television. They hugged each other tightly. Neither mentioned Alex's problems at Expressway. He and Maggie had never discussed such issues with the children, and he was not about to start now. Julie was only a kid, and the less she knew, the better.

CHAPTER 23

Tuesday, July 23

On Tuesday of the following week, Alex met with a placement counselor at Employment Services Ltd., one of the two firms Expressway had recommended. He was not happy that the man was Hispanic and spoke with an accent, but since Expressway was picking up his charges, he decided to take his chances. After discussing Alex's experience and career aspirations, they spent the rest of the afternoon preparing a résumé. It was agreed that Mr. Fernandez would inform potential employers that Alex's decision to leave Expressway was by mutual agreement because Expressway "lacked promotional opportunities" within the environmental department. The termination agreement Alex had signed stated that he agreed to accept a settlement package in lieu of filing for unemployment benefits from the state. He understood that the company would contest his application should one be filed.

After providing Mr. Fernandez with a list of prospective employers, Alex headed for Orlando. With Expressway's investigation underway, Cliff was nervous about being seen with him but agreed to meet in Kissimmee. In addition to meeting with Cliff, Alex also wanted to revisit Peter's neighborhood.

Later, as the two men sat having a beer, Cliff filled Alex in on the details of the ongoing investigation. Expressway's auditors had questioned his staff extensively about how gifts were handled on the company books. He had, of course, already instructed the key managers to explain that the only gifts made by the company were of very little monetary value, and that business related entertainment expenses were never included with customer billings. So far as he knew, no one had broken ranks.

They sat for hours, discussing Alex's employment options as well as the responses Cliff would make when he was questioned regarding reimbursement claims. As usual, Alex drank heavily while Cliff provided his usual doses of encouragement and advice. They'd been best friends, occasionally more, and each greatly valued their relationship. At Cliff's suggestion, Alex called Maggie to tell her that he would be staying in Orlando for a meeting with Joe Morgan early the next morning. As expected, she offered no argument.

Over the next three weeks, Alex spent most of his time contacting business associates in the hope of securing job leads. Most were cordial and assured him they would try to turn something up, but nothing came of the conversations. Many had been on the receiving end of his abusive management style and wanted nothing more to do with him, especially now that he was no longer in a position to reward them with Expressway's business. It was general knowledge throughout the environmental community that he had been fired for something having to do with SSI.

In the meantime, Mr. Fernandez scheduled several interviews, none of which resulted in a job offer. In the beginning, Alex had been optimistic that each potential employer would recognize his value and make him an even better offer than they had intended. After all, he had fifteen years experience in environmental management and had worked for two reputable companies. With each rejection, hope faded. And each fueled the fire of failure that propelled him ever nearer the edge.

After two months of fruitless searching, he sank into a perpetual state of despair. The severance check from Expressway had at first seemed large, but their bank balance was dropping at an alarming rate. Even though the possibility of a lengthy period of unemployment became an ever-increasing concern for Maggie, Alex refused to discuss the matter. The more she voiced her fear that without additional income, they could not continue to pay their bills, the more Alex insisted that he would not accept just *any* job. His new position had to at least be comparable to the one he'd held at Expressway.

As frustration over his employment search escalated, so did the stress between family members. Maggie refused to even consider relocation; she would *not* leave yet another good nursing position. Julie's increasing wildness and rebellion, while understandable given all that was happening in their lives, couldn't be tolerated. He loved her dearly, but what was she thinking? It was all Maggie's fault. If she were just willing to go to the ends of the earth with him—like she used to say—he'd be settled into a new job by now. Julie would be in a new high school and have plenty of time to make more friends with two years left before graduation. Why were the women in his life always such problems?

With each passing day, Maggie pressured him to accept any reasonable job offer in the Tampa area. He in turn pressured Mr. Fernandez to find something that would pay what he had been making at Expressway. All the while, Julie slipped farther into the throes of teenage rebellion.

Alex's method for coping, as always, was to drown his problems in alcohol. He started his morning with a beer and his day ended when he passed out in front of the television. Much of the time in between was spent on the phone. In addition to harassing Mr. Fernandez and various consultants, he began calling Cliff numerous times a day.

Why didn't his friend help him find a job or put him to work at SSI?

Once the investigation was initiated by Expressway, all payments owed to Scientific Solutions Inc. for services rendered were frozen. Expressway was SSI's biggest account. Even before the payments stopped, the company struggled financially.

Cliff teetered on the brink of exhaustion, working night and day to stay ahead of the wolves. Cycla-Corp was closely monitoring the investigation, and the sale of the company hung in the balance. They also requested massive amounts of documentation required by the due-diligence process. Alex called daily, each call more belligerent than the last. Irate creditors demanded payment. Cliff and a few trusted associates were frantically destroying evidence before Expressway's auditors discovered it. He had also received notice from the FBI that Expressway had advised of possible irregularities and that they were initiating their own investigation. As if that weren't enough, several key employees had jumped ship. It was anything but business as usual.

Maggie had returned to her job at the hospital the week after her short leave of absence. At first Alex expected the relationship between them to improve, as had always been the case. Instead, it had gone downhill. Arguments were their only means of communication, each one escalating more quickly than the last. Maggie seemed to have given up on the marriage. He suspected she was just biding her time.

Finally, their domestic war exploded. "Get up and get out of here, you drunken...slob." She stood in the doorway between the den and the kitchen after working a double shift.

Unshaven and unkempt, Alex lay sprawled on the couch. Beer cans littered the floor. "What'd ya say about a job?" Groggily, he pushed himself into a sitting position and labored to get his bearings in the glare of the television.

"I said I want you to get out. I'm not going to live like this.

"Get out? Hell, this is my house too!"

"It *was* your house, but not any longer"

"If you want to go, then get the hell out! I'm staying right here, so learn to live with it!" He managed to stand up, then swayed precariously.

"I've talked to my lawyer, Alex. It's *over*. We're tearing this family apart. For Julie's sake, if not for mine, you've got to get out!"

"*I've talked to my lawyer,*" he mocked. "What does *that* mean?"

"Just what you think it means! I've tried...God knows I've tried...to help you through this latest crisis, but I can't take it anymore. Either you go voluntarily, or I'll have you removed by the sheriff."

Like a drunken sailor testing his sea legs, he stumbled toward her. Without warning, he slapped her across the face, knocking her backward against the kitchen counter. Seeing the knife block in front of her, she grabbed a butcher knife and whirled around to face him, blood streaming from her split lip.

"I'll kill you if you come one step closer. I mean it, Alex. I'll kill you!" In all their years together, he had never struck her. "It's over! Get out *now*! You can get your stuff tomorrow while I'm gone, but I want you out of here tonight. Go to your pal Cliff, go anywhere, I don't care. Just get out!"

For a moment he just stood there, shaking his head and trying to make the sight of his injured wife standing there with a knife disappear.

Julie ran into the kitchen. "Mother, don't!" She threw herself against Alex, pinning both arms to his side and placing her body between them. "*What* are you doing?"

"It's okay, Baby," Alex whimpered. "I don't know what happened. It's my fault, not hers." He glanced forlornly at his wife. "I'm sorry, Maggie. I'm really, really sorry."

"Get out, Alex," she pleaded as she pressed a wet dishtowel against her mouth. "Just get out!"

Pushing his daughter to one side, he took a step toward her, but she backed away, keeping the island between them. The futility of the situation was clear even to him.

After years of struggle, their marriage had reached its inevitable conclusion. There was nothing for him to do but leave. He had lost his job, his self-respect, most of his friends, and now his family's support.

Moments later, the roar of his Blazer faded as he drove away into the night.

CHAPTER 24

Alex drove aimlessly for hours, stopping only to purchase a cold six-pack to drown his woes. Around midnight he parked at a construction site and, after finishing the last of his beers, passed out. He was awakened the next morning by the laughter of workers pointing at the pile of cans outside his window. After shouting obscenities at them, he started the engine and accelerated in their direction, turning aside at the last second as they dove for cover.

About four miles west of Temple Terrace, just off Busch Boulevard, he stopped at the Florida Shores and rented a studio apartment. It was the same place he had stayed the last time they'd separated. Any comparisons he might have made with the Tennis Exchange were too painful to consider and served only to remind him of how far he had fallen. The exuberance he had felt in those days seemed lost forever.

He arrived disheveled and disoriented, but the manager remembered him from before. After paying a month's rent, he drove to his house, cleaned himself up, and spent the rest of the day boxing up his belongings and hauling them to the apartment. It might take a while this time, but he was confident he could eventually make peace with Maggie and go back home, just like before.

Meanwhile, he'd have to tolerate the fourteen by twenty studio unit with the kitchen appliances clustered in one corner, a three-quarter bath in the other, and a small closet in between. In the main area of the nondescript room was a sleeper-sofa, an end table, two dilapidated armchairs, a small television on a wall shelf that swiveled, and one large picture of waves breaking along a moonlit seashore. Years of use had scorched the faded shade on the end-table lamp. Jammed into the kitchen area under a small circular ceiling fixture sat a plastic-topped table and three chrome-trimmed chairs.

Although the permanently soiled gold-shag carpet appeared to have been recently cleaned, he soon discovered it was still home to a colony of fleas. Settlement cracks at the corners of the two windows beside the front door had been repaired, but the beige touch-up paint didn't match the off-white walls. For efficiency units that could be rented by the week after the first of the month, this one was no worse than most and better than some. No matter…it wasn't meant to be home.

Overgrown ligustrum bushes restricted his view of the parking lot and blocked most of the sunlight which otherwise could have filtered in between the worn drapes. All in all, the depressing surroundings mirrored his gloom. The accommodations hardly met his minimum requirements, but for a man living day-to-day, they provided shelter, a semblance of privacy, and a mailing address.

In the weeks that followed, Alex vacillated between outrage and thoughts of suicide. After a few more unproductive interviews, he consoled himself with the belief that he was overqualified for the jobs. In the past three weeks, there had only been three interviews. The last was with a firm in Fort Myers owned by a friend of Cliff's. Although Alex by that time was operating at the fringes of sanity, even he could see that the interview had simply been done as a business favor. To add to his frustration, every telephone call made to sweet talk Maggie resulted in a dial tone.

While reading the *Tampa Tribune* one morning, he came across an advertisement that seemed too good to be true. It read:

> *Environmental consulting position.*
> *Degree in environmental science or*
> *equivalent required, plus ten years*
> *experience in project management.*
> *Send résumé to Drawer 127.*

His hopes soared for the first time in weeks.

Two weeks after sending in his résumé, he received a phone call from Nancy White, personnel recruiter for Frazier Environmental. Alex recognized the firm as a nationally known and respected environmental consulting company, exactly what he had hoped for. Ms. White explained that Frazier was the primary environmental consultant for Florida Sanitation and that an experienced manager was needed in their Tampa office. The position would be responsible for managing disposal of hazardous wastes generated at Florida Sanitation, the same type of work he had done at Chemtrac. Because Frazier worked with firms different from those used by Expressway, he hoped that the details of his recent employment problems would not be found out.

Fortunately, Ms. White's call had come early enough that morning for Alex to still be sober. She introduced herself by stating that she was in the human resource department and not personally familiar with the intricacies of hazardous waste regulations. Someone else would discuss those issues with him. She had called to verify certain information and to arrange for an interview. She told Alex that his experience was very impressive and seemed to match their needs. They agreed to meet the following morning.

His interview at Frazier went extremely well. Mr. Elliott, the engineer with whom he met, asked only a few questions relating to project management before proceeding to hazardous waste law. He seemed satisfied that Alex was the expert he claimed to be and made no effort to hide the fact that he was impressed. Alex left the interview brimming with optimism, certain he would be offered the job. It had come just in the nick of time, as their bank account was close to depletion. Although he had been served with divorce papers several weeks before, he and Maggie had continued to share the same checking account. He had to generate some income within the next few weeks.

Since moving out, he and Maggie had spoken only a few times by telephone. On each of those occasions, she had refused to discuss reconciliation, and when he'd persisted, she'd hung up on him. Having heard nothing more from her lawyer regarding the divorce proceedings, he assumed she might be having second thoughts. At any rate, no news was good news, and landing the job with Frazier would help him get back into her good graces. He was an expert at manipulating people, especially Maggie. His outlook brightened at the thought of being back on top and in control of his circumstances.

After moving into the apartment, he'd spent much of his time playing over in his mind the unfair treatment he had received at Expressway. He was baffled at how quickly his fortunes had changed. It hadn't been that long since he'd been the one pulling the strings, and David the one being jerked around.

With increasing frequency and clarity, he dreamed of getting even with those he held responsible. Each day his thoughts became more bizarre. Sometime along the way, he moved from talking to himself to hearing voices that whispered of the wrongs that had been done to him. Later, the whispers seemed to be jeering at him in ridicule. In time, the conversations with his demons became part of his normal routine. The voices insisted that justice be served. Why should he lose everything while Peter and David continued to prosper? At times, he could picture Peter and David laughing at him, and those visions pushed him ever closer to obeying the evil commands. As long as they were free to laugh about what they had done, how could he ever know any peace? That question echoed rhetorically in his head hour after hour, until he felt he could bear it no longer.

In time Alex began acting out his fantasies. He would park in the woods north of Expressway's building around quitting time and watch through binoculars as his former friends left their workplace. On some afternoons, he removed his rifle from its rack and carefully positioned the crosshairs in the center of David's forehead. To Alex, David's face bore a look of smug satisfaction, making it difficult not to pull the trigger ever so slightly. He could picture the small hole appearing about an inch above the bridge of David's nose while the back of his head exploded onto the people walking behind. It would have been so easy, as easy as bending his finger.

Fortunately for David, Alex's hatred for Peter took precedence over the hatred for him. Alex reasoned that had Peter not spilled his guts, David would never have been able to turn Landon against him and he would not be the victim that he was. It was Peter who had betrayed him out of sheer spite. David had merely reacted out of fear for his own job and as compelled by his own self-righteous, judgmental attitude.

On nights when his tormentors were more active than usual, Alex found solace by harassing David. He would place the calls from different pay telephones, waiting until he was sure the Colemans were asleep. The first two nights, David answered expectantly and kept saying hello until finally slamming down the receiver. On the third night David warned the mystery caller that the call was being traced. On the fourth night Alex whispered that he was planning to commit obscene acts upon Leah, knowing that David would then lie awake anguishing over her safety. When he tried to call the fifth time, he was informed by a recorded message that the number he had dialed had been changed to an unlisted number.

Alex was satisfied for the present. He'd made sure that David knew someone was out there in the darkness. And he was sure that David had begun to sweat.

He smiled as he fantasized about the conversation that likely ensued between Leah and David following his calls. Leah would ask David why anyone would want to interrupt their sleep at that hour. He would tell her it was just some crank caller with nothing better to do. Alex knew David wouldn't want to frighten his sweet little wife with prospects too fearsome to consider, yet he would be obliged to tell her that her safety could be in jeopardy. Eventually, they would both be living in fear.

Making David suffer gave him such pleasure. Inflicting fear was but the first step. He was dreaming of other ways to punish David, horrifying ways. The Colemans would pay dearly for what had been done to him. For the moment, however, Alex focused on the hope that he would somehow salvage both his career and marriage. That hope alone provided the only stability to his frazzled emotions.

Creating havoc in Peter's life was more difficult. His telephone number was unlisted, and he lived two hours away. Several months had passed since his departure from Expressway, and Alex assumed that, by now, he would have concluded that he'd gotten away unscathed with his treachery. When Alex was not thinking about David, he was planning revenge against Peter. During occasional trips to Orlando to break the monotony, he would stalk the man to learn his daily routine. He soon knew his routes to and from work, his weekly schedule, and his daily habits. Only on weekends did his routine vary, depending upon whether he went sailing with his father-in-law or played golf at the club.

Alex's wrath knew no bounds as he watched Peter hobnob with the upper crust—the place where *Alex* deserved to be—adding jealousy to his hate-filled heart. Killing him only once did not seem sufficient justice. In his mind's eye, Alex pictured himself killing Peter slowly, over and over again.

CHAPTER 25

Thursday, November 14, 1996

The alarm went off at 5:30. Peter reached over, tapped the off button, and sat up slowly to avoid waking Michelle. He could use another couple of hours' sleep, but since he had an afternoon golf date, he needed to get to work on time. After all, he should set an example for the underlings at Barrett's who might resent his early departure to play golf. And everyone knew that Thursdays were a golfing day. *Rank does have its privileges,* he thought, *and the sooner those losers get the message, the better.*

He always regretted his lack of moderation the morning after having partied too hard the night before. This morning was no different. He just needed a Coke™, a few aspirins, and a cigarette to soothe his pounding head.

Gingerly weaving his way down the hall to the kitchen, he removed a can from the refrigerator, lit a cigarette, and headed for the bathroom. He always used the guest bath, since there was less chance of waking his lovely wife. Beautiful or not, she could be very unfriendly in the mornings.

After his daily shower and shave, he went to the closet and selected his shirt, tie, and slacks. Quietly removing his billfold, keys, and pocket-change from the top of the dresser, he grabbed his shoes and returned to the kitchen. Then he checked to make sure Michelle had not been disturbed. Seeing that she still slept soundly, he headed for work.

On the way he pulled into a fast food drive-thru and ordered his usual two sausage biscuits with egg and cheese and a cup of water. Fifteen minutes later, at exactly six forty-five, he let himself into the office through the side entrance to make his customary but token appearance with the flooring crews who were receiving their assignments for the day from the foreman. Just showing up at that time of the morning reinforced the obvious: he was next in line to take over the business.

Working for his father-in-law was too good to be true. Peter was overpaid, had power and prestige, and could come and go as he pleased. He knew he could rely on the experienced supervisors to handle the day-to-day frustrations. The flooring business was not rocket science; he was fully capable of taking over already if necessary. The possibility that some employees saw him as a figurehead didn't bother him. What did they know about it? They were paid to do manual labor. He was a Harvard graduate and would be running the business when all of them were gone and forgotten. In the meantime, he might as well enjoy the good life. When the time came, he would be the man.

When the crews were dispatched, he went to the lobby and picked up the morning newspaper that had been delivered through the mail slot in the door. At seven-thirty he laid the paper aside, propped his feet up on his desk, and dialed home. He always called around that time just to be sure Michelle was up and about. Although she was the owner's daughter, she was also vice president of sales, and as such, needed to arrive at a respectable hour.

After chatting for a few minutes, he turned to the business section to check on some stocks he had recently purchased. With both of them bringing home fat paychecks, they couldn't spend what they had coming in if they wanted to, and dabbling in the market added some excitement to his life. On mornings when there wasn't anything pressing, he would drive around Orlando to inspect the local jobs. If he did happen upon a serious problem, he would use his car phone to consult the foreman for advice.

Although the job didn't challenge his intellect, he figured that in time he would learn to enjoy it, perhaps expand the business to

212

include interior decorating. He missed the excitement of managing projects and flexing his muscles with the consultants, but he consoled himself with the thought that success had its price and he had to be willing to make the sacrifice.

Peter grew up enjoying the life of a privileged kid and was accustomed to socializing with influential people. His parents were friends with the governor of Arkansas, not to mention other dignitaries who regularly attended parties in their home.

Peter was highly intelligent and excelled without effort in school. Although he accepted positions of leadership when they were forced on him, he seldom chose to pursue recognition. Somehow, he had acquired the notion that such self-promotion was beneath him. After all, he had no need to prove anything to anyone. He was an Everett, enough said.

One of the privileges that he enjoyed most was playing golf, and he was a natural. As with everything he did, he excelled in the game and had carried a three handicap as a senior on his prep school's golf team. Although he was offered scholarships by several local colleges, his father insisted that he buckle down and pursue a technical degree from a prestigious university. When it came time to select his major, the choice was easy. Geology had fascinated him for as long as he could remember, and he had been adding rocks to his collection since he was a kid.

The Everetts vacationed regularly in Colorado, often staying at the Stanley Hotel in Estes Park. After opening in the early nineteen hundreds, it quickly became the mountain retreat of choice for Presidents and other prominent people. Standing on its south porch as a small boy, Peter had marveled at the snow-capped peaks to the south. At night he could see the twinkling lights on the plains to the east. The enormous geological forces that had created such splendor captivated his imagination. Although it was assumed that he would eventually join the family's construction business, Peter was permitted to obtain an undergraduate degree in geology, but it was only with the understanding that his master's degree would be in business.

Peter enrolled at the Colorado School of Mines in Golden. This small, exclusive college met the academic expectations of his parents and gave them more reason than before to make periodic visits to the beloved state of Colorado. During his junior year, he studied abroad and traveled extensively. Following graduation, he entered Harvard and earned his master's degree, with honors. Peter desired to prove himself by working a few years elsewhere before joining his father's business. Since his father had been a fraternity brother of Steve Snelling and Steve had visited in their home many times while Peter was growing up, he contacted Pyramid and was offered several positions from which to choose. The one he selected was a project manager's position in Expressway's Tampa office. His boss would be Alex Carter.

A few years after joining Expressway, he met and was captivated by the beautiful, blue-eyed young woman whose father, Ed Barrett, happened to own the largest flooring business in Florida. Ed had taken over the business from his father when Orlando was just another undistinguished town in central Florida. In the early seventies, however, Orlando emerged as the host city for Disney World. Because of Disney's enormous success, the area took off and soon became a preferred conference destination for companies worldwide. Those visitors needed overnight accommodations, conference centers, restaurants, and other services, all of which required flooring materials.

No company was better positioned to capitalize on Orlando's growth than Barrett's Flooring. It was a hometown company, well respected, and commanded thirty-five percent of the commercial flooring business in the Orlando market. In addition to his company's success, Ed was a partner in numerous other investments. He once told Peter it took twenty years to make his first million, and ironically, his wealth had increased at least a million dollars each year since. Fortunately for Peter, Ed had only one heir, his gifted daughter, Michelle.

Peter met Michelle at the Seacoast Golf and Tennis Club, where the Barrett family held a lifetime membership. Peter had been invited to play in the annual invitational as a guest of Walt Whitmire, senior partner of SSI. It was well known within SSI that Peter was an avid golfer, and Walt was delighted to sponsor Expressway's young project manager in the tournament.

214

Peter placed third in the championship flight and was warmly applauded at the gala reception afterwards. When the trophies had been awarded, Peter retired to the bar to enjoy a few drinks with his new friends. Michelle simply walked up, took his hand in hers, and never let go. She soon moved to Tampa. Following a short but torrid romance, Ed Barrett threw a wedding for them that reportedly cost over one hundred fifty thousand dollars. She was a debutante and his only child. Peter was the son he never had and a perfect choice to carry on the family business.

It wasn't long before Ed made Peter an offer that he couldn't turn down. Ed explained that he was sixty-two years old and had worked seven days a week for most of his life. It was time he started relinquishing the business to Michelle and his new son. He told Peter that he wanted to spend more time playing golf, sailing, and spoiling the grandchildren that he hoped would be forthcoming very soon. Since he owned a large sailboat and a little place in the Keys, all he had been waiting on was the right man to whom he could entrust Michelle and, of course, the business.

Ed explained that Michelle would take over ownership of the firm in three years, with Peter serving as its president. Ed would continue to sit on the board of directors but not participate in day-to-day decisions. Even Peter's father could not compete with that opportunity and was quick to admit it. In fact, he even offered to invest his own money in Barrett's business. By that time, Peter welcomed any opportunity to leave Expressway, as long as it didn't place his father in an awkward position with Steve Snelling. When Michelle made it clear she had no intention of ever leaving Florida—but if she did, it would definitely not be to move to Arkansas—the matter was decided.

During his first few years at Expressway, Peter and Alex had gotten along very well. Both liked to party and often got together with others from Expressway after work. Peter provided Alex with strong technical support, making him look good to management. During the fall of 1994, their relationship deteriorated dramatically. Peter had accidentally picked up on Alex's telephone line one day and overheard part of a conversation between Alex and Cliff Hawkins. It was clear the two men were more than just friends.

As he began to discreetly investigate the matter, he uncovered more than what he had expected. He learned that Alex was receiving expensive gifts and perhaps monetary kickbacks. That discovery explained why Alex had encouraged him to award certain projects to SSI when other firms were better qualified and their bids competitive. The guilt of withholding that information from David, coupled with his own sense of morality, became unbearable. With each passing day, he grew more disgusted, and with it, more insubordinate to his boss.

Alex had initially enjoyed having Peter around because he could lord his authority over someone with a Harvard degree. He joked about his "yuppie" underling and enjoyed thinking he held the keys to Peter's career. At first Peter took the razzing good-naturedly, but he soon began to resent Alex's ridicule. Sensing that he was losing control over his young subordinate, Alex would on occasion berate Peter in front of others. His enormous ego could not tolerate someone of lower rank, especially a younger man, questioning his decisions and openly challenging him.

Joining the Barrett company gave Peter a good excuse for resigning his job at Expressway, which by then had become unbearable. Never before had he dealt with such stress, and the hatred he harbored for Alex was unlike any feelings he had ever experienced. For months he had debated what to do with his knowledge about Alex's unethical business dealings and his personal relationship with Cliff. Once he knew he would be leaving the company, he decided to act. He wanted to punish Alex for all the abuse the man had inflicted on him and, in the process, clear his own conscience for having been a silent accomplice. He could leave Expressway for a better opportunity, and in the process, get Alex out of his life forever.

Only *after* he had told David what was going on in all its sordid details had the thought begun to gnaw at him that Alex was not someone to antagonize. He hoped he wouldn't live to regret his decision.

Sitting in his office at Barrett's, Peter caught up on some correspondence and approved time sheets from the previous week.

Approving time sheets was more a formality than anything else, since the payroll clerk had already reviewed them. His approval was intended to encourage honesty. In theory, he checked for abuse of overtime. In actuality, he seldom looked at them.

At ten o'clock his phone rang.

"Peter Everett," he answered.

"Raymond here. Are we still on for today?"

"Sure, why wouldn't we be?"

"The weather report this morning said that Gordon is predicted to move on shore near Tampa later today. The weatherman said it could be raining by dark and getting pretty nasty. Not what I'd call an ideal day for golf."

Peter looked at his empty mail basket and considered his options. "Everyday is an ideal day for golf in my book. I like to play in the elements; it adds another dimension to the game. Like surfers heading for the beach before a storm. It gives the sport that added edge. They don't cancel golf at Saint Andrews for a little bad weather; they just play right on through. I'm for teeing off at three sharp. Will that work for you?"

"Okay, if that's what you want to do, but if it starts lightning, I'm history. And I don't really care what they do at Saint Andrews."

"You sissy. I thought you were a real man!" Peter laughed.

"And I thought you were halfway intelligent. Nobody in his right mind would tee off in the teeth of a hurricane!"

"Did I ever tell you about the time..."

"Save it, Peter," Raymond interrupted. "I've heard that story at least a dozen times, and I didn't believe it the first time."

"See you on the tee box at three o'clock on the dot, unless the weather really does turn bad. If we can't play today, let's shoot for tomorrow if it blows through, same time. By the way, how close is Goober, or whatever its name is, supposed to get to Orlando?"

"Pretty close, I hear, and its name's Gordon, you ignoramus. They don't know for sure. You know how squirrelly those things are. It could just as easily turn around and head for Mexico. But if it continues on the projected course, it's supposed to pass us a little to the north."

"How much wind is it packing?" Peter asked.

"Right now, old buddy, it's blowing about sixty-five miles an hour, but with half that much wind in your face, your puny tee shot wouldn't make it to the ladies' tee."

"I'm looking out my window as we speak, and it still looks pretty nice to me. If it hits while we're out on the course, and I for one hope it does, we'll have a good story to tell our grandchildren."

"Look, I'm the one with two kids. You have yet to prove that you can even reproduce. Michelle told my wife that you were only interested about two nights a month."

"I've already sired three sons. They just don't happen to know who their father is!"

"See you later, jerk!"

"Hey, Raymond."

"What?"

"Your wife told Michelle that—"

"Save it! I'll see you later."

After making a few phone calls, Peter headed for Ed's office to touch base, and then he dropped in on Michelle.

"You must be out of your mind to play golf this afternoon," Michelle said. "Haven't you heard that a hurricane is headed this way?"

"Honey, the other guys would never let me live it down if I begged off today. If it gets too bad we'll head for cover, I promise."

"Head for the bar, you mean. You're not fooling me. I'll bet you're sweet on one of those barmaids out at the club."

"I only have eyes for you, and you know it. If you died today, I'd be a grieving widower for the rest of my life. No other woman could ever measure up to you."

"Don't smile when you say that," she warned, her eyes twinkling.

They hugged for a moment, followed by a lengthy kiss, lengthy at least for eleven in the morning.

"Why don't we go home for lunch, and I'll just pamper you until time to play," Peter offered, half in jest.

"Can't do it, Sweetie. I've got a meeting at three-thirty out at Canaveral. The brass wants to re-carpet some offices, and Dad wants

218

me to meet with the bigwigs. He figures that with his little girl along, they'll figure some way to accept our bid whether we're the lowest or not. You men are all alike, aren't you?"

"Not me, Hon, and I represent, I mean resent, that insinuation."

"You just be home when I get there, Petey Baby! I took some steaks out for us to grill if it isn't raining. If it is, I'll cook them inside. I should be there no later than seven-thirty."

"I won't be home until about then either unless our game gets cut short."

"That's fine," she said as her phone rang. "I'll see you tonight, okay?"

Peter went back to his office and started reviewing a bid for MGM that they would be submitting the next day. He looked around his office and smiled. *Nice, really nice!* he thought. *Another world from the box I had at Expressway.*

His spacious corner office overlooked a large grassy area bordered by flowering bushes of various kinds. Inside, prints of famous paintings graced the walls. Peter had specified that the color scheme be green and burgundy with walnut paneling and furniture. The interior decorator had taken his idea and run with it. The striped wallpaper above the chair rail perfectly complemented the furniture and paneling below. A computer and oversized monitor sat on the credenza. A leather sofa, two arm chairs, a coffee table, and an enclosed, fully equipped entertainment center completed the furnishings. To add a touch of home, a brass lamp with a green glass shade sat on his desk.

If only my friends at Expressway could see this setup, he mused. *Maybe I'll invite them over for our Christmas party. I'd love to see Alex's face when he sees my office. Maybe I'll send them a Christmas photo of me sitting behind my desk. My pals would appreciate having a picture, and Alex would look at it out of curiosity if nothing else.*

At eleven forty-five he initialed the bid and pitched it in his out basket. He was having another great day. They had all been great since moving to Orlando, and if he played his cards right, life should just get better and better for the Everetts, assuming it could get any better.

CHAPTER 26

Alex woke at five a.m. after passing out sometime the evening before. A muscular redhead in purple tights was leading a group of middle-aged women in aerobics on the tube. His head throbbed as usual after too much booze. He got up, stumbled to the bathroom, and returned to the couch to mindlessly flip from channel to channel. Finding nothing of interest, he turned off the set. His frustration had already begun to build.

By 5:30, he could wait no longer. He picked up the phone and dialed his home. After the sixth ring, Maggie answered.

"Maggie, it's Alex. I need to talk with you."

"What do you want? Do you know what time it is? It's still dark outside, for goodness sake."

"Please don't hang up. I have to talk with you," he pleaded.

"I have nothing to say to you, Alex. It's over! *We're* over! *Through*! Why can't you get that through your thick skull?"

"How's Julie?"

"You didn't call to ask about Julie, but she's doing fine. Much better since you and I are no longer at each other's throat."

"I'm getting my life back together, really I am. You'd be proud of me. I haven't had a drink in weeks and don't even want one anymore. It looks like I'll be going to work for Frazier Environmental pretty soon as their hazardous waste specialist, reporting to one of the top guys. I expect their offer any time now. But Maggie, I'm miserable without you, and I want to come home. If we could just get together, you would see for yourself that I've got things under control. If we could just meet and talk, I'm sure we could work things out. I know it was all my fault. Just give me one more chance, that's all, just one more chance. Let's just meet for lunch and—"

"Stop it, Alex," she interrupted. "It's no use! Can't you understand, I don't *want* to make it work!"

She was fully awake now, her heart racing wildly. Just hearing his voice unleashed a flood of memories, most of them bad. For the past month she had been meeting weekly with Dr. Jacobs and had only recently come to terms with the realization that their marriage was over. The counselor had described it as an "extremely destructive" relationship that could only be improved if Alex obtained professional counseling for an extended period of time, and success even then was by no means certain. Maggie hadn't had the strength before to deal with the truth, but this time was different. She never wanted him back, not under any circumstances. She no longer trusted or respected him, and without those, there was no basis for a healthy relationship. Besides, she now was convinced that he was mentally unstable and, to be honest, she was terrified of him. And according to Dr. Jacobs, she had every reason to be.

"Alex, I'm through talking. You need professional help...with someone like Dr. Jacobs. I'm not the one to give you that kind of help."

Before he could catch himself, Alex lashed out in anger. "That quack has probably told Coleman everything you two have talked about. He gets his kicks from nosing into other people's personal stuff. He's just a degreed whore who's on Expressway's payroll, or had you forgotten that?"

He heard a click, and she was gone. When he redialed, he got a busy signal. As he slammed down the handset, the phone slid off the table onto the floor. In a fit of rage, he kicked it halfway across the room.

After opening a beer, he collapsed into a chair and sat staring at the streetlight in the parking lot. He hated not being in control, and Maggie hanging up on him was like a slap in the face. He wanted to kill her. She deserved it for kicking him out of his own house like some mongrel dog. He sat there rigid, fists clenched, eyes bulging.

221

His heart raced, and his head pounded worse than before. He didn't need her. He didn't need anyone, except maybe Cliff. All of his friends had turned their backs on him. After a while he was able to pull himself together and start thinking more rationally. At eight-thirty and another beer later, he telephoned Cliff's office.

"Good morning, Scientific Solutions, Incorporated.

"It's Alex. I need to talk with Cliff."

"I'm sorry, Mr. Carter, but Mr. Hawkins is in a meeting this morning. May I take a message for him, or would you like to have his voice mail?"

"How long will he be tied up?" Alex snapped.

"He should be available around ten-thirty," she answered softly.

"Give me his voice mail then."

After a few seconds Alex heard Cliff's recorded message. He hated listening to the same message he'd heard a thousand times before.

After the beep, Alex started speaking softly, doing his best to sound calm. "Cliff, Alex here. I'd like to hook up tonight if you're not too busy. It's been weeks since we got together, and I'm going stir-crazy sitting around here waiting for something good to happen. Could you please give me a call at home...no...I mean my apartment, when you get a chance? I'll stay by the phone until you can call. Have a good one." He slammed the phone down.

He dressed and hurried the two blocks to a convenience store to buy a newspaper, then rushed back to the apartment so he wouldn't miss either Cliff's call or the long awaited call from Frazier Environmental. After scanning the front page, sports section, and classifieds, he read the business section just to keep current with local announcements. On the second page was a section entitled "Personnel Announcements." The first paragraph caught his eye.

Mr. Ed Barrett, president of Barrett's Flooring based in Orlando, recently announced the promotion of Mr. Peter Everett to vice president of operations. Mr. Everett joined the

*firm earlier this year after having
held several executive positions with
Expressway, a division of Pyramid
International.*

He clenched his teeth and tried to quell his shaking body. *How could that good-for-nothing have been promoted to vice president? He doesn't know a damn thing about the flooring business. He was no executive at Expressway, just some two-bit flunky who worked for me. That release was printed just to justify his existence.*

Alex seethed. Peter's laughing face flashed before him. He jumped up, ripped the newspaper apart, and threw it around the room like a crazed reveler at Mardi Gras. The image of Peter's grinning face wouldn't go away. No matter where he turned, it was in front of him, laughing, jeering at him. *That worthless low-life was born with a silver spoon in his mouth. If he'd had to earn a living, he wouldn't know where to start.* Slowly, Alex became aware of his frenzied behavior. He forced himself to calm down and regain what little sanity he had left.

After pacing the room for a while, he went to the refrigerator for something to eat, but except for the beer and some molded bread, it was empty. He hadn't showered, shaved, or even changed clothes in three days.

At ten o'clock, he walked to the cluster of mailboxes at the parking lot entrance, leaving his door open so he could hear the telephone should it ring. Inside his box were two envelopes. The beige one was from Frazier, but the plain white envelope bore no return address. The one from Frazier felt thin, suggesting a single page...not a good sign. Dread jerked at his guts. Although afraid of what he would find, he frantically tore it open. In one glance he knew it was bad news. The letter was only three sentences in length.

Dear Mr. Carter:

We regret to inform you that we do not have a suitable position at this time. Your application will be retained for six months, and you will be considered

*should a suitable position develop. We appreciate
your interest in Frazier and wish you every success.*
Sincerely,
Marjorie White, Recruiter

Unwilling to believe his eyes, he reread the letter twice, three times, hoping somehow to change the words into the glowing offer he had expected. *Perhaps they made a mistake and sent me the letter intended for someone else. Yes, that's it...that has to be it.* Frazier was his last hope. Without opening the other envelope, he entered his apartment, slammed the door, and feverishly dialed Frazier's telephone number.

"Good morning, Frazier Environmental. How may I direct your call?"

"I want to speak to Marjorie White," he answered, his voice pitched higher and his speech much faster than normal. After a short wait, she answered.

"Good morning. This is Marjorie White. How may I help you?"

"Ms. White, this is Alex Carter. I interviewed there about three weeks ago for an environmental position. It's the one where experience in managing hazardous wastes is required."

"Oh, yes, Mr. Carter. I remember you now. I believe you had previously been employed with Expressway in their remediation group, and as I recall, and with another firm in Georgia prior to that."

"That's right." The way she so quickly identified him with Expressway confirmed his suspicion that she had spoken with someone there who could have given her damaging information about his termination. He tried to keep his voice from revealing his growing panic. "Ms. White, I received a letter this morning that I think was sent to me by mistake. The one I got says that I was not selected for that job."

"Yes, that's correct, Mr. Carter. I'm sorry but—"

"How could you have hired someone else?" he blurted out. "I'm the most qualified person you could possibly find for that job, and you know it. I don't know what Expressway may have told you but whatever it was, it's a damn lie. I want to talk with Mr. Elliott. I'm not taking this bull from some broad."

"I'm sorry, Mr. Carter, but Mr. Elliott is not accepting any calls this morning."

"Listen, you stupid bitch. I said I want to talk to him, and I want to talk to him now, dammit! If I have to come down there to talk with him, that's exactly what I'll do."

"I'm sorry, but Mr. Elliott has left explicit instructions that he is not to be interrupted."

"You tell that bastard to go to hell!" he screamed, slamming down the receiver. His breath came in gasps, like the elasticity had abandoned his lungs. All of a sudden he became a mad man, swinging his arms wildly in the air and cursing uncontrollably. *Peter! Peter did this to me!* He stormed about the apartment like a cougar caught in a trap. Back and forth he stalked, at times bumping into the walls and furniture. His thoughts raced in all directions—disconnected, incomplete, and irrational.

"I've got to get control of myself. I've got to get control of myself. I've got to get control of myself," he repeated over and over like a mantra.

Finally, he could take a deep breath, then two, and three. The veins that had popped out in his neck and face began to recede. He opened another beer and drank it without stopping. Finishing that one, he opened another. Everyone else seemed to be controlling his life. David, Maggie, Peter, Dr. Jacobs, and now Mr. Elliott. What could he do with everyone in the world against him?

The room began spinning around him. He felt himself going down.

The next thing he knew he was staring at the ceiling overhead. Why was he lying on the floor? Had he tripped and fallen? Or passed out from the stress that was tearing him apart? The spinning room had slowed to a stop.

Then he remembered the other letter. He turned his head and saw it lying on the floor nearby. After fumbling in vain to open it carefully, he angrily ripped off the end and scanned its brief message. He wondered what else could go wrong...then he knew.

November 12, 1996

Mr. Carter:

    The check used to pay last week's rent is attached. As you can see, it was returned from the bank marked insufficient funds. You are hereby advised that you have until noon, Friday, November 15, to pay your rent in cash. If you fail to pay, we will be obligated to have the utilities disconnected and eviction proceedings initiated. Please tend to this matter immediately.

                      The Manager

There must have been some mistake. The last time he'd checked their bank balance, it still showed over three thousand dollars. *Surely, Maggie would not have withdrawn the money, my money, without telling me. How can I possibly get hold of any cash in twenty-four hours?* He checked his billfold. He only had twenty-one dollars in cash. His thoughts ran helter-skelter. *Cliff! Cliff will loan me the money. After all, he has given me a hundred times, a thousand times what I need for the lousy rent. What's a couple hundred dollars to somebody like Cliff?* It was ten-fifteen when he dialed Cliff's number.

"Good morning, Scientific Solutions, Incorporated."

"It's Alex. I need to talk with Cliff."

"I'm sorry, but Mr. Hawkins is still tied up. Would you—"

"What do you mean he's *still* tied up? How the hell would I know he was tied up?"

"But Mr. Carter, you called at—"

Furious, Alex again slammed down the phone. Cliff had become increasingly difficult to reach over the past few weeks. Why? Cliff was the only one he could turn to, his last hope.

The room was spinning again. His mind jumped from one disconnected thought to another. Lights flashed before his eyes. His head throbbed. Thoughts from the past bombarded him like an old movie on fast forward. His mother stood naked before him. If only

226

he could look away and never have to see her that way again, but he couldn't. He felt her warmth and remembered.... The scoutmaster hovered over him, fondling him without restraint. Suddenly, center stage in his mind, was Peter's jeering face. His mouth was moving, but no sounds were coming out. Then Bill appeared, whispering in his mother's ear, and she was listening, nodding, and smiling. Then came David sitting behind his desk like a king on his throne, pompous, self-righteous. Maggie suddenly appeared, standing before him with a knife in her hand and fear in her eyes. If only he could talk with Cliff...Cliff would be able to somehow deliver him from this never-ending nightmare.

Finally, the images faded. Exhausted and wet with perspiration, he grasped for some semblance of sanity. As his thinking cleared, he picked up the phone. For a moment he couldn't remember the number he had dialed from memory so often in the past.

Hearing the receptionist's familiar greeting, he was at first unable to speak. After she had repeated the greeting a second time, he stammered, "It's me. I've got to talk with him. I don't care what he's doing! Just tell him to answer the damn phone."

A few moments later, Cliff's voice came on the line. "Hi, Alex, what's the problem?"

Hearing his friend's voice was like a lifeline thrown to a drowning man. "I know you're busy, but I really need to see you. The job at Frazier didn't work out. Someone at Expressway must have shot their mouth off, probably David. Anyway, they turned me down."

Cliff didn't reply immediately, irritating Alex by his silence. He had expected to hear a word of encouragement. "Cliff, are you still there?"

"Yes, I'm here. I'm just listening."

Even in Alex's frazzled state of mind, he could detect a different tone in Cliff's voice, one he had not heard before. Normally, he was warm and friendly, and he always put a positive spin on things. Not this time.

"I need to borrow two hundred dollars," Alex blurted out. "Maggie pulled out all the money from our bank account, and the check for my rent at this dump bounced. If I don't come up with the money by tomorrow, they're going to throw me out. If you can let me have a loan for a few days, I'll drive over this afternoon and pick it up." Again Cliff made no immediate reply. "If you can just loan me the money, I'll get it from Maggie this weekend and pay you back." More silence. "Hell! Say something, Cliff. I'm not going to sit here begging."

"Alex, I have never loaned or given you money before, and you know it. I suggest you call Maggie and get it from her. My finances right now are a bit of a disaster. As you may know, we haven't received any money from Expressway in over three months. Four of my key people have quit, and we've lost several major accounts in addition to Expressway. I wish I could loan you the money as a friend, but I simply can't."

Alex listened in disbelief, unable to read between the lines and unwilling to admit that his best, and now only, friend was refusing to help. "Look, Cliff, you can't afford not to help me. With what I know—"

He heard a click, then silence.

The last thread connecting Alex to the real world snapped. Whatever traces of normalcy had existed only moments before were irretrievably lost. Caught in the eye of his own storm, Alex's thoughts swirled around him in chaos and destruction. The rage that he had bottled up for so long was suddenly unleashed. He had nothing left to hope for…and nothing left to lose.

Instead of reacting in a fit of violent anger, as had become so common, he felt a strange sense of calm settle over him, a peace he had not known in a long time, perhaps never. He carefully replaced the receiver in its cradle. His face, flushed and distorted only moments before, returned to normal. No longer confused and at war with himself, he knew exactly what he must do. All his life he had been on the receiving end. Now came his turn. It was payback time.

The inevitable day of retribution had arrived. When it was over, he would begin a new life someplace far away, where he would be respected and appreciated, and perhaps even loved.

Liberated. Yes, he thought, *I'm liberated from this rotten world.* All the fantasies that had invaded his thoughts before now began to merge into a plan, an intricate plan that would forever silence his enemies and rid him of the dreaded visions.

He went to the small closet and pulled out the boxes he had brought from home, searching through them until he found the one he wanted. He removed and put on a one-piece camouflage coverall. Then he secured his hunting knife in its scabbard on a military belt at his waist. A small flashlight and leather gloves went into the pockets at his thighs. He stuffed boxes of cartridges into his duffel bag. From his trousers, he removed his wallet, keys, change, and handkerchief, placing them in the pockets of his coveralls.

Smiling with pride at his cherished hunting bow, he lifted it from the nail next to the picture of the seashore. For a moment he stroked it as a violinist might a Stradivarius. Then he removed the quiver from a coat hook in the closet. Next he retrieved his 30-06 rifle. Going to the daybed, he took a forty-five caliber, army-issue handgun from under the cushion. Finally, he removed a Styrofoam cooler from the closet, transferred to it all the beer from the refrigerator, and covered it with ice.

After checking the parking lot for activity, he carried his weapons to the Blazer. With hunting season open, there was nothing unlawful about what he was doing, but his purpose demanded that he exercise caution. He placed the ammunitions pouch, bow, and quiver in the back seat and the rifle securely in its rack. Removing the pistol from its holster, he laid it in the passenger seat beneath a hand towel. After placing the cooler on the floor in front of the passenger seat, he returned to his apartment.

He was ready. Very carefully, one last time, he went through a mental checklist and smiled. Before leaving, he went to the bathroom to relieve himself and take one last look in the mirror. From a pocket at his chest, he removed a small jar of eye black. After lightly smearing some of the cream on his cheeks, he drew a darker line down the middle of his face with diagonals extending from it in opposite directions like branches from a vine. Satisfied with his appearance, he locked the door and hurried to his vehicle, so focused on his mission that he didn't hear his phone ringing.

Starting the engine, he headed for Orlando. For the first time since leaving Expressway, he felt like his old, cocky self. It was almost noon, and he was only a hundred miles, two hours at most, from paying an unexpected visit to the new vice president of operations at Barrett's Flooring.

CHAPTER 27

Waves of fierce gray clouds rolled across the sky as Alex entered the flow of traffic on Interstate 4. Most of the other travelers were escaping the oncoming hurricane. For the lone hunter heading east in the dark blue Blazer, that storm didn't even exist. Driven by his own private forces, he was on a mission. While he may have been at war with the world about him, he was finally at peace with his demons. The turbulence on the horizon in his rearview mirror was a fitting backdrop. The world would soon be a far better place because of him.

Careful to stay below the posted speed limit, he watched others fly past him, casting looks of disdain in his direction. Now was no time to be stopped for a traffic violation. While he wouldn't hesitate to use the pistol beside him, neither did he want anything to interfere with the completion of his mission. Removing a beer from the cooler, he opened it and slugged down half the can.

He'd quit asking himself why his best friend had rejected him. The answer was simple. Cliff had used him, like so many others had in the past. Alex shook his head. He should've known better than to believe the jerk really cared about him.

Cliff sped west on Interstate 4, heading directly into the storm. He hated that he had hung up on his friend, but Alex had given him no choice. The FBI had stepped up their investigation and he couldn't rule out their tapping of his telephone lines. He feared that any comments with Alex could be used against him, and against Alex, too, for that matter. But Alex would understand. Once he got in touch with his friend, he would explain the situation and offer whatever help was needed.

After giving his secretary hasty instructions on how to re-arrange his afternoon appointments, he'd driven to a nearby telephone booth and placed a call to Alex. When he received no answer after letting it ring repeatedly, he hung up and headed for Tampa. He wanted to apologize and just be there to comfort his friend. It never occurred to him that Alex would soon pass by headed in the opposite direction. Only later did he reflect on what might have been—had the two met.

Orange Avenue, once a busy four-lane street used by both local residents and tourists, was now used primarily by commuters and parents hauling their kids to and from the private schools in the area. An east-west expressway constructed in the mid-seventies had diverted much of the traffic away from Orange Avenue.

Grove Park Estates had been developed in the sixties to provide housing for managers and support personnel associated with Cape Canaveral. It was expanded in the seventies to accommodate the arrival of Disney employees, and a six-foot masonry wall was later built along Orange Avenue to provide privacy for the neighborhood. To soften the stark appearance of the wall, oleanders were planted on the outside. The bushes had since grown well above the top of the wall, totally concealing it except at the traffic lights where streets entering Grove Park Estates intersected Orange Avenue. Most property owners had planted similar shrubs and trees inside the wall, many of which exceeded the oleanders in height. Since the area's covenants did not permit privately owned fences, Peter had screened his pool area by planting bottlebrush along his property lines.

Parkway Drive, the street on which Peter Everett lived, ran parallel to Orange Avenue. Interior streets branched off Parkway toward the center of the community, and traffic from Parkway had access to Orange Avenue every four to six blocks. Peter's house was third from the corner at one of these spur streets; his yard backed up to the masonry wall.

232

At exactly two o'clock, Alex parked on the grassy shoulder along Orange Avenue, next to the hedge of oleanders. Checking his watch, he figured he should have about fifteen minutes before Peter arrived home, if he still intended to golf that afternoon as usual. Alex was prepared to wait until nightfall, if necessary, to do what had to be done. He turned on his emergency blinkers, got out, and raised the hood. It was clouding up, and the wind was stiffening. To the west he could see a darker sky, but never once did it occur to him that the oncoming storm might alter Peter's weekly routine.

To those passing by, Alex's Blazer would appear to be just another redneck's vehicle that had most likely run out of gas. He wasn't worried about a Good Samaritan stopping to render assistance, since most Florida residents had been frequently warned about the potential danger of such situations. Once lured out of their cars, they could be robbed, beaten, or even killed, and their vehicles stolen.

Alex reasoned that should a police car happen by, the officer would see the raised hood and assume the driver had gone for assistance. Even if his vehicle were to be ticketed, it would make no difference. After today, a delinquent parking ticket would be the least of his concerns.

The light amount of traffic passing by was about as he had expected, having been there many times before. Once the schools let out, the traffic would get much heavier, but by then he should be gone.

While driving over from Tampa, he'd fantasized about killing Peter. For the first time his prey would not be a dim-witted animal, but an intelligent human being capable not only of self-defense, but also of striking back if given the opportunity. He had no intention of allowing that to happen. *I'm going to pay that traitor back in spades for what he did to me.* He smiled at the thought.

Getting back into his vehicle, he checked his reflection in the rearview mirror. The image he saw met with his approval. Waiting until no cars were seen in either direction, he got out and removed the bow and quiver from the back seat. He then closed and locked the door and hurried around the end of the wall, disappearing into the tangled foliage.

Between the shrubbery and the wall was an opening just large enough for a person to pass in a crouched position. No dogs threatened to betray his presence because the leash law in this neighborhood was rigorously enforced. Within moments he was behind Peter's house, about ninety feet from the back door.

He positioned himself directly across from the pool and the table where he knew Peter would sit for his pre-game drink and cigarette. After weeks of careful stalking, Alex knew the man's routine down to the minute.

Of all his weapons, the bow was his favorite. Anyone could position the crosshairs of a telescope and squeeze off a round from a high-powered rifle. But bow hunting was an art. Alex had spent endless hours honing his skills, hours that most hunters were too undisciplined or too busy to devote. Bow hunting required expert tracking and the ability to creep undetected within killing range of one's prey. It was also primitive, almost spiritual. Using an arrow to kill was the ultimate achievement that any hunter could reach.

The actual moment of taking life couldn't be adequately described. Alex's heartbeat increased, his senses sharpened, and he experienced an exhilaration that approached sex. In the past, hunting boars had provided him his ultimate high. A wild boar would attack when cornered or wounded, using its large tusks to gore the victim. Alex had faced attacking boars before and had succeeded in killing many. He never tired of the rush it provided. If anything, he longed for a more intoxicating kill. At no other time did he feel his manhood more, nor did he feel more in control.

His vantage point was perfect. Given his camouflaged attire and blackened face, he was truly one with his surroundings. Propping himself on one knee, he drew back the arrow into the shooting position. Finding that the foliage hampered his aim, he broke off a few limbs to provide the clearance needed. After rehearsing the maneuver several times, he waited for Peter's arrival. His heart raced, as it always did before a kill. As the long-awaited moment approached, his breath came in fast, shallow pants. Never before had he experienced anything comparable to this. It was the moment for which he had waited and prepared. He was ready.

At two-fifteen, he caught a glimpse of Peter's car turning onto the spur street. Fifteen minutes later, Peter appeared at the back door, drink in hand. As he stepped onto the deck, it occurred to Alex how much Peter resembled a peacock in full plumage—yellow shorts, matching yellow, green and purple Polo shirt, and leather sandals. He looked smug, cocky, arrogant, spoiled, and worthless. At that moment, no man on earth could have hated another more. If Alex's life had been lived without distinction, what he was about to do would be his finest hour. Like the eyes of a serpent an instant before the strike, his unblinking stare was riveted on Peter's every move.

Peter placed his drink on the table, glanced at his watch, and sat down facing in Alex's direction. Lighting a cigarette, he leaned back in the chair and closed his eyes. He straightened up every few minutes to check his watch and sip his drink. Once he looked up and stared at the darkening clouds, and then, as though amused, appeared to chuckle and resumed his relaxed position.

Alex remembered Peter's boasting at different times that he had a rule against having more than one drink of hard liquor before golf. He would go on to say that a single drink helped to steady his putting stroke, but more than one loosened him up too much. Peter stared again at the clouds, then threw back his head and swigged down his drink. He took the last few draws from his cigarette before dropping the butt into the empty glass. Anticipating his next move, Alex slowly raised the bow and drew back the arrow.

Peter stood and turned toward the house. Before he could take a step in that direction, a searing hot pain exploded just above his left knee. In the next instant, he crashed hard onto the pavement. As Alex watched from his hiding place, the fallen man stared with horror at the arrow protruding through the front of his leg. Tendons and strands of muscle fiber erupted around the shaft like an exotic flower with petals of red and white. A thin stream of blood trickled down his leg and dripped onto the concrete. Nausea swept over him as his senses sought relief by slipping toward unconsciousness, then instinctively fought back.

"Alex...Alex!" What was intended as a shout came out as a wail. "I know you're out there. At least have the guts to show yourself."

For a full minute no sound except the wind could be heard.

"Damn you, Alex!" His voice had weakened. "You'll never get away with this. Never!"

Again there was silence.

Peter had been caught completely off guard by the attack. For the first few months after leaving Expressway, he'd lived in fear of a reprisal. But as time passed, he'd convinced both himself and Michelle that Alex's anger toward him had abated. He had always believed that Alex was long on talk but short on action. Too late he realized that his mistake in judgment could prove fatal.

Rolling over into a crawling position, he supported himself on his right knee and hands, his left leg extending grotesquely behind. With every ounce of strength he had left, he struggled forward to escape his assassin.

Alex smiled broadly. His white teeth contrasted starkly with his blackened face. The shot, intended only to cripple his victim, couldn't have been more perfect. He relished Peter's agony as he writhed in pain and, no doubt, comprehended the coming horror of his death. Satisfaction permeated the hunter's entire being. Peter knew the identity of his executioner. The arrow had served as his signature.

Nodding his approval and filing away Peter's every move for future enjoyment, he took aim with another razor sharp arrow. Had the setting been more isolated, he would have toyed with his wounded prey, a cat playing with a mouse. But sensing his own vulnerability, he quickly sent a second arrow into the back of Peter's neck. Pleased with his shot's accuracy, he imagined his prey's dying breath as the air slowly escaped around the arrow's shaft. Then he sent four more arrows into the fallen peacock, never once missing his mark.

As Alex stared at the motionless body, he was reminded of the pincushions his mother once used. Too bad Mr. High-and-Mighty Peter Everett couldn't see himself now. The ecstasy of the moment was beginning to wane, but the killing of Peter had far exceeded his expectations.

Propping the bow against the wall, he hurried across the yard and around the pool to retrieve his trophy. He grabbed Peter by the hands and quickly pulled him across the grass and into the bushes next to the wall. The body lying at his feet was viewed no different than that of a deer or any other big game. As he had done so many times before, he knelt down and field dressed his kill. Returning one last time to the pool, he washed off his hands and knife. After using the glass to rinse the blood from the pavement, he tossed it into the water before running back to where he had entered the bushes.

He waited for the traffic to clear, then walked quickly to his vehicle, unlocked the door, and placed the bow and quiver on the back seat. After lowering the hood he got in and switched off the emergency blinkers.

Pleased with a job well done, he treated himself to another beer. Peter's execution had been appropriate for the crime committed. Alex grinned at the thought of his groveling on the pavement in his purple, green, and yellow outfit. So who was the better man now? *They'll all know before long who the real man is,* he thought, *all those stupid fools at Expressway who thought they could push Alex Carter around.*

He only regretted that it had been done so quickly.

CHAPTER 28

At one forty-five in the afternoon an announcement over the intercom instructed Expressway employees to clear the building in fifteen minutes. David called to see if Leah was home and breathed a sigh of relief when she answered. Running through a driving downpour, he chastised himself for leaving both of his umbrellas in his van.

How typical of Expressway, he thought as he jumped in behind the wheel and jerked the door shut, *to squeeze every moment possible out of its people when they could have just as easily sent us home at noon.* At least Leah was safe. He eased his way into the bumper-to-bumper traffic that crawled through the torrential rain. Two hours later, he pulled into his driveway.

For a while he and Leah sat together on the back porch, rehashing what had become referred to around the office as "the Alex affair." Although the hurricane had increased in intensity, the porch on the leeward side of the house was protected from the full force of the storm. After dinner they retired to the Florida room to follow the storm's progress on television. When the lights began to flicker, they turned everything off and, side by side, stared out the windows as nature flexed her mighty muscles.

"So has Landon cleaned out his office?"

"Not yet, but his last day's next Friday. I guess when Snelling heard that he had refused to heed my concerns due, at least in part, to his friendship with Alex, Steve had no choice in the matter. Rumor is that he was given the choice of accepting a demotion to Houston or resigning. I've heard he's joining a firm he worked for while in law school. He's avoided me for the last week, so we haven't discussed his plans. And you can rest assured we won't."

"What does all this mean for you?"

"My job is safe if that's any consolation. They would've fired me when they fired Alex's staff if they'd thought they had a strong enough case. Most folks seem satisfied that I wasn't involved, although some are obviously guarded around me and others are downright unfriendly, especially Jim Hargrove. I guess in time things will be okay. It's not going to be easy, but... I just hate that in Steve's eyes, I probably let him down. Maybe someday I'll get the chance to explain my side of the story."

"Many of them must know you were caught in the middle. You do still have some friends there, you know."

Getting no response after a few minutes, she continued, "What's next in the process?"

Her words pulled him back from the awesome spectacle outside to the reality of their lives. "The FBI should wrap up their work at our office in the next few weeks and be able to devote more of their resources to SSI, if they haven't already. I'd be willing to bet Expressway's not the only company SSI has bribed."

"How long will that take?"

"I have no idea. SSI has most likely destroyed a lot of evidence, but it's impossible to destroy everything. I would guess that somebody at SSI, and probably Alex as well, will end up going to jail. When it's the FBI asking the questions, most people will tell everything they know. Those who are key witnesses will try to make a deal to save their skins. The FBI promises immunity to the little fish in order to land the trophies."

"How could all this have happened in a company like Expressway?"

They'd had similar discussions before, but there were just so many facets to the answer. He knew it was hard for her, being outside the business, to understand how things worked on the inside.

"One contributing factor is our management system. The company assumes that our own employees are honest. Internal audits

239

are designed to uncover careless mistakes rather than crooks who are stealing from the company.

"As I've said before, it's impossible in the beginning to accurately estimate the total cost of a remediation project. There are too many variables. Change orders are used to update the original scope of work and the budget. With an accomplice inside the client's office, the consultant can inflate charges using change orders as long as they don't get careless. They don't do it on every project as that would be too obvious, just some of them."

"Could you have caught Alex by comparing the cost of his projects with those of the other project managers?"

"That's a *real* good question, Hon. Maybe you should have my job. Unfortunately, it's the nature of this business to write a lot of change orders. Alex periodically exchanged projects among the managers, including some of his own. Two or three guys might actually manage one project during its lifetime. With the projects changing hands, in addition to our turnover in project managers, Alex soon figured out how to cover his tracks."

"That sneaky rascal. No wonder you didn't catch him."

He didn't respond to the soft, wet kiss she gave him, or the playful teasing of her finger on the back of his hand.

"Doesn't Expressway ever audit companies like SSI?"

"We audited them last year. But that audit focused on billing errors. We checked to see if the charges shown on the invoices matched the rates we had agreed to in the contract. Nobody verified the accuracy of the hours shown on the time sheets with SSI employees."

"So, the FBI will be looking for doctored time sheets?"

"Partly, but other areas may amount to more money than falsified time sheets. One involves equipment rental. On every project the consultants use expensive equipment that's billed to the customer at so much per hour or per day. While each piece may or may not be used, the customer gets charged for it anyway."

"What else? You mentioned other ways."

"This *isn't* what I had in mind to talk about tonight. I'd much rather forget this mess and…be together, if you know what I mean." With that, he slipped a strap off her shoulder.

"Not so fast, mister," she said, a twinkle in her eye that belied her firm tone. "You're out there everyday where exciting things are happening, and I have to beg you for a report. So go ahead, finish telling me what you were going to, or you'll end up sleeping on the sofa all by yourself and only dreaming of whatever it was you had in mind." She removed his hand and pulled the strap back up.

"You drive a hard bargain." Just then a bolt of lightning struck nearby, and Leah grabbed him about the neck. "That's more like it," he said, as his hand went quickly to the strap and this time held it at her elbow.

"Stop that," she scolded. "I'm not that kind of girl, in case you've forgotten."

"Sorry, my dear. I thought for a moment you were a fraulein I once knew."

"Who would want a fraulein when they could have me?" Licking her lips, she gave him a come-and-get-me look. "Now, tell me another way SSI cheated you?"

"You really are a tease...you know that, don't you?" he said, trying again to get a kiss.

"Just be a good boy, and tell me what I want to know. Then, *just maybe*, I'll become the fraulein of your dreams."

"Okay, fraulein, you win. Just for good measure, I'll give you two scenarios, both of which, I'm sure, SSI used on us." He noted that she'd left the strap hanging loosely at her side, a good sign of things to come.

Another thunderous burst rattled the windows. The lightning flash that occurred simultaneously announced that a nearby tree had been struck, and she snuggled against him. He felt secure and at peace just being next to his woman in the safety of their home.

"A consulting firm creates a subsidiary that assembles equipment systems needed for the clean-up projects. The parent company buys the finished package at an inflated price; then they add a mark-up when they sell it to the customer. They make a killing on the equipment, plus they receive a fee. It's a win-win for them if they can pull it off. A couple years ago I put a stop to Expressway's being caught in this trap by refusing to purchase equipment without at least three competitive bids."

He looked at her. She was listening to him, he knew, but she seemed intent on watching her fingers as they softly traced the veins on the back of his hand.

"Some consultants also bill multiple customers for the same hour of work. All projects require the consultant to send people to the job site to check equipment and collect groundwater samples, among other things. One such inspector can visit several sites during the same trip. Each customer gets billed for the entire trip rather than for their fair share. Customers get cheated. States get cheated. Taxpayers foot the bill through higher gasoline taxes."

She looked thoughtful. "So Alex, or someone like him who's willing to approve the inflated invoices, is the key."

"That's the way it works. And once they get a person to bend the rules even a little bit, they own him."

"What a mess."

"I agree, but I think the FBI will uncover everything, and somebody will go to jail. It'll also put SSI out of business."

"And good riddance," she replied. "What about the states? They must be aware of this investigation."

"That's where it gets a bit tricky. I've informed officials in the states where we do business. Because we took the initiative and involved the FBI in our investigation, every state has agreed to try and keep this matter out of the papers, at least for now. The FBI has also instructed everyone involved to keep this matter confidential. The states don't want the embarrassment either."

"Fat chance!"

"You're right, Hon. I'm surprised that it hasn't made the news already, but it will, that's for certain. It could happen any day, but hopefully not until the FBI has concluded its investigation. Even then, we'll be limited on what we can disclose so as not to jeopardize the FBI's case against those indicted. I'll be a prominent player when the media does report this story, that's for sure, and I'll be made to look pretty bad."

"Do you think Alex will be indicted?"

"For sure."

"The publicity will really hurt Expressway's reputation won't it?"

"That's putting it mildly. The press will crucify us. Even though Landon got the hook, I could still be forced out down the road, you know. Right now they need me to maintain some semblance of control over the work being handled by my department, or what's left of it. But when this blows over..."

"Don't you worry about it," she said in her most consoling tone. "We've always wanted to move back to Colorado, and that would give us a good reason to do it." She gave him a reassuring smile. "You know I'd still love you, even if no one else did."

"Maybe I should let the kids know that Dad may soon crash and burn. I'd hate for them to open the paper one morning and see my ugly mug on the front page."

"Oh, David, don't talk like that." Her fingers quit tickling his hand.

"Honey, with the FBI involved, we haven't seen anything yet. You can be certain that most of our competitors have, knowingly or unknowingly, committed fraud. If the investigation is expanded industry wide, it could be the worst scandal to hit the oil industry in fifty years, and you know how the public feels about big oil. This isn't like the charges made by politicians from time to time of price fixing, which are never proven. This case will send people to jail. I can only imagine what the press will make out of it. Reporters would kill for a story like this."

She lifted his hand to her lips and kissed it.

"I couldn't have made it through this without you," he said taking her hands in his. "I'm so thankful for you."

"And I'm so proud of you," she replied, tearing up a bit. "I never once gave a thought to the possibility that you'd done anything wrong. You're the best man there is on the face of this earth as far as I can see. We've always had each other and we always will."

She reached up and covered his mouth softly with her fingertips.

"Speaking of having each other," he said, as he undressed her with his eyes. "How would you like to..."

"You haven't finished your story yet," she interrupted with a scolding tone.

He sighed. "Even if I don't get fired, there's a good chance I'll be reassigned to someplace like Siberia."

"They'll have to ship me there, too." The twinkle returned to her eyes, and she gave him a come-hither smile. "You bad boy. I bet you're all talk and no action!"

With that invitation, he pulled her against him. "Just you wait and see."

"Mister, are you suggesting we turn in early?" she asked, her eyes sparkling and a grin twitching at the corners of her mouth.

"You bet I am." He pulled her to her feet. "Go on up. I'll be there in a minute."

She slipped the other strap off her shoulder, catching both at her elbows. Just for good measure, she stopped in the doorway and wiggled her hips. Then in obvious delight, she gave him one last look over her shoulder and disappeared around the corner.

"Did you lock up," she asked sleepily an hour later, "or do you want me to do it?"

"No I didn't, but I don't think we need to worry about that. Nobody in his right mind would be out on a night like this."

CHAPTER 29

Alex pulled into a convenience store to gas up and get directions to the nearest hardware store. Huge drops of rain began to fall as he climbed into his Blazer a few minutes later.

He switched on the radio just in time to hear a weather report. The storm had passed through the Keys and moved out over the gulf, gaining momentum as it went. During the day it had turned north with winds of seventy-five miles per hour and rising. By the time it made landfall, it promised to be the worst storm to hit the bay area in fifty years. According to the announcer, Gordon was now moving in a northeasterly direction straight for Tampa. If it continued on its present course, the eye would hit around midnight with gusts in excess of one hundred ten miles per hour.

He cursed the traffic closing in around him. Bumper to bumper vehicles lined up in both directions as far as he could see. He hated waiting in lines almost as much as he hated David Coleman. After sitting at an intersection through three light changes, he began blowing his horn and muttering curses under his breath.

An hour later he finally merged into the westbound lane of Interstate 4. The oncoming cars had their windshield wipers and headlights on. To the west, the sky was bluish charcoal, unlike anything he could remember ever having seen.

A few miles west of Orlando the traffic again came to a complete stop. As he waited, his thoughts went back to Peter. It was over so quickly; it almost seemed too merciful in view of what he could have done. No, make that *should* have done. He replayed the details over and over, savoring each one as he envisioned it in his mind's eye. Then his thoughts turned to the Colemans.

He'd always liked Leah, but David had no doubt turned her against him. So she was expendable. The fact that she was David's wife was reason enough.

His thoughts became confused again as he made his way through his jungle of fantasies. He saw himself creeping into the Coleman's home, surprising Leah in the kitchen. It would be so easy. He'd been there when David had discussed the security system layout with the contractor. The tightwad was too cheap to put out the extra bucks for the fail-safe system. Instead he had opted for the basic package, saying he could add the remote signaling option later. Alex had only to cut the phone line, and no intruder alert would be sent. And nobody would hear any screams over the noise of the storm. The weather gods had smiled on him. He returned that smile.

The vision became crystal clear in his mind. He would take Leah at knifepoint to the garage and then rape her before forcing her to go ahead of him up the back stairs. Once they were in the bedroom, he would force her to confess to David what they had done in the garage...and how much she enjoyed it. Another smile spread across his face at the thought of what that would do to David and his almighty principles that he tried to impose on everybody else.

A honking horn pulled him back to reality and urged him to move ahead. Traffic inched forward as the rain beat heavily against the windows and the wind buffeted his Blazer. The radio station had become mostly static, but that was inconsequential. The voices were back. He didn't need any outside input now.

Another hour of stop-and-go driving brought him to the Lakeland exit. He decided to pull off. Although he had been drinking all day, he couldn't remember when he'd last eaten. At any rate, he needed to go to the rest room and grab a sandwich. After circling the packed parking lot, he came to a halt in front of the dumpster. He frowned as he read Florida Sanitation stenciled on its side. The sting of the letter from Frazier Environmental he'd received that morning came fresh in his mind. Or was it the day before? He couldn't remember.

246

Getting out into a driving torrent, he waded through the water streaming across the pavement. The rain revitalized him, made him feel clean and good. For the first time in years, he *knew* he was doing what he'd been destined to do. He was balancing the scales. He was making things right. His smile of satisfaction obviously startled the frowning cashier as he popped inside along with a huge whoosh of rain and wind.

After finishing a burger and fries, he waited at the doorway to see if the rain would let up. A lady in a nearby booth pointed him out to her husband, and his first impulse was to curse her for talking about him. When he realized that she might be commenting about the black streaks on his face, he decided to make a dash for his jeep. As he bolted through the doorway, he ran into and flattened a little girl who was running toward the door from the parking lot. "That'll teach you to get the hell out of the way next time," he yelled down at her while her mother watched with a look of shocked disbelief. Several customers stood at the window, pointing to his Blazer as it skidded out of the parking lot, while others consoled the sobbing child.

By the time he reached the exit to I-75 north, just east of Tampa, it was after seven o'clock. The rain accumulated on his windshield faster than his wipers could clear it. Some cars were pulling off along the shoulder while others seemed to have stalled in the traffic lanes. He could only guess where the road was as he maneuvered his way through the islands of vehicles. The wind pushed his Blazer to the right, requiring him to consciously steer to the left. He felt energized rather than intimidated by the force of the storm and relished the challenge of competing against its fury.

The few cars still traveling north had slowed to a crawl. By the time he reached the exit for highway 301, he was exhausted. When he turned eastward, the wipers kept up a little better, and the wind to his back propelled the Blazer forward. Visibility was so bad that he missed the entrance to David's subdivision, and he had to turn around and go back. There were no other vehicles in sight.

After a quick stop in front of the Coleman's driveway, he turned into the graveled cul-de-sac a few hundred yards past. Since there were no houses nearby, only woods, he parked in the middle of the turn-around area. Reaching into the cooler, he drank one beer after another, alternately brooding over the past and anticipating the future. Each time he thought of Peter's body lying on the ground with the rain splashing off his remains, he felt a surge of power. His day of retribution had so far exceeded his wildest expectations. He'd been up to the match, and he'd won the first round. Laughing aloud, he slugged down another swallow. One of his demons had been laid to rest.

The radio station that had faded out in the storm once again transmitted clearly and updated the progress of the hurricane. Travelers were warned to get off the roads and take appropriate precautions. Those living along the coastline were urged to vacate their homes and move inland. Those already marooned were advised to fill their bathtubs with water. Cans of food, flashlights, blankets, and clothing were to be taken someplace protected from flying glass. According to the announcer, it was already too late to batten down the hatches.

Interspersed with the announcements were the names and addresses of schools, community centers, and other locations designated as emergency centers. Gordon was a stronger hurricane than the national weather center had predicted, and it was making landfall just south of Tampa, directly over Bradenton. Sustained winds in excess of one hundred twenty-five miles per hour were being recorded, with gusts up to one fifty. Twelve inches of rain were expected before it was over. Low-lying roads had already flooded and would only worsen. The urgent message of the night was repeated over and over: Seek cover.

A smile spread across Alex's rain-streaked face. *If anyone needs a safe haven tonight,* he thought, *it's David and Leah.*

Amazed at the intensity of the lightning, at times bright enough to read by, he became one with the storm. During the flashes, he saw branches and clusters of moss flying through the air. Vines, which normally hung to the ground, appeared to be groping in the darkness like tentacles from a giant sea monster. The roar of the storm was deafening.

As had happened so often in the past, and more frequently in recent weeks, Alex's thoughts roamed helter-skelter through the ravaged landscape of his childhood. There she was, his caretaker and protector, defiling his young mind with her nakedness. Her warm whiskey breath caressed his face, and her soft lips kissed his cheek and then his mouth. If he only could have forgotten, perhaps he could have forgiven her. Now she was gone.

In the next instant he could see Peter sitting in David's office. Their mouths were moving, but he couldn't hear what they said. They were talking about him, of that he was sure, and they were laughing at something they'd done to him. But he couldn't make out what it was. Then came Bill's smirking face, whispering in his mother's ear while his hands caressed her seductively. They were both looking at him. For the first time during such reflections, he noted tears streaming down her cheeks; the more she cried, the more Bill laughed. He was a child again, back with his mother, and then in the strong, groping hands of the scout leader.

"Please God, make it end," he pleaded, pounding his forehead against the steering wheel. "Just make it end."

After finishing his business at the Coleman's, he intended to drive to Bill's and spend the rest of the night making him regret the day he was born. There was nothing now to prevent him from doing to Bill what he had wanted to do for so long. First, he would make Bill repent for his sins and grovel for forgiveness Then he would make him suffer long and hard. As much as he despised Peter and David, that newer hate paled in comparison to his loathing for Bill, a hatred that had festered and spread for over twenty years.

On rare occasions Alex allowed himself to admit that David had never ridiculed him in front of others as Bill had done. But David still had to pay. Otherwise, he would always be tormented by the voices reminding him of David's complicity in his undeserved termination. That could *not* go unpunished.

"Yes," he said aloud, "justice will be served. And I'll be doing the serving."

During a lull in the storm, he got out and relieved himself. Before getting back in, he removed the rifle from the bracket and propped it against the front seat. If by any chance a policeman stopped to inquire why he was parked in this fancy neighborhood, he would simply explain that he was returning home from a hunting trip and had taken refuge, just as instructed by the radio announcer. If that didn't suffice, he would use his pistol to put an end to the questioning.

Shortly after one o'clock in the morning, Alex started the engine and switched on the headlights. It was time. Slowly he eased forward. The damage from the storm was worse than expected. Uprooted trees lay strewn about like the sea monsters he had imagined earlier, washed up from the deep. Some were lying across Forest Drive, forcing him to veer around and then through the brush.

Searching for the Coleman's house in the eerie darkness reminded him of a ship at sea seeking a lighthouse in dangerous waters. Then he saw the faint glow coming from their floodlights. He sneered at the uselessness of the lights on a night like this. Stopping just past the entrance, he shifted into four-wheel drive and accelerated, driving over saplings and tangled brush until he was even with the house. Normally, he would never have inflicted such damage on his beloved Blazer, but tonight he was lost in his vendetta to bring punishment to those who had so unjustly punished him. No longer a thing of value, the vehicle served only as the means toward that end.

Judging from the distance traveled and the glare from the floodlights, he knew he was far enough into the woods not to be seen by any patrolman stupid enough to be out making the rounds that night. He switched off the headlights, then the ignition. The time had finally come—*his time* to be judge, jury, and executioner. The memory of Peter lying dead at his feet no longer filled his thoughts. Just as before, his breathing was becoming shallow, more like that of a panting cat, and with each breath his senses seemed to sharpen.

No matter how unlikely it was that the Colemans had seen him crashing through the woods, he took no chances. Had he been willing to risk being detected, he would have parked at the entrance and walked down the driveway. Even in his crazed state of mind, he never considered such a brash action. No, this was a time for caution and for patience, for waiting, for watching, and when the time was right, for action. He knew that the longer he waited, the greater the chance that the Colemans would be asleep. The night was his. What he was there for would not take long to finish.

CHAPTER 30

Alex pushed hard against the door of the Blazer, but the gale-force wind held it tight. After several more futile attempts, he scooted across the seat to the passenger side, repositioned the rifle, and placed the pistol in the holster on his belt. Then he pulled the handle.

The door had moved only a few inches when the violence of the storm ripped it from his grasp with such force that it sprung the hinges. Torrents of rain hit him full force, stinging his face like tiny spears. Fumbling blindly for the rifle, he bent over and forced himself through the wall of water and driving wind onto the ground. He had underestimated his adversary. The added complications brought on by the elements should have panicked him. Instead, he mentally shook his fist in the face of God, defying the superior forces of nature that dared interfere with his mission.

Finding that he couldn't stand upright in the powerful wind, he crawled forward allowing the wind to push him toward the house. Gripping his rifle with both hands and using it as a brace against the ground, he moved methodically forward, pushing aside the undergrowth that hampered his progress. Water covered the ground, flowing over his hands as he groped his way along. He realized that the rising river would drive the alligators and snakes to the same higher ground that he now inched his way across. This danger could not be discounted, but he'd spent much of his life hunting in situations where he'd been exposed to similar dangers. Having succeeded then heightened his sense of invincibility now.

He maneuvered himself into an area where the undergrowth had been cleared except for some thick clusters of palmettos and

251

wild rose bushes.   The glare from the floodlights illuminated the ground a few feet ahead, and he migrated toward their glow like a moth to a flame. Another forty yards and he would reach the clearing that encircled the house. The rest would be easy.

After checking his bearings, he resumed his belly crawl. The cold rain lifted the stupor that had permeated his senses during his long wait. Thorns tore his face and clawed at his eyes, but he felt no pain. The storm's fury, now reaching its crescendo, served only to intensify his resolve and focus his hatred on the man sleeping peacefully inside the house.

When he reached the clearing twenty minutes later, he stopped for a moment to catch his breath. His exhausted body screamed for relief from its battle against the storm, but he couldn't permit it that luxury. He was in the hunt, driven by the most primitive instinct known to man. The taste of his own blood trickling into his mouth as the rain flushed down his face fueled his vengeance. It was as though David were personally beating, slashing, and resisting his advance. Resting just long enough for his eyes to adjust to the brightness of the lights, he crawled across the clearing and into the bushes alongside the garage. Once he rounded the corner, he was shielded from the main force of the storm and able to stand.

Directly in front of him, just as he'd pictured it, was the conduit leading up the wall to the junction box. Following the pipe downward to the ground, he found the exposed orange telephone cable and cut it. Raising the window would activate the security system, so Alex used the butt of his rifle to break the glass, clearing its sharp edges from around the frame. Confident that the noise from the shattering glass could not be heard above the thunderous storm, he quickly climbed through the opening.

As soon as he was safely in the dimly lit garage, he sank to the floor. He was exhausted, cold, and soaked to the bone. Directly in front of him was David's minivan. Next to it sat Leah's sedan. Rising to his feet, he moved around the cars to David's bass boat. Inside it, next to the motor, he found a large can of gasoline. On the wall in front of the boat hung shovels, rakes, and other yard tools that had been neatly arranged. *Just like an engineer,* he thought.

Everything in his life has to be organized just the way he wants it.
His sneer grew into a smile. That was about to end!

The door in front of Leah's car led to the house. In the far corner was a long, narrow storage room. He recalled from earlier visits that it housed the water heater, furnace, electrical breaker box, and, most importantly, the controls for the security system. The room was also where David's golf clubs, shotguns, and fishing tackle were kept.

Moving quickly to the utility room door, he tried the handle and, as expected, found it locked. The room had been added at the last minute because of an unexpected building code requirement. Due to the restricted area available within the room, the door had to swing out into the garage, placing the hinge pins on the outside.

Putting the recently purchased screwdriver under the head of the top hinge pin and using the heel of his hand, he tapped upward on the handle. The pin popped loose and fell to the floor. After removing the other pins, he lifted the door from its hinges, leaned it against the wall, and stepped inside the utility room. With the removal of the door, an unheard alarm instantly sounded inside the house. A moment later, he severed the wires to the backup battery for the security system and removed the main breakers from the electrical panel. All power and communications to the house were now dead and the security system disabled. Using his flashlight, he surveyed the garage again, this time more carefully than before.

He had assumed he would have to break out a living room window to gain entry into the house. Almost as an afterthought, he tried the doorknob leading from the garage into the house. To his surprise, it opened. Relishing in David's act of carelessness, Alex lowered his own guard ever so slightly.

The warmth of the house welcomed the uninvited guest, as did the faint aroma of food, bringing back vague recollections of happier times in his life. He closed the door behind him and stood in the darkness for a moment, getting his bearings and listening for any sounds of movement. Except for the noise of the storm, he heard only the ticking of a clock. He remembered that clock well. It had once belonged to David's grandmother and was very special to him.

If David were going to be around in the morning to mourn its loss, he would have dashed it against the floor. But that wasn't the plan. Swinging his light in the direction of the ticking, Alex fixed the beam directly upon it—sitting on the mantle in the study.

The room, somewhat small to his way of thinking, invited visitors. On the wall opposite the doorway stood the marble fireplace with bookshelves to either side. David's pipe rack, humidor, and lighter sat on a table to the right, next to the loveseat. To his left was an antique roll-top desk and matching swivel chair. *Nice, very nice,* he thought. *Too bad he didn't have more time to enjoy this. Too bad it won't be this nice where he's going.*

Across the hallway from the study was the living room. For an instant he considered slashing the upholstered furniture, just for sheer pleasure, but the thought vanished as quickly as it had come. He eased down the hallway toward the kitchen, leaving puddles of water standing on the hardwood floor with each step. Glancing up the rear stairway intended for the private use of the family, he nodded in recollection.

Taking a few more steps, he found himself standing in the doorway to the kitchen. White appliances next to the hickory cabinets looked like a picture in a magazine featuring homes of the rich and famous. He assumed they were hickory because the grain was finer than the oak cabinets in his and Maggie's house. White lace curtains framed the windows, and a cake sat under a clear glass cover on the counter. *Not bad. So this is how the big shots live.* After a brief inspection of the other rooms downstairs, he returned to the rear hallway. *If it hadn't been for David Coleman, Maggie and I could have had a setup like this.* He'd seen enough.

Heading upstairs, he gingerly placed his weight on the first step and then the next. No squeaks. Halfway up, a landing redirected the steps toward the front of the house. A moment later, he reached the hallway at the top.

To his left, only a few feet away, was the door to the master bedroom. The almost-photographic memory that kept haunting him with vivid abuses from his past now served Alex well. He could picture the floor plan, thanks to the grand tour David had given him before they'd moved in. Flashing his light around the balcony over-looking the floor below, he could see that all the doors were the expensive, six-panel kind, not the cheap, hollow-core ones that had been used in his home. *It only takes money*, he thought. *That's what everything takes in this lousy world.* To his right an open doorway led up another flight of stairs to the attic. The cool, damp air flowing past him toward the upper level made him shiver.

Pocketing his flashlight, he removed the knife from his waist and turned toward the master bedroom. He'd waited a long time for this moment.

Once again, his heart pounded. His breathing came in labored pants. He trembled with anticipation.

CHAPTER 31

They had been asleep for a couple of hours when David was awakened by Leah shaking his arm. "Honey, wake up. Something woke me—a beeping noise of some kind. Whatever it was, it's stopped."

"Where was it coming from?" he asked, propping himself up on his elbow to face her while still trying to get his wits about him.

"From that thing on the wall," she said, pointing across him in the direction of the bedside table.

"You mean the keypad for the security system?" Turning in that direction, he saw that none of the lights were on, all of which had been glowing when he had armed the system earlier. Even the green power light was dark.

"I think so, but I'm not sure," she said. "By the time I woke up—"

David jerked himself into a sitting position and placed his hand firmly over her mouth.

"Shhh," he whispered, instantly grasping the implications of a dead security system and the darkened room. The fringe of light from the outside that normally framed the windows behind the drapes had disappeared. "The floodlights are out, too."

In one motion, he was up with the bedside telephone to his ear. No dial tone. The hurricane could have knocked out the electrical transformer for their neighborhood, but not likely the telephone service as well. And there was not one chance in a thousand they would have lost the security system at exactly the same time, since it had its own backup battery system.

"What's wrong, David? Is there a problem?"

"I think we have a visitor." He quickly removed the thirty-eight-caliber revolver from under the mattress. When the Alex incident had occurred, David had replaced its bullets with new silver-tipped, high-powered cartridges. The shells he'd removed had been in the pistol for over thirty years, and he wasn't sure they would still fire. He'd never even shot the pistol.

"David, is someone in our house?" He heard the panic in her voice.

"Hush," he replied, reaching out and pressing his finger to her lips. Tiptoeing to the bedroom door, he quietly turned the dead bolt, expecting that the intruder would burst through the door at any moment with every intention of killing them both. Breathing a sigh of relief, he chastised himself for being so careless. Since receiving the obscene phone calls, he had been faithfully locking the bedroom door, but that night he'd had other things on his mind.

Although David's initial fears about Alex had lessened somewhat, he still felt the man to be a real and dangerous threat. And he knew that it had to have been Alex who made those threatening telephone calls they'd received a few weeks earlier. He also knew that Alex was very capable of doing something like this. He'd let his guard down. Now he had to deal with the consequences. His heart pounded as adrenaline coursed through his body. With the door temporarily secured, he returned to Leah who was sitting on the edge of the bed.

Raindrops hammered against the windows, driven by the wailing storm outside. Limbs broke and crashed to the ground. For a moment, his engineer's mind debated whether the windows might implode into the room, spraying them with shards of glass. That thought was quickly displaced by the more immediate threat.

"Are you sure it's not just the storm?" Leah whispered hopefully.

"I'm sure."

"Is it Alex?"

"My gut says yes." He pulled her by the arm. "Come on, get up."

"Do you think he's already in the house?"

"If he isn't, he will be. We don't have much time, Leah. You need to do exactly as I tell you."

David didn't have time to explain what had already been processed by his mind. When the system had given the last beep that Leah heard, the intruder would have still been in the storage room. He couldn't remember whether he had locked the door to the garage, but anyone desperate enough to be out in that storm would not be deterred by such a minor inconvenience. They had only moments, possibly just seconds, before the attack would come.

"We don't have much time," he repeated as calmly as he could, trying not to alarm her anymore than necessary. "Put something on, get into the bathroom, and lock the door."

"What are you going to do?" she asked, already slipping into the sundress hanging on the bedpost.

"I'm going to wait out here until he tries to open the door, and then I'm going to blow him to hell where he belongs." Opening the top dresser drawer, he removed the small pistol that he had taken into work on Alex's last day. Before handing her the gun, he injected a shell into the chamber and checked the safety.

"Here," he whispered, placing the gun in her hand. "All you have to do is pull down on the little lever, the safety." He took her left index finger and pulled the lever downward. "Did you feel it click? Just slide it down, aim, and start pulling the trigger. I think it holds six or eight bullets, but I'm not sure. I've never shot it. If anyone tries to open that door, just start shooting. Don't ask questions, just shoot. Is that clear?"

"Yes, but why can't I stay out here with you?" she pleaded. "Why can't I—"

Realizing that every second was precious, David took her by the arm and began pulling her toward the bathroom doorway. "Just do it!" he whispered. "We don't have time to talk. *Please*, do as I say."

"But—"

With that, he literally shoved her through the doorway into the bathroom. "Lock the door and keep it locked." He pulled the door to and held it closed. A second later, he felt the lock engage.

With her secure for the moment, he slipped into the shorts he'd discarded only hours before and positioned himself in front of the bedroom door, lying flat on his stomach. Pointing the revolver at the door, he rested the grip on the floor to steady his shaking hands. His father's reply when his mother had suggested he pray just before facing a major surgery suddenly popped into his mind.

"Alice, a scared prayer ain't worth a damn."

David whispered a prayer anyway.

He'd do whatever had to be done to protect Leah and himself. When Alex entered their home, he'd crossed the line. No moral decision had to be made. At the first sound of movement outside the door, he would shoot to kill.

At the moment Alex disabled the security system in the storage room, the beeping alarms from the keypad in the hallway outside the kitchen had stopped. When he'd reached the upstairs hallway, he'd dropped to his knees and begun crawling toward their door. It was an instinctive maneuver, something he did when sneaking up on unsuspecting game. He inched forward, listening for any suspicious sound that might put him at risk.

When Alex was directly outside the door, he reached up, groped for the knob, turned it, and gently pushed. When the door didn't immediately open, he pushed again, a little harder that time, hard enough that the dead bolt bumped ever so slightly against the strike plate, causing a faint click.

David had been lying on the floor for what seemed like an eternity when he heard something at the door. At first, he wasn't sure. The hurricane raging outside sounded like a freight train threatening to blast its way into the bedroom at any moment. The house creaked and groaned under the brunt of the storm.

But the second time he heard the same sound, David opened fire. The explosions were deafening in the enclosed room. Assuming

259

that Alex would be standing, he fired three rounds chest high. At the sound of the shots, Leah screamed.

Caught off guard with the element of surprise no longer his advantage, Alex dropped to his side and rolled away from the door, which was exploding just inches above his head. Particles of shattered wood rained down on him. His arm hit the door and his foot bumped the wall. Then he deliberately kicked the floor and let out a loud groan. After a few seconds, he groaned again. Then nothing. Even the storm seemed to pause in anticipation.

"David! David! Are you all right?" Leah called out.

"Yes, I'm okay. I think I got him," he yelled back. "Stay put, do you hear me?"

"Please be careful."

He waited, listening for any sound that might betray the condition of their attacker. Hearing none after several minutes, he inched his way to the door and stood up. His knees felt as though they might fold beneath him. His shaking hand could hardly grasp the dead bolt.

Surviving the first barrage of shots unharmed, Alex retreated on hands and knees down the hallway toward the front of the house. At the corner of the front stairway opening, he wheeled around to face the master bedroom, sitting on the floor, hands resting on his knees. Holding his revolver with both hands, he aimed into the darkness and waited.

David eased the splintered door open just enough to peer around it into the hallway, but he could see nothing in the darkness. Opening it a few inches wider, he stuck his foot out, hoping to feel a body. Feeling nothing, he swung his foot in a wider arc. As his foot completed the arc, it struck the wall to the left of the door. Hearing that faint thump, Alex opened fire. One of his shots struck David in the left arm, knocking him backwards to the floor. As he fell, more slugs whistled past his head. Now it was Alex who heard a groan.

David managed to push the door closed with his foot. Thirty feet away, Alex removed the spent clip and inserted another.

Leah heard the shots and the groan. She flung open the bathroom door and ran out into the darkness.

"David, where are you? David? Honey?"

"Over here, by the door," he answered, just loud enough to be heard above the storm. "I'm hit, but I think I'm okay."

He reached over with his other hand and felt the warm, sticky blood that ran steadily down his arm. The burning sensation at the wound was now joined by a throbbing ache.

Sensing her approach in the darkness, he cautioned, "Stay down and be quiet. He's still out there." He'd managed to squirm his way over toward the bathroom, somewhat out of a direct line of fire should Alex begin shooting again. In the next moment she was kneeling beside him, her hair brushing his face. Reaching up with his right arm, he pulled her to the floor beside him.

"How bad is it?" she whispered. "Can you move?"

"Yes, but I'm bleeding a lot. It's my left arm, above the elbow. I don't think the bone's broken, but I don't know if I can move it."

"We need to get you into the bathroom," she urged, as she lifted his shoulders and got him into a sitting position. From there she helped him to his knees so he could lean on her for support. With her help, he knee-walked the short distance to the bathroom. She closed and locked the door.

Removing a terry cloth sash from a robe hanging beside the shower, she wrapped it tightly around his arm. "That should stop the bleeding. Does it hurt too bad?"

He winced. "Don't ask. Where's your gun?"

"Right here," she said, picking it up from the bathroom counter and placing it in his hand.

"I dropped mine when I fell."

He sat on the edge of the tub, fighting to maintain consciousness. Following her instructions, he leaned over and placed his head between his knees as she draped a cool, wet towel over the back of his neck. After a few minutes, he straightened up. She was waiting with aspirins and a cup of water. Within a few minutes his strength returned.

"You'd better put on some different clothes. We might have to make a run for it." Without comment, she eased the door open and slipped back into the bedroom. Lightning flashes in the distance punctuated the darkness.

In a few moments she returned. "Look what I found," she said proudly as she handed him his gun.

Taking it, he handed her back the smaller of the two, the one that had not been fired. As she again dampened the towel and checked on the bleeding as best she could, he laid the gun aside and placed his right hand on the inside of her thigh.

"I can tell you're going to live," she quipped as she backed away and pushed his hand to the side. "Your sense of direction in the dark is still uncanny."

With no further sounds coming from the hallway, David wanted to believe the worse was over. But all his instincts told him otherwise. They'd survived the surprise attack, thanks to Leah being a light sleeper. But he knew Alex wouldn't stop until he'd finished the job he'd come to do. He had to believe they could defend themselves against the next attack.

"Do you think he'll try to come after us in here?" Leah asked, speaking softly but no longer in a whisper.

"I doubt it," he lied. "He might even decide to leave and wait until later, when he can catch me in the open. Who knows, he could be wounded himself. Let's just sit tight."

"It almost has to be Alex, don't you think?"

"That would be my guess. But whoever it is, he's here for only one reason, and it isn't to steal your diamonds," he said with a touch of sarcasm. "It almost has to be Alex. I'm just surprised he hasn't done something like this before now."

"Are you feeling any better?" she asked as she loosened the tourniquet for a moment.

"Much better, thanks to you."

She touched his arm at the elbow. "At least the bleeding seems to have stopped."

Pain shot through his shoulder. "But it still hurts like crazy. I'm not going to lie to you about it."

She began preparing a sling for his arm using a scarf she'd retrieved from her dresser. "Dave, I'm sorry you're hurt, but thankfully it *is* only your arm. I wish there was something more I could do."

"I'll be okay. We'll just wait him out." He tried to push himself up, but his weak knees wouldn't cooperate. "I need to relock the bedroom door."

"You stay put," she began. "I—"

"You'll do no such thing!" he interrupted. "Stay away from that door, Leah. We *don't* know where he is."

"The door can't be relocked," she said after a moment, "so I pushed a chair up under the knob when I went in there to get dressed."

He reached out with his good arm and pulled her to him. "That wasn't safe, and you know it," he scolded affectionately. "What am I going to do with you?"

"You're going to let me help you get us out of this, that's what."

They had waited in the bathroom for what seemed like hours when they heard the faint sound of the battery-powered smoke detector going off downstairs. A moment later, the upstairs alarm also began screeching. Within seconds, Leah detected the acrid smell of smoke, and then David did as well.

"That lousy, no-good...," David muttered under his breath. "He has set the house on fire!"

With his original plan foiled, Alex quickly conceived another. He quickly went to the garage to retrieve the can of gasoline from the boat and the rifle he'd left there earlier. He then piled pillows from the living room furniture and chairs from the breakfast room in the rear stairwell and blocked the doorways leading from the entrance foyer into the rest of the house. After dousing the pillows and chairs with half the gasoline, he poured the remainder on the foyer carpeting. Then he set both areas ablaze and opened the front door to create a draft. If the Colemans were to escape, they would have to use the front stairway. He would be waiting.

Running from the house with rifle in hand, Alex crossed the drive and assumed a shooting position under the big oak tree.

Although the rain was letting up somewhat, the wind was still very strong. He waited expectantly, resting his elbows on the ground to form a tripod to support the rifle. Peering through the scope, he centered the crosshairs on the open doorway with the stairway beyond. There was no way he could miss them at this range. They would be dropped in their tracks while coming down the stairs, only to be incinerated by the inferno within.

The air drawn in through the front door supercharged the fire, spreading it at an incredible rate. Within moments, smoke engulfed the foyer and flames raced up the rear stairway. Alex could already see a glow through the second-story windows.

Adrenaline overcame David's weakness, and he pushed himself to his feet. Tiptoeing across the bedroom, he moved the chair Leah had propped against the door and opened it slightly. Smoke billowed into the room, and an eerie orange light flickered in the blackness of the house. The roaring inferno raced up the rear stairwell, around the open doorway and up the stairs to the attic. A swirling, howling tube of unbroken flames, it would consume everything in its path within minutes.

His first instinct was to grab Leah and run for it. But even as his mind formulated their escape route, he realized that was exactly what Alex expected them to do. No doubt he waited out front to ambush them as they fled the house by the only route available.

As though reading his mind, Leah shouted, "Let's climb out the window onto the porch roof. From there we can jump into the pool."

From his vantage point, Alex could see the front of the house, garage, and Florida room. Lost in anticipation of the pending kill, he blocked all else from his consciousness. He didn't even notice the car that slowed to a stop at the end of driveway, then accelerated into the night.

Now living in a world of madness, Alex had metamorphosed from a personable, handsome man into a demented maniac whose fiendish expression reflected his tormented soul. The incessant rain had plastered his hair to his forehead. His blackened face looked like a map of bloody roads etched by the thorns and bushes. Waiting in giddy expectation, he breathed in frenzied gasps. At any moment, he would see the Colemans burst from the house, perhaps as human torches, escaping from one hell to another. He chuckled to himself.

Before opening the window, David put his good arm around Leah's neck, his pistol pressing her cheek, and kissed her. "Be careful. And stick as close to me as you can. Once we're in the pool, stay next to the house and follow my lead."

"I will, but *you* be careful. It's *you* he's after, and he'll stop at nothing. I love you."

"Still have your gun?"

"Just call me Bonnie," she said, removing the pistol from her waist.

"Bonnie?"

"I'll explain it later, Clyde. Just be careful, please."

As they climbed onto the roof, David was thankful for the rain. Not only did it offer them protection from the heat, but it also partially obscured them from their attacker. Keeping low to the roof, they scooted to the corner nearest the garage, directly above the deep end of the pool.

"Jump as far as you can!" David shouted over the wail of the storm and the hissing of the burning house. "You've got to clear the sidewalk!" Although he was yelling and her face was only inches from his own, he wasn't sure she could hear him. He started to repeat his warning but stopped when she acknowledged his instructions.

Alex rounded the garage just as they dropped into the pool. When they had not come running out the front door, he realized they would never leave by the stairs, nor would he risk climbing out one of the front windows over the entry. The only option left was the one they had taken. Once again he had underestimated his adversary. He jumped up and ran toward the garage.

* * * * *

265

The shock of the cold water and the sudden impact from the fall caused Leah to relax her grip on the pistol. It instantly slipped from her hand and sank to the bottom of the pool as first one and then another shot hit the water, ricocheting off the far wall of the pool and into the night. David fired twice in return.

Alex froze in his tracks, then sprinted back around the corner of the garage. He now faced an enemy that could take his life. David Coleman wasn't going to be the sitting duck that Peter Everett had been.

Huddled against the near side of the pool, David tried to think. As best he could recall, he should have one bullet left in his pistol. But with his left arm in a sling, he couldn't even reload using the bullets in his pocket. Flames engulfed the house, and the pool area became brighter by the moment. In the distance he could hear the laboring wail of a fire engine. He hoped that help, any help, was on its way, but doubted it would reach them before Alex did.

Realizing they would soon be fully visible in the glow from the house, he pushed Leah toward the shallow end, using the edge of the pool to shield them. Pulling her head next to his, he shouted, "Give me your gun. I'll keep him busy while you make a run for the woods."

"I dropped it."

"Forget it," he shouted back. "We've got to get out of here *now!*"

The illumination from the burning house moved across the pool like a searchlight, its bright fingers spreading outward between the pool and the woods.

"Go!" He pushed her up the steps. Once out of the pool, they were fully exposed, and David tried to keep himself between Leah and Alex. At any moment he expected to feel another hot bullet pierce his back.

Rounding the corner just in time to see the Colemans dash for the woods, Alex took quick aim, but his shot went wide of the moving targets.

"Now I've got you," he said with satisfaction as he watched them disappear into the trees. The woods were a second home to

266

Alex. He knew the Colemans wouldn't get far before he had them in the crosshairs of his sight. "I'm going to kill you, David, you son of a...." His words faded into the roar of the night.

A fire engine screeched to a stop in the driveway. Firemen began jumping off the truck, axes and hoses in hand. Because the front of the house was too far gone to enter, two of the firemen ran around the Florida room toward the rear. As they rounded the corner, Alex took aim and fired. Both men fell in their tracks. At the sound of the shots, the other firemen dropped their equipment and came running.

Stymied by a stand of impenetrable palmettos a short distance into the woods, Leah and David came to an abrupt halt. They whirled around when the second volley of shots rang out and, in the bright glow of the burning house, saw the firemen fall. Pushing her down to the temporary safety of the ground, David started back toward the house.

"No!" she shouted after him.

"I have to warn them! Alex'll kill anybody who gets in his way!" He took a step into the clearing and waved his arms to attract attention. "Go back! Go back! He's crazy!" Another shot rang out. The bullet whistled past his ear.

The other firemen raced for cover as David dove into the brush and began crawling toward Leah.

Abandoning all caution, Alex came running toward him, stumbling forward and screaming obscenities. In seconds, he was within a few strides of their hiding place.

"Run! Run!" one of the firemen shouted as Alex fought his way through the brush.

He was within an arm's reach of the two crouched figures when the shouts came. Stopping in his tracks, he looked back over his shoulder toward the house. In that instant, David leapt to his feet, jammed the pistol into Alex's chest, and fired.

For a split second their eyes met. David saw the panic on Alex's face. Then he fell spread-eagle to the ground.

A huge sense of relief overwhelmed David as he jerked the rifle from the dying man's grasp. The face that only seconds before had radiated hatred now froze in an expression of horror. As the rain beat down on them, David could only stare in shocked numbness. Blood bubbled from the corner of Alex's mouth. He appeared to be trying to speak. Falling to his knees, David bent over, his ear only inches above Alex's lips. His last utterances were a mixture of garbled sounds interspersed with mumbled words. Then his facial muscles relaxed, and he took on a look of childlike innocence.

David stared into the unseeing eyes, then gently closed the lids and whispered, "I'm sorry, Alex. I'm so, so sorry." And the emotions of the moment overtook him.

Leah and David walked slowly around the burning shell of their beautiful home while firemen, policemen, and medics seemed to be everywhere. Lights blinked, police radios squawked, and the paramedics tended to the fallen firemen. The house, along with all of their family treasures, collapsed in a heap of smoldering rubble.

The day of retribution had ended.

Epilogue

Dawn broke and the sky cleared. David's wound had been dressed and his arm placed in a real sling at the hospital before he and Leah were escorted to the police department and provided with dry clothes and hot coffee. He knew they were both still reeling from the horrors of the night. Right then all he wanted to do was touch her, feel the warmth and suppleness of her skin, and reassure himself that she was alive and safe. Yet, he felt a peace he hadn't known for years. One of his dad's favorite admonitions floated through his mind, stopping just long enough to leave its mark before descending again into his subconsciousness for safekeeping.

"Remember, son, each day is a gift. Some are gifts of plenty, others are gifts of work, and still others are gifts of trial that help us appreciate tomorrow."

After a detective took their statements, the night sergeant told them they could go.

They stepped through the doorway into the bright new day. A sanitation crew had already begun cleaning up the debris left behind by the storm. In the distance, a siren wailed. A breeze blew in from the bay, and the palm trees along Bayshore Drive swayed gently in response. All things considered, it was a great day to be alive.

To passersby, they could have been mistaken for a pair of street people being released after a night's incarceration...except for one thing. This couple had a special look. They radiated a profound joy of life seldom seen in the world around them.

"Honey, what did Alex say last night?" Leah asked, turning to face him.

269

At first he didn't answer, his stare locked on something in the distance. Then, looking down at her, he said, "I'm not sure. It was too garbled. But I think he was trying to say, 'Tell mother that I—' something. Maybe it was 'tell mother that I forgive her,' but that doesn't make any sense. His mother died sometime back. I guess we'll never know. In the end, I think he regretted hurting so many people...at least that's what I *want* to believe."

"Oh David, I feel so sorry for him, and for you too. I know how much you cared . . . and how you tried to be his friend. If only he had given you a chance...."

David shook his head wearily. "Let's go home."

"We don't have a home to go to," Leah replied with a playfulness that surprised him. "But we still have each other, and that's *all* that really matters."

She smiled and he responded, the first genuine smile for either of them in what had been a very long night.

"What are you going to do now?" she asked.

"Who knows? I've had enough of corporate life to last several lifetimes." After a pause, he added, "Maybe I'll write a book about this whole ordeal. Think anyone would buy it?"

"They just might. I know I would, so you can at least sell one copy." She was grinning again.

After a moment, he nodded. "I would never have chosen to go through what happened to us, but it has made me rethink a lot of things. I've never been more grateful for the gift of life than I am at this moment. I feel like the weight of the world has been lifted off my shoulders." With his good arm he pulled her close, and they kissed as younger lovers do who have been too long apart.

Then they turned and, hand in hand, headed toward the bay. Together they would face the future...whatever that might be.